FEARLESS II

MMA SPORT & RUSSIAN MAFIA ROMANCE

AMARIE AVANT

PROLOGUE

Vassili Karo Resnov

Never get angry. Never get...too angry. And keep my fucking chill when outside of the octagon. I agreed to be a softy to make my marriage work.

I'm wide-legged on a leather chair, so fucking big and plush, it was made for me. A massive flat-screen is before me. I'm on display, slaughtering my opponent with a roundhouse kick. The other fighter is knocked out in midair and fell onto the blood-painted canvas like a rock. The KO segues into another one of my Killer Karo approved highlights. This time, my tactic is a raw submission. I had Hauser in an ankle hold that broke his shit clear in half almost two years ago.

While I stare at my first love, I fist my iPhone in my hand, waiting for my greatest love to answer. The images keep flickering of me in beast mode, going for the kill. I'm too good at this. Too good at being bad.

She finally answers.

"Hey, baby," Zariah says, breathing a tad heavy.

Her intake of air causes me to pull some into my lungs too. Damn, I realize my body was overdue for oxygen during the wait for her to answer. Last month, my wife was pressing the "away" button repeatedly and disregarding my calls.

My greatest matches fade from before my eyes, as I speak to my slice of heaven on earth. I ask, "Zariah, beautiful, you on your way?"

"I'm trying. Your child refuses to walk." Zariah's voice sounds muffled. "I opened the garage. Forgot something. Now I'm headed back to the garage with Natasha on one hip, her favorite juice spilling on me."

Tilting my head to the shiny chandeliers above, I silently thank God she forgave me. "That's Natasha, mayhem with apple juice."

From my peripheral, I notice my cousin, Yuri, has dropped his cane and is leaning against the doorframe. This fat, *mudak*—asshole—is eye fucking the pin-up doll for a maid. So far, she's done more bending over in my face because some idiot blabbed about my impending match.

"Send me a pic, Zar." I chuckle a little. "I don't mind a wet t-shirt contest—with you, girl. Even if you're soaked through with her juice."

"Whatever, Vassili. I don't have time to be abused by your mini-me."

"Oh, you don't?" I break into a grin. Our one-year-old is part of the reason I'm forgiven now.

Yuri turns around. "See, *kuzen* I told you Zariah is all talk. You two are good."

My wife continues with, "I'm all sticky, and we have less than an hour to..."

My eyebrows knit as I focus on the background noise with my wife.

Yuri winks. He thinks all is good. That I'm out of the doghouse.

But something changed in a split second. Zariah's tone is stricken with fear, and her voice lowers, "We —we have..."

My head tilts, facial expression darkening as Yuri stops leaning against the doorframe. He turns his attention from the slutty maid to me.

I ask, "Zariah, girl. What's wrong—"

"Mrs. Resnov, you've taken everything from me..." I hear a Latino male voice in the background.

Zariah scoffs, "Mr. Noriega... wh-what are you doing at my house? How do you know where I live?"

"Zariah," I shout into the phone. "Who is that!"

"Oh, is your husband on the phone?"

There are muffled noises. Yuri silently asks me what's going on. He mouths Zariah, and I nod.

"Mikhail will be at your house in a few minutes, kuzen," Yuri whispers.

I yell into the receiver, "ZARIAH, WHO IS—"

"Tell him."

She's trembling. Fuck, I can feel it light-years away.

Zariah begins to speak into the receiver, "It's Juan Noriega. He-he is—he's a Loco Dios. I'm representing his wife in their divorce," her voice scales down. And then she's pleading with him. Begging him to allow her to put our child in the house so they can talk. And I'm... useless.

Juan motherfucking Noriega? A knife has slid into my bones. Without fail, I've always forced Zariah to provide me with a rundown of every case she picks up. Regardless of it being family law, I refuse to have my wife in a dangerous situation. There was no mention of this mudak, Noriega. I'd have refused her request to take on any case that had anything to do with the infamous Loco Dios gang member. Shit, shit, shit. Whomever she represented against Noriega was more than deserving of justice. Instinct slams into me and churns sour.

This is revenge...

"Does he have a gun?" My voice is tapered. Her fucking

3

answer, 'yes' is enough to feel two slugs piercing into my heart. But I continue to stay calm as Yuri sends out a message.

"Put him on the phone," I command, lips growing tauter with each word.

"Okay," Zariah says, her voice wrapped in terror that I've never known.

"The infamous Vassili Resnov," the man's voice is callous to the core.

"Who. The. Fuck. Are. You?"

"*Ay Dios Mio,* you sound scary," he laughs. "But I know you, mi amigo. You can knock my fucking spine lose, eh? Make me go goodnight."

I glare at the television screen. There's so much fucking blood. I'm massacring my opponent. My gaze fixates on the fighter's eyes, which cloud as he taps out in my arms. I glower so hard that the visual blurs before me.

"Nyet, I won't dislocate your spine. Not at first, piz'da," I grit out. My voice is calm and collected. Too calm for the fighter in me. "Keep talking to me, so that you don't have to die a slow, painful death, Noriega. You let my wife and daughter go. You can keep fucking talking to me about whatever Zariah has done to piss you off. We're both men," I pause for a beat. Fuck, he's not a man. A real man would've brought his grievance to the woman's husband in the first place.

"Sounds like I'm talking to the motherfucking Terminator. You scare me, Karo. I dunno if I want to talk to you . . . or your wife. Mrs. Resnov is so pretty. It's easier to speak to pretty people. Your daughter too."

"Don't," I growl.

"Aye, all I meant to say is I'm Juan Noriega. I take it you know of me. But no worries, mi amigo, I'm a nobody these days. I know all about you, though," Noriega says. "Ex

Welterweight UFC champ. Loved by the masses. I also know you're a fucking Resnov. Your family isn't to be fucked with."

The luxurious hotel had faded into oblivion. All I see myself doing is tearing this man limb from limb, killing him with my bare hands. His bones will fracture, turn into powder, to dust and then become nothing. Painting my hands with his blood until my knuckles break.

I gulp down the lump in my throat. "Then I don't need to inform you of my capabilities. My family's capabilities?"

"No, hombre. I'm dead already," his voice sours. "My parental rights were terminated for my ninos because of *your bitch.* My bitch upped and took my house, my cars, everything I have, also because of *your* bitch. At this precise moment, I've got a nine to *your bitch's* head. But don't worry, like I said, the bitch took my wife and my two kids. I heard *your bitch* is pregnant. I prayed to God the two of you *were* having a boy. So, the little nina and the baby in her tummy will meet the same ending."

"Noriega." My blood slows to a freezing point. I know that Yuri's in the background compelling me to keep this cunt open. To keep him talking. But I'm not that person. I'm not the fighter who has words for someone because my mind goes straight to how they're dealt with. All I can do is keep sight of my heaven. My Zariah, my Natasha, my baby in her belly! My fucking family that I'd go to hell for.

I beg God for sanity, hands balled into tight fists. It's the moment I need for composure. "Listen to me, if you touch my wife or my daughter, you will die a thousand deaths. I will beat you with my bare hands. That's already in the motherfucking cards. You've already consigned yourself to that. But do you want me to fucking murder you and revive you a thousand times, all to have me tortured and murder you again?"

"You're capable of that, Mr. Resnov. The only problem is, I no longer have a heart. Adios, mi amigo."

Click!

My 190 pounds of muscle are shot. I stand, on limbs that want to fail me. But sheer drive keeps me going as I storm through the suite. "Where are my keys? Yuri, where the fuck are my keys?"

My cousin starts arguing with me. A lamp goes crashing. I toss a chair against the wall to get toward the front door of the suite. Finally, he halts my bulldozing through the room by grabbing my shoulders.

There's pain behind his eyes. Yuri's still favoring his one leg. But he grits through it and says, "*Nyet*—no! Vassili, *brat*. Everything will be good."

My world has tilted on a spindle. My head is chaotic, crazed. I'm seeing red. And I'm about to serve him the left hook he got when we went to jail a little while back. My bark is hard, "Yuri, move. I will fucking murder you to get to my wife, blood or no blood, bitch!"

He flinches, holding his palms out. "I can't. You can't. We can't fucking do anything for them no matter how much we—"

My forearm slams against his neck. Yuri is no longer my cousin. No longer family. He's part of the problem.

Fat cheeks reddening, Yuri bites out the words, "Va-Vassili, we are in Australia."

My eyebrows crinkled. I. Am. In. Australia. My title match is tomorrow. I'm a world away from my fucking heart! I let him go and grip at the top of my head. There's no more Mohawk to tug. My shit is all buzzed down. "Fuck the belt, Yuri. I don't want it."

Yuri rubs at his neck. "Okay, *kuzen*, but—"

"I need to get home!" I punch the wall next to him. It's all

6

marble. My knuckles crush against the glossed stone. The skin has pulled back and blood smears, leaving a trail.

"That's impossible, Vassili. We are too far away. We're in fucking Australia! I have a crew on the way..." My cousin is speaking, though I can't understand the words. All I see is myself becoming a monster.

"You'll have a heart attack. We will handle this. Mikhail promised to keep them safe. He is on the way to your home right now," he argues through gritted teeth. But Yuri's words hardly penetrate. I concentrate on God. Over the years, having faith hasn't been easy. I toss up a promise. This day will mark the end of my relationship with Him if the worst occurs.

1

Vassili
Four Months Ago, Brazil
(The morning after the winning Match with Tiago)

"You sure you want this chocolate?" Zariah's voice is filled with laughter. All those dark-brown curves of hers peek from where they're tucked into the sheets. The hotel bed is so heavily scented with our sex I almost didn't get out of it this morning.

I arch an eyebrow. Her gorgeous smile pops in and out of view. I continue with the repetition of push-ups I'm completing on the floor at the foot of the bed. I grunt out, "You'll save me a piece?"

"I guess I could." She places another chocolate truffle to her lips and then says, "How hard will you work for it?"

"*Nyet—no*, girl, I don't work hard unless I want to. I'll eat you instead," I tell her.

"Whatever, Vassili," is her snarky reply.

I can hear her muttered chatter, damn, but that sound is good to my ears. While preparing for our daughter, Natasha's first birthday, my wife has offered arguments and snide remarks. Zariah is a lawyer, what can I expect? But I was on the opposite side of the defense team, and we were butting heads every day of the week. Yet, there's a smile in her comment about me eating her "*if* she lets me."

"Get the fuck outta here, baby, with that '*if you let me*' shit." My voice is playful. I almost crack a smile, I'm so fucking happy. The next strain to my bicep is met with a truffle she's tossed at me. It lands yards away. Instead of picking up the piece of chocolate she sucked at throwing, I continue with isolating my biceps. "Zariah, girl, why do I have the feeling that this is my only piece out of the entire box?"

The next view I have while mid-push-up is her lovely curves, breasts bouncing. She falls back into the goose pillows in a burst of laughter. An undertone of cherry permeates her mahogany cheekbones before I can no longer see her. She's pulled a pillow over her face to stifle her laughter. Damn, she can't get away with anything.

I get up from the floor, sweat glistens down my skin from the repetitions I've completed. "Zariah, get up, sweetheart. You enjoy all those chocolates."

I pick up the now empty box of six. There's a single piece left, the one she threw at me. "There's only one chocolate that I crave. So, eat it all, baby. Get yourself sweet for me."

She slides the pillow away, and I'm blown away by what I see. The world's most gorgeous face. Her sparkling eyes slide up and down my muscles, and my gaze locks onto her pouty lips. She knows how to screw with me.

Zariah licks that pout then says, "Um hmmm, candy isn't required to get me sweet for you."

I cock an eyebrow, running my hand over the tattoos at

the side of my neck. "Then you'll give your husband some love? You'll love me now..."

She sits up. The sheets tangle over her frame, covering those heavy breasts. Yet with that shape, it can't hide much. "I'll always love you, Vassili. My heart isn't set up any other way. But, I will *love you* after your shower."

"That so, counselor?" I reach down, grabbing the meat of her ass and hips. The image of her on our first encounter will forever be embedded in my brain. The most beautiful sight. I never imagined she could be more gorgeous than when she sat in front of her mirror, virgin pussy splayed out for me. After having Natasha, Zariah had added on in the weight department. She is so damn thick. My palm squeezes on the flesh of her ass, and I swear my cock becomes titanium, hard like never before. I paw and then grab at it before quickly placing another hand under her arm and scoop her up.

"Yuck! Vassili, let me go!" Zariah argues as I bring the soft masses of her curvy naked body to my hard, sweaty chest.

"No. You once said I smelled good when I'm all sweaty."

"I plead the fifth," she chortles.

"You can't. I'm your husband. You said you loved my sweat."

The mock disgust erupts into a broad smile, white teeth kissing her dark red lips. "That was after sex sweat, not dripping like a dog sweat. Besides, you loved me crazy, boy, so I was probably bragging on you. Now, I'm at a loss for words, so stop badgering the witness!"

"You're my witness." I nip at her lip with my teeth. My growl causes her to shiver in delight against me. She's so soft and even after having my daughter, still so innocent.

We've had a hard seven months due to my torn patella. Yesterday was my first time returning to the cage. It was met with celebration and taking out a worthy opponent, Tiago.

Slaughtering him has solidified my place back in the UFC world and elevated me closer to my fucking belt.

I reposition Zariah. Her thick legs wrap around my waist.

"Oh, so you don't listen?" She squeezes her legs tighter around me.

Squeezing her tighter, I ask, "Girl, what are you talking about? My sweat smells like cologne."

"Ughhhh..." she bites her lip while eyeing my mouth.

"You want a kiss, sweetheart?"

"I guess." She squeezes again. "I'm dirty by association anyway."

"Dah, well I was going to take my kiss regardless." I nibble her bottom lip. The warmth of her pussy stamps her wetness against my waist.

"Oh, you'll take it?" Her tongue slithers with mine. "How?"

"Just like this," I tell her, holding onto Zariah with one arm while pushing my boxers down. My teeth sink into her lips. "You belong to me, girl."

Grabbing her by the hips, I position her soaking kitty at the head of my dick. The instant I slam into her, Zariah gives this haughty little chuckle. Her pussy creams onto my cock.

"Why you laughing, baby," I cock a brow. "I'm going to tear this pussy up!"

"Oh, *yes!* Vassili, tear it up, baby," she groans.

"You want this pussy beat?" My ten inches are glossed with her sweets, and Zariah is angled out toward me.

"Fuck me, baby!" Zariah pleads as I slam into her. The onslaught of my cock bruising every sweet corner of her insides has her bucking and begging. "Yes! Yes! Vassiliiiiiiiiii!"

Zariah unwinds her legs from around me, leaving them transfixed in a V-shape. This offers me free reign as my biceps bump her up and down. My feet plant into a wide-legged stance, causing me to gather traction on the plush carpet. Her cunt is sopping wet, tight. Every time my cock bruises at her insides, her wet walls try to grab ahold of my dick.

Her titties, with their hard chocolate nipples, bounce up and down as I toss her in the air and slam into her over and over. My cock burrows deep inside Zariah, and I hold her there. I've met heaven right between her thick thighs and it's begging me to come hard. My balls are against her asshole, but my cock dominates deep in her pussy.

She grabs my face, kissing me hard and rough. "Fuck me, Vassili."

In the past, she worried that I wouldn't like her pussy after she gave birth. That couldn't be further from the truth. It's fatter now, silky soft and rains like the Lena River, the longest river in Russia. Thinking about it drives me to the brink. I slow down, not wanting to nut too fast.

"Fuck you? You want me to beat the fuck out of this pussy?" I arch an eyebrow, this time my biceps push her up and down slowly.

"Beat the fuck out of my pussy, Karo," she grins.

One inch at a time, my cock gets a taste, savoring the perfect mold. Damn, she's gushier inside than I imagined, as I continue to tease her insides. "Thought I was getting you all wet, and sweaty."

"Shit... shit..." she purrs. "Vassili, if you fuck me harder. I'm gonna... I'm gonna cum..."

My cock glides in and out. I lay her on the edge of the bed, position her legs over my shoulder. Then I place the crown of my piece against those thick, throbbing lips, gliding around in her sugar.

"Ohhh..." she tries to reach up. In her position, she's useless. Her eyes narrow. "Harder, Vassili ... I love you..."

"Oh, you love me." My cock is swallowed by her pussy for

a second and then out, heavy stiffness dragging over her clit and lips.

"Don't play!"

I slip inside again, pull out and fuck with her clit. "Don't play? You ate all the chocolate. I can play."

"I hate you, Va—" Zariah ceases her usual rant as I get to my knees and taste.

2

Zariah

Never thought to beg for sex until I met Vassili. Hell, I never made it enough of a priority to give it up for the first time until I met Vassili. This year has been tumultuous at best. We are a stubborn pair. My headstrong demeanor parallels with Vassili kicking ass in the octagon. Yesterday, when Vassili and Tiago were annihilating each other, I froze. Then I ran.

Now, I realize that MMA has a special place in his heart. The game is so important to him, no matter what promises he made to get the hell out of dodge when a match wasn't going too well. I had forced Vassili into a corner when he was putting a hurting on every man he stepped into the cage with. I learned that in our marriage, there will be ups and downs—on that damn canvass—and I have to ride it with him no matter what.

I cannot believe how easily Vassili has forgiven me for my faults. Since I apologized for running out of the convention center, we are magnetized to each other. We've transitioned back into the same greedy lovers that we've always been in the past. His body, cut and ripped with muscles and dipped in gold and tattoos is the most beautiful sight. Second only to his cock. Minutes ago, as he bounced me in the air, and that thick, long, shaft crashed into my pussy, I grew hypnotized.

Vassili is now kneeling before me. I'm at the edge of the bed. My second set of lips is pulsating with the *Hulk Smash* he performed. Now, Doctor Jekyll has become Mr. Hyde. Vassili seductively bestows butterfly kisses against the pulse at my neck.

"I hate you, Vassili," I grumble, attempting to grab at the long wavy hair of his mohawk while he kisses a trail down my chest. His response is to nip harder at my nipple. Shit, it hurts, but the pain has nothing on the way he screwed me. It felt good. Soaring through the air and slamming down onto his cock was freedom, liberation, and erotica all wrapped into one sexy ass bow.

A warm, wet trail glides down to my belly button. I tug at his hair again, but he pushes my hand away and continues toward his goal.

When his lips meet my clit, the aggression, the anger, the addict in me dies instantly. A humming sound vibrates my tonsils. He hates when I cry, so I hum in happiness.

That gorgeous chocolate brown wavy hair of his rises. Vassili's sinful dark orbs connect with my gaze. He growls, "Fuck, Zar. Keep making that sound. It makes me want to slide down your throat."

I'm torn.

His cock in my mouth.

Or his lips against my clit.

I grip the sheets, unable to determine which titillating act I prefer. *"69!"* The thought pops into my head, like those old dreams I had of being a mute, naked and about to commence my closing remarks in a courtroom. I'd finally shout something inaudible. But apparently, Vassili can read me, or I'm not so far gone that my words didn't penetrate.

Like we're on the canvass, Vassili's hard body clambers over mine. He positions his cock against my face. And before I can even begin to taste, he's devouring my pussy!

Damn, this is hilarious. I'm speaking in tongues; his crown is spearing the side of my cheek and he's eating me like an animal.

Vassili growls against my inner thigh.

Oh, yeah! He acquiesced to my begging. I grab his cock with one hand and gobble it into my mouth. But Vassili works my sex like an 'all you can eat Las Vegas buffet.' Once again, I'm humming, grinning, and floating at the gates of euphoria.

"Zar!" His voice is testy.

I'm a little too greedy for this reciprocation stuff, and he's doing it too damn well.

I slide my tongue along the hard, smooth steel ridges of him and recall how much I love his dick. Then I suck and suck until Vassili's seed comes roaring all the way down my throat.

Our one week-shy of a year old, Natasha's fat little paws slap at the coffee table as she gains leverage. Her chunky legs are locked straight. She's taken a few steps before, but she's too damn eager to get around.

"She's making room," my mom speaks up, right behind Natasha.

Pursing my lips, I offer her the same pettiness by saying, "Um-hmm."

"Making room?" Vassili's eyebrows come together. "Walk, sweetheart," he tells her as she shuffled to the side.

"She's making room for a new baby," Mom says.

"Humph, that's a pain I still haven't forgotten yet. I don't know how anyone goes through it and..." I start laughing at Natasha's movements. She's using the table to dance now. Though her diaper is fresh, she drops a little and brings it right back up. "Okay, maybe I understand how mothers endure labor more than once."

Mom is right there as Natasha starts to fall. Usually, she cries for Vassili in frustration, but my mom refuses to let her hit the floor.

"Mom, she has all that diaper back there—"

"Child, this is a hotel. I don't care how luxurious of a room we're in, Natasha isn't falling on the floor."

Vassili takes Natasha in his arms. He sits on the low seated chair. "Daddy was beating some ass last night."

"Daddy be... be... *ass!*"

"Vassili," I chide as my mother bursts into laughter. I swear I recall a day when she had no sense of humor. My father hardly allowed her to be comfortable in her shoes. I can't be mad at her, so my reprimand comes with a smile. "How do you allow this baby to cuss?" I ask her as Vassili's voice lowers. He's having a sidebar conversation with Natasha as he often does. When *they* talk matches, I know he cusses a storm. And Natasha giggles in response. The shirt he's wearing clings to his buff biceps as he does a jab into the air with her in his other arm.

Her head tosses back, she gives a wide-toothed grin, or should I say gums. Three teeth up top and two at the bottom.

I glance at myself in the mirror, and then I look at my mom's reflection. Hell, it should be me in "mommy" sweats. My mom needs a new love. She didn't get over my father until I jumped the broom. I can still recall her asking about my dad during my last two years in high school. Her inquiries never stopped, even after I moved to Atlanta, near her, to attend Spellman. Now, my mom is over a year solid all alone. And that's speaking volumes since she divorced my cheating, abusive father a decade ago.

Last night, Vassili and I disappeared early, leaving her with Natasha. It's almost dark again. So, guilt lines my stomach. I saddle up to her and ask, "Mama, are you sure you don't want to have a night out? We're on vacation in a new place."

"Nope. I have Natasha. Everything I want to do is at a respectable hour." She glances back and forth from me and Vassili and adds, "Tsk, my version of respectable. Y'all two have blurred the line."

"Dang!" I sound like the teenager she used to know me as. My cheeks warm. I'm twenty-seven years old, yet my mother doesn't need to know of the freak Vassili has made me into. He winks as I pick up Natasha and burrow my face in the fat rolls of her neck.

"No! No! Nooooo!" Natasha argues as I kiss her caramel skin. I smack kisses on her neck and start to blow, causing my baby to cackle with laughter. It's the sweetest sound, and it makes this bulky husband of mine soft for a fraction of a second.

"I don't mind y'all disappearing at all hours of the day and night. Long as Natasha becomes a big sister soon," Mom says, on the topic I attempted to skirt around.

I dance around that question with, "Hmmm, we have to get you a man."

"I have one, thank you very much. Now go enjoy—"

"Who? Since when?" I ask. Natasha tugs on my shirt for attention, but I stare my mother down waiting on her answer. The guilt that lined my stomach disappears and now concern rides there instead. My mom's too nice. I ask, "Does Martin know about him? Who is he?"

"No, you and your brother, Martin, need to stay out of

grown folk's business. Mind you, my relationship is new. I won't ruin it by chatting. Go out, drink, and try to have a good time. Because the two of you mix like oil and water. Have fun before being forced into returning to reality..."

"Well, damn, mama, tell me something I don't know."

She catches my gaze. "Honey, as long as you keep God first in your marriage, you two can continue clashing and loving. Contrary to the example you were provided as a child, a little rebellion makes love stronger if Jesus is in the mix."

"This is the treatment we get when your man wins against one of the local legends," Taryn, my Asian and Somali friend, grumbles. We are invisible to the bartender, who has an imaginary 'Team Tiago' stamp on his forehead. The guy put up a fight and lost, and now we lose out on good drinks.

I sigh, waving at the Brazilian. He catches my eye and continues to flirt with a young woman. "Yeah, I'm surprised the bartender doesn't add a little something extra to our drinks by way of bodily fluid."

"I will sue, and then still kill him. You can be my attorney, right? Because I don't plan to pay you a retainer or the going rate either."

I chuckle. "I guess I owe you one, Taryn. If you hadn't dragged me back into the stadium, I wouldn't have seen the ending of the fight."

"You can pay me back in Valentino." Taryn drums her hands on the scuffed wood counter.

I scoff. "Your ass needs a job, Taryn, a j-o-b."

"Ugh!" She shakes her long hair. "Gainful employment isn't in my vocabulary."

"Is love?" I play it cool, still waving for the bartender's attention. "Hello…"

"Is what?" Taryn stops batting her eyes. She then attempts to gather the server's attention by leaning across the counter with her tiny tits. "Zar, what?"

We step away from the bar, and a crowd of natives engulfs the spot we just had. The bartender comes over to them. I look her in the eye, and ask, "Love? You, Yuri."

She glances back at the high-stool table where our guys sit. There's no denying the sparkle in her eye. Yuri gestures for us to come back over with the cock of his beer.

Whereas Vassili is all muscle, in jeans and a shirt, Yuri is every bit as thick in the arms with a gut that slims beneath a custom suit.

"Girls, I need some fucking water here, my tongue is as dry as sandpaper." Yuri corners Taryn into his space. She's so much tinier than him. A pretty roasted almond color to his paleness. Yuri isn't a lover of working out nor is he much a fan of the sun.

"Oh, you want water, do you?" Her voice is dripping with sex. "Their vodka isn't as good as your family's. I've got something better for you…"

They proceed to caress each other's tongues in the middle of the bar.

Vassili kisses my neck and grabs his beer. Sometimes I swear, he is a super fan of public displays of affection, like the first time we screwed in a car. There's no way in hell I'll fuck him with an audience, those token times he devours my mouth outside of the bedroom are rare. I live for every second of it. His dark eyes sparkle. He wants to eat me. I swear even after being married for over two years, he still treats me like a virgin in front of others at times. If you don't count the ass pawing. Every few minutes, he squeezes one of my ass cheeks like his life depends on it.

21

Sometimes I want him to grab me in front of a crowd of people. Set aside my education and the entitlement my father instilled in me. Set aside his tattooed, gentleman qualities. There's no denying that I belong to him. Yet, I realize that on those occasions where he is *too respectable,* he is thinking of something. Perhaps how his father, Anatoly, treated his mom. Yeah, that must have something to do with his level of pause. I hope...

3

Vassili

How the fuck do I respond to her? Zariah turns her head away from me. She takes my lack of willingness to fuck faces as if I'm dismissing her. I went from slamming my cock into a different pussy a day, sometimes more, to my wife. Zariah satisfies me in ways I cannot begin to explain. I can't slobber her face. Not here.

Shit, I didn't even know I was starving until Zariah became mine. But with my parents on my mind, I am in the wrong headspace for PDA. Because I'm amped up on adrenaline, and maybe because I'm paranoid about a few things like my fucking father.

Zariah starts to sway to the music. She snaps her fingers and closes her eyes. All the restraint in the world is holding me back from her right now. No need for ass shaking, my girl is too fucking beautiful being herself. She doesn't even know that it's the little things that send my cock to a heavy rise and my heart drumming in my chest.

"Dance with me?" Zariah asks out of the blue.

Fuck, can't say I don't dance because Natasha jiggled around even as she crawled to music. I dance, but in the few years that Zariah and I have been back together, we've only attended the VIP section in clubs. And I would bash a man's skull in for looking at her at The Red Door. There's never been a time we were dancing in the lounge when it's been open to the public.

My eyes keep zipping around. Have I gone paranoid, obsessively anxious like Anatoly? Someone is here...

Zariah glowers, expecting an answer. She doesn't know that I'm scanning the room with my peripheral vision because that would lead to more questions. Like the truth. So I take the dick way out...an excuse. "You don't know the words to the song. We don't know the words. Why dance?"

There. On the side, left corner, a man who resembles one of my many brothers sits, nursing a shot glass. My muscles tense.

Zariah rubs my bicep. "Vassili, baby, dance with me. Who cares what the singer is saying? The melody is perfect."

My eyes lock onto hers. "I don't fucking dance." My voice is as hard as ever, iced over due to hate from a past life. And dammit, I need to see what this guy wants. My mouth tips at the edge to soften the blow. "I don't dance. Okay, love?"

Zariah cuts her eyes and glances away from me.

Yuri slaps a hand on the table. "What the fuck," he asks in Russian.

My middle finger goes to the air as I toss back my beer.

As if on key, my cell phone vibrates in my jean pocket. I pull it out.

"Is that my mom?" Zariah asks. She'd left her phone with her mom and Natasha since her mother's cell won't hold much juice.

"It's..." I glance at the screen. *Anatoly.* "Nobody."

"Nobody," she breathes the word.

"Hey, Zar," Taryn cuts in and saves the day. My wife's mouth was set for a comeback. Yuri's little friend says, "There's a new bartender. Let's see if we can get a good old' fashioned Cosmo? Beer is not my fancy." Taryn lifts her empty glass. The girls rise and head toward the bar.

"That your pop?" Yuri asks, our language changing back to Russian now.

"*Dah!*"

"So besides being a fucking dick, is Zariah aware that the two of you are talking again? Because I've seen you just about pawing Zar's pus—" he stops and gulps. Changing his phrase out of respect. "I've seen you two go at it, Vassili, many times. So is that why you've hardly touched her tonight?"

I rub the scar along my jaw with my thumb thinking about how Anatoly called me seven months ago. The first thing out of his mouth was 'disrespect.' That the MMA fighter, Louie the legion Gotti, disrespected me in the cage by tearing my patella. I laughed at his ass until he promised that The Gotti only had seconds to live. Meaning that one of my brothers, with a particular motherfucking set of skills, was probably a hundred yards away from Gotti. The fighter had to be in plain view. After calming Anatoly down and saving Gotti's life, the piz'da and I continued to talk.

"Tell her," Yuri warns.

I shake my head, and respond to my cousin, "Nah, she doesn't need to know."

"He came to you with a peace offering... you declined," Yuri says of the unnecessary hit on Gotti. He shrugs. "This is the longest period of time that you and Anatoly have talked to each other. He wants something."

No shit! I'm aware of exactly what that mudak wants. "Okay, *okay?* What the fuck, Yuri, am I stupid now?" I bark, still keeping an eye on the guy in the corner. There's a shadow masking much of his face, but the resemblance is all too familiar.

Yuri snaps, "First, you didn't want Zariah around me. *Me.* I'm more than blood, Vassili! I'm your *brat!* We are brothers. Then my pops, Malich, and the family were off-limits. Okay, I saw that coming. Zariah loves Malich and the family *now.* But now Anatoly is in your ear and you're acting... Will your morals slip with him, too?"

The familiar stranger who I was staring at stands up. My hand goes into the air, and Yuri stops talking. This idiot thinks I'll up and allow Anatoly to come around my wife and kid one bright sunny ass day! Fuck that! And he's too stupid to realize that I'm about to tear this motherfucker across the way a new one. "Do I need a lecture from you, Yuri?"

He kisses his teeth. "*Nyet.*"

I glare through Yuri. Then I start toward the hallway that leads to the restrooms where the man in jeans and a hat went. He has to be one of my *brats*—brothers. Anatoly keeps popping up. If this is my blood, he's getting the blood bashed out of him.

In the hallway, my pace slows down. There're two guys between me and the other Russian. Lines are leading to both the men and women's restrooms. With my hand in a fist, I bite my knuckles and glance over my shoulder. The girls are sweet-talking a new bartender for a sugary drink. From their location, they'd be able to see me bash this mudak's head in.

A revolving door, reading *'Cozinha'* which means kitchen in Portuguese, is a few yards before the crowded restrooms. When the doors swing open, I cock a grin. The line shuffles forward.

"You should tell her," Yuri says over my shoulder.

A deep breath funnels into my lungs. Shit, he followed me over here. "What?"

"You and Zariah are *good* until your dad sneaks his ass

26

into the States. He has you worried and treating Zariah like—"

In a few quick steps, I'm around the two people and close to the other Russian. My palm stiffens the side of his shoulder, and he goes stumbling into the kitchen.

My left hook goes out, targeting his nose. It's powerful enough to slide him across the room. At the last instant, I raise my elbow. My bone catches the face of the Brazilian line chef who is holding a butcher knife to the side of my face. His jaw is dislocated. He's out cold. He hits the ground, his knife clattering besides him.

Fuck, there are seven more cooks and kitchen personnel where he came from, all ready for war.

"What the hell?" Yuri asks behind me as he catches an angry dishwasher with a jab to his eye.

"This guy is my—" I slam my foot into my enemy's chest. The Russian's eyes widen. But his gaze isn't dark like mine —ocean blue. And come to think of it, he doesn't look shit like me. He is no family of mine. This mudak isn't even Russian!

The stranger's voice is off when he clutches his chest and says, "What the fuck, mate!"

He's Australian. His dialect, the confusion on his face, all of it is pure comedy.

"I thought I knew you," I tell him, as I press my arms against the shoulders of another Brazilian chef. My knee slams against his junk. Fuck it, they have weapons. I'm playing dirty. The knife in his hand falls.

"Oh, I thought I knew you, too," the Aussie chuckles, with effort while regaining air into his lungs. "You're the fighter, Karo?"

Now, he's gripping a frying pan in one hand. I brace my forearm, but he slams the damn thing right over my left shoulder. It sends another man sprawling.

27

In seconds, all three of us have taken out the guys in the kitchen.

"I'm the fighter." I shrug, taking a deep breath, licking the blood from my busted lip.

"Okay, wanker, can I get your autograph?" He asks. "Also, mind telling me what had you acting like a *fuckstick?*"

His choice of words goes over my head. I was in the wrong and this is as close as we get to an apology on my part.

"Sure." I shrug, grabbing a tab and pen from the apron of a server Yuri put down.

"Dah, I'd like to know, too?" My cousin smooths the lapel of his suit.

We chat for a few minutes. The Aussie shares that his girl is in their hotel room sick, so he came down for a drink, At least I think that's what he said. He tosses words out like *spiffed* and *chockers* and I pat his back.

A waitress heads into the kitchen. She stops in her wake, sees all the guys on the ground, and then glances at the three of us. She grabs a plate on the counter and goes back to her business.

"We better get the fuck out of here, before they wake up," Yuri says.

"It was fun, mates." The Aussie heads for the door.

I start for it.

Yuri's shoulders lift in defeat. *"Brat,* I'm not wasting my fucking breath again, but tell her that Anatoly is coming around."

Without responding, I press my hands against the kitchen door and allow it to swing open.

Nothing, aside from my marriage, is off-topic. Yuri always understands where my head is at. He was a little bitch when I told him to stay away from Zariah, but in the end, he respected that. He was right. Zariah loved the family. The half that Anatoly uses his fucking puppet master antics on from across the ocean. My uncle's side of the family is closer to me than anything. Uncle Malich has always been more like a father to me. His sons, especially Yuri, are more brothers than the football team of half-siblings I have.

For the longest time, I couldn't give a fuck about my father. Anatoly held me in the same regard. But after losing my belt to Gotti, it was in my father's blood to intervene. And I haven't told Yuri the extent of Anatoly's interest in my life these days.

It has nothing to do with him.

And it sure as hell doesn't have anything to do with Zariah. Although she was willing to meet Malich, Yuri and the rest of them, she will never cross paths with my father. I won't allow it.

I have to get Anatoly Resnov out of my fucking face.

4

Zariah

Mom's right. We honestly don't mix at all. Like bad pancake batter that you try to make crepes with but in the end, it results in something even worse. That's the first analogy that came to mind the instant we returned to our reality. Los Angeles.

Planning Natasha's first birthday was a horror story before we left for Brazil. We fought about everything. We simply don't mix. He likes Russian food, I have certain favorites. However, most of it I loathe. He loves squeezing the forearm conditioner when we are arguing, and that's pretty much how we got to Brazil. His jaw tensed, mine set in a line too, sitting in silence in first class.

Now, it's the perfect first day of summer, a Saturday morning, to be more precise. Donning a colorful maxi dress and Vera Wang sandals, I apply makeup while Vassili steps out of the shower.

"Damn, girl, bring that ass over here," he orders. Water glistens over mounds of muscles and tattoos. I woke up earlier than him. There are a few surprises for Natasha's birthday that in retrospect will be quite the surprise to Vassili and his pockets soon.

One, I might have blown the bank for Natasha's first birthday. Two, there's a petting zoo on the way to our home, with the clown he and I compromised and nixed.

While brushing the waves in my long hair, I start with a little deception, saying, "Um, I'm going to finish getting dressed."

Vassili opens the glass door and steps out of the shower. "Good, good, you can do that after I get you undressed."

I make the mistake of looking at his body. The impeccable art that was carved into his chiseled chest. The way his abs stop at a V-shape which brings my eyes lower.

Before I can make a mad dash to the exit, he wraps his arms around me, his cock hardening by the second.

I breathe in his fresh scent and say, Vassili, whether it's a shower or sweat, you love to screw with me."

"I do." He nips at my earlobe. "You had my baby, Zariah. And I have to show my appreciation."

"Mmmm," I moan as he turns me around in the mirror, my ass pulled against his hard rock. His hand slithers into my low-cut dress, tugging at my nipple. I groan, "Vassili, I hate you. Don't do this to me. You'll ruin my dress!"

"I miss your pregnant belly." He says planting my hands on the counter. "Those titties full of milk use to fucking spill out of your bra when I fucked you from the back."

The lips of my pussy are dying for him.

"And when you had my daughter, shit, Zar, no woman in the world could touch how beautiful you were that day. Not before it, not since. You are my queen."

"You are trying to play me for a piece of ass," I chortle.

Although he has me precisely where he wants me. All the sneak purchases for our baby girl have flown from my mind.

The second he commands me to be wide open for him, that is exactly what I do.

He starts to descend to his knees behind me. His mouth is muffled against my ass, as he says, "Shit, you and this long ass skirt. I don't like it."

I chuckle. "Whatever, Vassili, I have things to do."

His face is against my ass, and he holds me there. Damn it if I don't want to come out of my panties and this maxi dress for him. I can feel the warmth of his breath through the material. My thong is drenching with each exhale. All he has to do is issue a command—

DING. DONG.

My eyes close instantly. My head falls back.

"That was nothing," he says, voice stifled. The wetness of his tongue starts to seep through the material and leaves me breathless.

"I have to go, baby," I murmur. He's wrong, it's a whole lot of something. Like I said, it might be the clown and the zoo, but it may very well be bayou Princess Tiana. The Princess and the Frog themed birthday was what Vassili agreed upon. He isn't aware that I chose a celebrity chef and hand-selected the food.

People say that planning weddings are filled with stress. It brings with it as much tension and irritation as tears of joy. Planning Natasha's first birthday rivaled that strain. Yet, we've managed to come home from vacation, and right now life is good.

So, I hustle away, leaving the sexiest man alive on his knees, naked in the bathroom.

My mom has been given the task of ushering the various vendors to the different parts of our vast backyard. A quaint cart is decorated in the appropriate Princess and The Frog theme. A baker stands next to it, handing out freshly made beignets and other similar desserts.

The pony ride area is at the farthest corner of the backyard. Children of all ages are seated before a movie screen. The width of the screen is almost as nostalgic as an outdoor movie theater. With theater popcorn in hand, the children watch clips of Princess and the Frog.

There's a canopied section with linen tables and a DJ. Natasha is in the photo booth with friends and cousins who all want to share the special day with her.

"So why didn't I get the memo, Samuel?" I nudge my chin to my husband who is talking to his uncle. I'm standing next to my mentor and employer, Samuel Billingsley. They're both wearing t-shirts with Natasha's photo on them. Heck, my mom's zipping around the backyard, and I could've sworn she had a shirt in her hand, too. Yuri is fixing my best friend, Taryn's, silky straight hair, as Taryn places a shirt over the tiny tee she was wearing.

"C'mon, you're a designer girl. Besides, your outfit matches cutie pies," Samuel chuckles. It's on the tip of my tongue to tell him that Taryn is even more about the labels than I am. But he reads me so well, inquiring, "You still worried about Maxwell's arriving?"

My father has been in the back of my mind for a while. I ask, "You can tell?"

He nods.

I sigh. "We've been at odds for long enough. Heck, I don't care if we continue to clash, but today is about Natasha. Our baby's birthday has nothing to do with us or his dislike of my husband."

"Call him already," Samuel begins to back away. "And whatever his response is, breathe."

I sidestep a few happy children heading to the petting zoo and pull out my cell phone. My father answers the call on the first ring.

"Good afternoon, princess." His voice is contrite at best.

"Dad, you RSVP'd last minute to the party. I didn't even argue with you about bringing Berenice." I keep my eyes on Yuri and Taryn. He's like a polar bear next to her thin, model-type body. They're glancing into each other's eyes as if there isn't a gang of children running around them. Be happy is what I tell myself. I cut my monologue short with, "So, are you coming before the cake is served? This is your granddaughter's first birthday."

"Zariah, I do not require a reminder. There was a bank robbery on Century and Normandie."

"So, what? You are the Chief of Police, and very capable of delegating assignments to the proper unit."

"Due to your current *employment,* I am not sure if you keep up to date on *current* events." My dad never fails. When he can toss shit in your face he will. Maxwell Washington has so much to be disappointed in me. It's a wonder we were engaged in conversation this long without him pulling out daggers. Samuel Billingsley is one of his oldest friends and ex-Chief Deputy District Attorney. My childhood mentor was the reason I chose law school. Let my father tell it, and I chose to become a lawyer and follow the DA route as an homage to him. It must've busted Maxwell's bubble when I chose to work at Billingsley Law firm, which is family law. Samuel switched career routes a few years ago.

I scoff. "I work for your best friend."

He disregards me and says, "This robbery seems similar

to the one that occurred two months ago, Zariah. Therefore, the department must be on one accord. We must determine if this is an isolated incident, or should we have the public complaining? Princess, putting work first is exactly how I raised you. Or attempted to, rather."

My anger begins to rise. A vivid image of us arguing at the mall while I was pregnant with Natasha comes to mind. I'd been so livid that I'd fainted while snapping at my dad. Samuel's advice barely permeates as I force myself to suck in air.

I scale down my tone, yet my words still have a bite as I say, "Oh! It's an election year, isn't it? Let's not piss off your friends who want an office repeat and have helped you get to where you are. Do them a solid, since they're good as family."

I click the off button. Samuel walks over with a beignet. "We cannot allow others to ruin our mood, but we can allow food to pick it back up."

I laugh at him and shake my head. I'm still unable to fathom how Samuel and Vassili befriended each other. Samuel once warned me to steer clear of riffraff like Vassili. But Samuel gave my husband a chance and learned that he's much more than the last name Resnov. A name I once feared. Samuel is the greatest father-figure anyone could ever have. Sucks that I have a willing father, Maxwell Washington. He is *willing* to welcome me home with open arms if I divorce my husband.

Vassili comes up to me, holding out my shirt.

"Oh, you are awful. Made me wait until last." I shake my head. "This shirt is awesome!"

"That pose was supposed to be mine," Samuel says. "Love that photo."

"Sam helped me choose the photos for each shirt," Vassili says.

Each of our shirts is different, but all have Natasha's

gorgeous photo on them. Mine also has the writing, "The bully's mama." I recall the exact moment this photo was taken. Natasha stood for the first time, for a fraction of a second. Her hands were balled into fists. In retrospect, it looks like she was ready to go to war, cute face to boot.

As I slip the shirt over my head, Vassili kisses me. "Now, I have something for us all. The people who design my Karo gear and these shirts put together a video. You promise not to cry if I show it?"

I mock pout, though my eyes are burning with happy tears. "Oh, baby."

"Nyet. Don't 'oh baby' me, girl. No crying. Can I use the large screen you snuck and rented?"

My face breaks into a smile. "You knew I'd go behind your back and rent it anyway!"

"I did. Instead of it playing clips of a movie we have seen a trillion times, I have something in my email that I need to pull up."

The tears of happiness continue to swell in my eyes. My husband beats strong men into submission. He's someone to be feared, but he is incredibly thoughtful, too.

Vassili pulls me to him. "Girl, you better dare not cry." He kisses me hard on the lips again before walking away.

5

Vassili

I head over to the attendant manning the big screen. Children are seated before it, watching the scene were Princess Tiana turns into a frog.

"Where's Uncle Malich?" I ask Yuri as he catches up with me. Malich is all about family, so this will be the highlight of his day. He'd gotten his t-shirt and went to change, but I haven't seen him since.

"Igor was eating everything in sight," Yuri says of his brother. "Dad took him home. Anna is staying here with their kids."

I shake my head. Why does it take Malich to keep his grown ass son from trying to kill himself? The idiot, Igor, has diabetes. His wife, Anna, is good at keeping him on track. The attractions around my home must've kept her too busy with their children to watch her husband.

"Are you putting that video on now?" Yuri asks.

The email app on my cell phone pings with a new

message. I start to click on the one titled "Baby video," when I notice a new email, the title in all capital letters.

FRANK GASPAR.

I'll never forget the name.

The sea matched the pitch black of the night. My heart rate was at a resting pace as I jogged through the sand. My gaze narrowed, a dark figure stood at the stairs that lead up to my Venice beach house. He stood in the shadows of the wooden pillars, blending in well with the stairs. Pretending to be oblivious, my eyes shaded somewhat, I caught sight of a badge. It was one of those "to protect and serve" motherfuckers.

With a hard frown, I played stupid, continuing at my current pace.

The outline of a baton went to his side. In the last second, the cop lifted it, saying, "A message from—"

The baton slammed against my hands so roughly, it broke the skin on my palms as I grabbed it from my skin.

"You're gonna fucking hit me!" I whacked him across the head with the stick determined to break the damn thing. Then I gripped him by his neck, slamming him against a pillar. His feet dangled.

"What is it?" My wife's concerned voice breaks through the memory. Where did she come from? My gaze tracks across the wide-open spaces. Children are running around with cotton candy and parents are chomping on beignets. Balloons fly in the wind. I rationalize where I am.

Fuck, fuck, fuck, she can't know about him. Zariah and I have our secrets. Big ones. The first one went by the name Sergio. I murdered him slowly to get Zariah's attention.

In a fraction of a second, I've deleted the message without opening it.

Yuri catches the slight look in my eye. "Um, the email, maybe it was sent to me instead of you?" He catches on. "Don't worry, kuzen, let me check."

Zariah sighs, "Oh no, I hope you guys find it soon."

Yuri pulls out his phone, toggles the apps for a second and then says, "Nope, don't see it. Let's go make a call, Vassili. This is my god baby's birthday. The director had better come through."

Director? My cousin sounds like a liar. I shake my head, and we head to the sliding glass door.

I cock my head and he follows me to the downstairs office. Inside is memorabilia from my previous MMA fights. My first shirt with the Killer Karo symbol is framed above the back of my desk. I head to my leather chair, claiming it with a heavy heart.

"We need water?" Yuri asks, hesitantly.

I nod. From the inside of his suit jacket, he pulls out a bottle of Resnov vodka and opens it.

After he takes a swig, I grab the bottle and toss it to the head, downing much of it. Wiping my mouth, I ask, "Do you remember maybe two years ago or so, I called you over after a run near my old home in Venice?"

"Nyet."

"Some cop came out of nowhere. You popped him underneath the stairs to my home."

My cousin's eyes flit around with a bewildered look.

"You came over, whining about not sucking on your old lady's tits. And you capped him and hauled him away."

"Oh, you'd dumped the cop beneath the stairs by your home. I see those are the stairs you were referring to. I came and finished him because you were being a pussy?" Yuri tosses back.

"No Sherlock, I don't murder mudaks for no reason. I thought we'd figure out who he worked for."

"My dad," he says of Malich. "Your dad, or Zariah's."

"Ring-ring-ring," I nod, sarcastically.

"So, who did the cop work for, brat!" He grits out. "I was

going to start with his family. If the piz'da had a wife or kids, we would've known!"

My eyes bug out. "Are you serious right now, Yuri. You killed him before we could get that far."

"You were my accomplice."

"Kuzen," I gesture, "I'm not wearing a fucking wire, we need to figure this out!"

"Okay!"

I reach up and grab my cell phone from my back pocket, open the email account and view the "deleted" items. Then my thumb mashes onto the email entitled with the cop's name. I open it up for the first time, and as I suspected, the dead man is there. Someone exhumed his body, and in the photo, the stiff is near a muddy area. A close-up photo of his Los Angeles Police Department Badge shows that he's none other than Frank Gaspar. Now, I have two bodies to my name. I slide the phone over. Yuri glances at it in disinterest.

"So?"

"Some-fucking-body pulled him up from the LA River, and all you've got to say is 'so'?" I nudged my tense jaw at the phone. "Who did this?"

"Well, my pop didn't. I remember everything now, Vassili. You were ready to start pointing the finger at all of us. Malich didn't do it."

"Tell me something I don't know, Yuri," I grit through tensed lips. Although I still feel bad for thinking so negatively about my uncle, he's more than a father to me.

"It leaves one of two people. Vassili, we can't take out Anatoly, but we sure as fuck can go murder Maxwell Wash—"

I reach over and slam my hand over his mouth. "Don't fucking say that, Yuri! Not in my house. My wife is that bastard's daughter!"

Yuri pushes my hand away.

"And again, Vassili, I say 'so'?" He holds out his hands. "She doesn't like his ass anymore. One crooked cop off the streets is no sweat off my back."

"Maxwell Washington is the Chief of police. Bet your ass that the entire division would search for him, unlike they did for Gaspar."

"Can you stop saying his name?" Yuri inquires. "I'm not a fan of mentioning the names of people that I... you know."

I scoff, "But you have no problem adding to the list?"

"Better them than me, Vassili. You have always been luke-warm in this game. You're not in the Bratva, but you'll ask me to get some motherfucker in a basement to get the attention of a piece of pussy!"

I slam my forearm along his chest. All the air expires from his lungs. I growl, "Say something else, mudak! That was my wife. I never asked you to help me torture for anybody but—"

"Dah, and you got whatever the fuck that Italian guy's name was in the basement for Zariah, as you requested. I don't have a fucking problem with helping you. What I recall is, a certain someone telling me to stay the hell away from his woman in not so nice words."

"We weren't even married when I said that." I shake my head. "You're bringing up old shit? I have a wife for that!"

"Fuck, kuzen, you have always been *moy brat*—my brother! So, forgive me if I recall bullshit that still hurts. Then you call me to get rid of this cop, I do it. You call, I do it. Oh, and before this, you sent me to Atlanta to follow Zariah around like a stalker while she attended college. I still had my assignments for Malich."

"I get it, you were busy," I counter.

"Nyet! You don't get it. You say, *manage the fucking situation.* I had a long list of things to do. To top it off, I've managed your MMA fights, Vassili. Where the fuck is my

41

thank you for once? You know what holiday is in October?"

"Halloween," I grit out, testy.

"Nyet! Boss Day. Where the fuck is my Hallmark card, huh?"

"Yuri . . ."

"You call me inside to—to argue with me about some cop on the beat. This is my god baby's birthday! Fuck him, fuck that Italian dude, fuck you! I'd say fuck your wife, but I like her, and she's family now. You, I don't like."

I hold my tongue. Shit, I have another assignment for him. He'll be in Atlanta for me by the end of the week. He doesn't know it yet.

"Yuri, you are more than a fucking *brat* to me, okay?"

The fat ass almost smiles at the thought of us being brothers. "And..."

"And." I gulp down the tension in my throat. Shit, I've only said sorry a few times in my life. In all cases, it was to a female. Zariah, Sasha and my mother. "We will figure out who dug up Gaspar's body and emailed me."

"You said, we? *We work together?*" His eyebrow bunches, Batman and Robin, no doubt, permeating his mind.

I stand up. This fool is pushing it. I rub a hand over my face. "We work together."

"And if it's Zariah's father? Do we get to kill him? Shit, if you want to do the honors, I'll dump."

"Well, fuck that. We need to get back to my baby's first birthday. When that's done, we'll figure out if it's Washington or Anatoly that is behind this email. Afterward, we'll deal with it accordingly."

Zariah

These last two weeks have been a whirlwind. Watching Natasha as she bulldozed her smash cake was the highlight of it. Second only to me promising Vassili that I will always be there, regardless of how scary his matches can be.

We had a great time in Brazil after the fight with Tiago. His confidence brings me life. Yet my mind continues to roam to the night after the fight. When we went to the bar with Yuri and Taryn.

Sitting at Billingsley Legal, I click the top of my pen, listening to the rapid sound. My room isn't the biggest in the building, but it's cozy with a custom suede couch and pictures of my family all around.

I haven't been to work in over ten days. I'm fixated on how Vassili gave me the cold shoulder at the bar. We did have a fuck-marathon before and amazing sex afterward. *All I wanted was one dance!*

Usually, I can't get his hands off me, not that I'd ever want to. But every once in a while, I'm stuck with the cold shoulder. We can be out, holding hands. There are certain instances where he won't kiss me. But I swear, the second we are behind closed doors, he's all over me...

I guess I hadn't noticed it in the past couple of months because, hey, what can I say? We have argued about his return to the cage after the loss to Louie Gotti the Legion. The Italian fighter reminded Vassili of a man he murdered for me when I was seventeen.

We rarely talk about his parents. Damn, am I trying to make a connection here? He becomes distant after mentioning something despicable his father did to his mother. But Vassili hasn't talked to his father since the night we woke up married in Vegas. He told the bastard never to call again... So that leaves me.

I glance down at myself in a designer, peach-colored pantsuit. There's a little pudge to my stomach that I haven't been able to vanquish. But I always assumed that my after-baby hips weren't too big. Heck, ass and hips are a good thing. And the thug of a man that I married has never had a problem with it.

I need to work on this tummy. With that consideration, I click faster, unable to concentrate on work. At 175 pounds, I am twenty pounds over what I was when Vassili and I met.

"I trick people well with custom suits and high heels, but damn, not in the bedroom." My thumb moves in rapid succession with the pen.

Samuel pops his head inside my lilac-walled office. His thick eyebrows arch before he steps into the room, a cream suit pops against his dark brown skin. The smile on his face fades. "Why so down?"

"Nothing, nothing." I place the pen on the table.

He assesses me a second longer then offers a confident smile. Samuel says, "Meeting in a few. We have a new—"

"Uncle Sammy, that new guy is a dream," Connie sneaks into the office behind him. She's a redbone with a slim shape. She's also too starry-eyed when it comes to love. She's the woman I never wanted to be until I met Vassili.

"Who's this new guy?" I ask, aware that whoever he is will be the topic of discussion at Pokilicious. The sushi restaurant is our go-to once a week. She *got her entire life back* when she found out that the sushi restaurant hadn't poisoned me. Since finding out I was "just" pregnant, it's Connie's favorite place.

Samuel regards his niece with a look. "You two can chat about Mr. Nicks after hours. I don't want him meandering down the hall, hearing anything that can cause him to file for sexual harassment. Zariah, how's Mora?" His inquiry ends the previous discussion but presents an array of questions of my very own.

"She's... good... as usual," I begin. My eyes narrow in thought. Samuel always asks about my mom and he has the nerve to use her nickname, Mora, short for Zamora. Something my dad never agreed with.

"Tyrese Nicks," Connie butts into my thoughts. Her light brown eyes have a faraway look.

It's on the tip of my tongue to tell Connie to stop playing 'high school' and go for the goal. But Samuel sings about lawsuits again on his way out. He can half carry a tune.

"Counsellor, leave him alone before you catch a *case*," I joke.

With a tiny giggle, Connie leaves me to my own devices.

———

An hour later, Vassili texts me, "Lunch?"

Samuel has squeezed in the 11 am meeting, and I'm not certain how long it will take. Especially if he has to introduce "Tyrese Nicks." I bite my lip and respond.

I text back, "Make it late??"

Outside my office, an island of cubicles is in the center of the firm. With Billingsley Legal, a new and upcoming law firm, there is room to grow. Larger offices surround the perimeter.

I head to the conference room, chatting with my assistant, Lynetta, about an upcoming mediation for a case. I had started listing off tasks when I feel someone watching me. Not with hatred or anything, but with intensity.

Lynetta turns around as I do. She bats her fake eyelashes, saying, "Oh, Tyrese! Please let me know if you'd like any help until a new assistant can be assigned to you,"

The man before us nods politely at her, although his gaze never leaves my own. Tyrese is a cool six feet, with creamy brown skin. The brother has a serious pair of dimples. I can tell by the quality of his suit that he blazed through law school. Like me. More power to my black brother for coming from a well to do family.

"Welcome to the team, Mr. Nicks." I extend a hand.

"Zariah Washington, you don't remember me?"

"Resnov," I correct him with my award-winning smile. "Can't say that I recall…"

His brown orbs cloud at the sound of my last name. Shit, so now I can't place Tyrese Nicks. Nevertheless, what I do recall is the fear that slammed into my chest the instant Vassili told me he was a Resnov. Mommy didn't raise no fool. Tyrese is also aware of the name.

To make matters worse, he doesn't associate the name

with anything good. He stops eyeing me like chocolate pudding to sneer at the surname I married into.

Lynetta heads into the conference room, as he says, "Your father and mine were partners a very long time ago. I'll never forget how... inspired you looked when sitting in on the Sullivan case. You looked at Samuel ..."

The way you're eyeing me? With hunger?

"I heard my name," Samuel cuts in.

"I was reminding Zariah about Sullivan."

Samuel offers a grunt of disgust for the highly decorated cop who murdered four women.

"I was about to tell Ms. Resnov," Tyrese begins, gesturing to me. "That you restored my faith in the justice system during his extensive litigation process."

Mr. Dimples smiles at me and the lingering gaze of his slowly slides away.

Samuel pats his back. "It's trials like those that made me leave the DA office. Us defense attorneys need the police to assist with evidence. I had to gather evidence against Sullivan."

My mentor pats my shoulder as well. Damn, that was a dig at my father, who wasn't too keen on cuffing his own, but every word Samuel said was fact.

My phone buzzes as Tyrese holds the door. That's a saving grace. Like hell do I want him ogling my ass as we walked in. I step a few paces away and they head inside.

Vassili has replied to my text message with, "Meet at 2?"

Grinning, I send the 'thumbs up' emoji, then stuff my cellphone into my pants pocket. Skipping a meal will counteract my *extra* thickness. But lunch with my husband and daughter is the cherry on top of the cupcake I shouldn't have.

7

Vassili
Venice Beach
An hour earlier…

The Ukrainian who I've sparred with for almost fifteen years, Nestor, taps gloves with me. We're in the cage at Vadim's Gym. This is my first practice match since leaving Brazil. Adrenaline slamming through my veins, on my toes I go, keeping a tight profile.

"Tighter, tighter," Vadim, my trainer, shouts. "You're not the champ no more. Keep your chin down, elbows tight!"

My eyes narrow, although I keep them on Nestor. I cock my head for him to make the first move. He punches at my chin. Air zips past as I step to the side. I jab for his nose. My thirst for blood isn't lost on him. In a split second, Nestor saves himself from having to reconstruct his nose. His forearm zips out, tucking across his face. I issue swift body shots to his lungs. If it weren't for the gear he's wearing, his ribs would've been slaughtered. He lurches to the left and the right, with each hit. Catching his footing, he comes back with a right hook that slides across my chin.

"Stay on him!" Vadim shouts in Russian. "Vassili, pen him."

Then I catch him with a left, right, left. Nestor's knees buckle, he grunts and slides back onto the ground.

"C'mon!" I wave a gloved hand. "Get the fuck up. I'll put you down again, I promise."

"Don't get cocky," Vadim threatens, reminding me once more that I'm no longer the champ.

Nestor claws the ground. I step back to my corner, not taking my eyes off him. Like a yoyo, Nestor jumps up to his feet. He shakes out the pain and disequilibrium.

We go back on our toes, chins down, fists at the ready. I let him feel me out and imagine Alvarez, no Karsoff, that motherfucker will be my next match. Might as well have ambitions. Nestor tosses a low kick toward my shin. It's one of those filler movements to see where I'm at. Nestor thinks he's closing in on me, bringing me back to the clinch. The confidence is all in his eyes. He reaches low and targets my chin. My hands press the back of his neck, bringing his chest forward. My knee slams into his gut. The padding along his abdomen saves him from the type of "knee" that realigns organs in a fighter's stomach.

"That's what the fuck I like to see!" Yuri shouts out from the seating area.

While Nestor rests, Vadim gives me the body ropes for conditioning. Today, my coach is gunning to break my body down until I'm resurrected. Newer. Harder.

An hour later, Vadim grips the back of my neck. "You are a beast! Your comeback is now, Vassili. Your grandfather's blood is on fire in your bones."

I dip my head at his compliment.

"Who am I murdering next?" My glare roams from him to Yuri. "I need a fucking date. I'm dying here."

Yuri's fat ass all but swallows the folding chair as he sits forward. "Alvarez's team hasn't responded—"

"Fuck Alvarez, I want Karsoff. Put that shit on the calendar so I can go play tea with my daughter already."

My cousin gives a huff as Vadim goes to the runner stroller where Natasha is currently sleeping. He smiles in at her. "Vassili, you got a win the weekend before last. Give people a chance to respond. And like you said, enjoy your beautiful little girl."

I grab the hand towel from Yuri, stretch it and pop him. "You, manage the fucking situation or I score my fights. Fuck the middleman."

"Oh yeah?" Yuri's voice raises until he looks over toward the stroller in concern. Nobody wakes my daughter. She has more guts than I do.

He whispers through gritted teeth. "You called Alvarez outstanding on your own two feet in Brazil. Now, you want to step over him for Karsoff? Everyone calls me stupid, though."

"Yeah, you are, mudak. Get me Karsoff or La—"

"This guy is out of his mind?" Yuri tells Vadim.

My coach glares at me while addressing Yuri. "He has aspirations. All he sees is getting the belt back."

My fist slams against my chest. "My motherfucking belt."

Vadim flicks my ear. "Close your cunt. Get the fuck outta here, Vassili. My other fighters love to talk shit when you stay a moment longer. And no matter how cute Natasha is, that baby is also meaner than a—"

"*Volk*—wolf," Yuri finishes.

"You're the Godfather, Yuri, and you say that of my child?" My face is hard but my thick accent rings with laughter as Vadim agrees to his metaphor.

I grip the handles of the stroller and head past the workout gear.

"Yuri, anything on the email?" I ask him.

He shakes his head. Throwing a thumb over his shoulder, Yuri asks, "You want a ride? I'm parked in the alley."

"*Nyet.* I parked a few blocks away. Natasha loves to watch the singers and dancers and shit, and I'll get a little cooldown."

"Fuck? Kuzen, you haven't worked out enough?" Yuri asks, pulling a candy bar from the lapel of his suit. He laughs at me, then shakes his head.

While Yuri heads toward the back of the gym, I start for the Venice Beach exit.

Outside, the sun blazes across the beach. Not one spot along the coast is left as families and couples enjoy the beautiful summer day. I start for the trail, picking up a jogging pace. Off in the distance, a young Michael Jackson wannabe is gathering a crowd. My baby girl will wake up soon. This is how you wake up a bully without getting into a world of trouble... music.

The boy, panhandling about twenty yards away, has the moves to boot.

The umbrella is shielding Natasha, but she kicks out her foot. Her baby shoe somersaults into the air. She's awake.

"Girl, do you know how much I spend on your shoes?" Tone playful, I stop to retrieve the expensive, stylish tennis shoe that Zariah always complains about. She purchases those ugly "stride" shoes, mentioning how they assist in walking. Our baby is too pretty for that.

The name brand tennis shoe is wedged into the sand. When I turn around, a man stands before the stroller, kneeling eye-level with Natasha. In a flash, I'm there.

"Who the fuck..." The threat is lodged in my throat.

A pair of eyes the same as mine smile back at me.

Grigor! One of my many little brothers barely fills out a power-suit. He looks ready for Wall Street, but here he is in Venice, California. I grip his lapel. "Why are you here?"

"No hug, brother?" The idiot still has a silly smile on his face.

"Daddy! Daddyyyy!" Natasha pounds a fist onto the table before her. Organic fruit puffs tremble with each hit.

"Aren't you a beautiful little girl." Grigor reaches out, and I slap his hand. He bares his teeth, shaking out the pain in his hand. "Vassili, you don't have to be so rude."

"Fuck You. Your cunt of a mother was such a simple piece of pussy, it doesn't mean you have to be —"

Grigor interrupts my comment with a dose of seriousness. "Vassili, dad wants to talk to you."

"Where's Semion?" I ask of my father's sister's son. Of all the damn kids Anatoly had, he only wanted me for the Bratva. And he only utilizes that ugly fuck, Semion, as his lap dog. There has to be logic in that because Semion is so fucking ugly, you'd have to be crazier than the devil to cross him.

"At the car." Grigor nudges his head to the side. Along the tiny one-way street is a Maybach. My cousin, Semion's enormous square face bobs as he leans against the side of the car. Inside the car, is the back of another head, which must belong to my father.

"You came a long way for nothing, *brat*," I toss over my shoulder.

It's 12:15 pm, and I need to shower and dress. Natasha and I have our routine. She takes a two-hour nap during my training, as well as during the drive to and from Vadim's gym. Usually, I play hard with my child in the afternoon to tire her out for the night. We'll be pushing it as it is to pick up Zariah by 2 pm.

Natasha is pointing to seagulls squawking in the water as

I jog past. At least she will get a good night's sleep. Now, I'll have to improvise to wash off all this sweat. Grigor's impromptu arrival throws me off my game for a moment, and I almost pass the street that I parked on. In Venice, with all the million-dollar homes and tiny streets lining the ocean, one could get lost. But I owned a home in the area prior to getting married and settling down.

I move the stroller off the pathway since the street I parked off, the sidewalk doesn't connect with the pathway. The wheels navigate over the sand then wedge into the earth's ground.

I ask, "Where you want to go for lunch, beautiful, huh?"

"Daddy, da-daddy," she slobbers.

"Oh, you're happy today, no teething?" I unlatch her from the seat, hoist her onto my arm, folding up the stroller, and then heft that beneath my other arm. "Daddy stinks, sweetheart," I tell her as she begins to slobber on my shoulder.

We head through the sand and onto the sidewalk. I lean the stroller against the front door of my Mercedes SUV, open the backdoor and place Natasha in her car seat. While climbing into my car, I glance back at my beautiful daughter and my mind is on the woman who made her so gorgeous. Zariah.

Forty-five minutes later, the sweat has salted against my muscles and my damp shirt clings to my chest.

"Dad's a fuc—Dad's a mess," I tell Natasha as I place her on my hip, and we enter the kitchen.

"Eat, eat," she growls.

"Yes, this is where we eat, but not yet, girl. Let me shower," I reply.

I'm a little too excited to hold a conversation with my

child. There was a time I could go days without talking. But that was before sneaking a peek at Zariah's pregnancy books. It taught that the more I talk to Natasha, the more vocalized and intelligent she will become. Becoming an MMA father like me is Natasha's destiny, but there will be times I prefer her to use her words and not her fists. "You want French fries?"

"Yeah!"

"Okay, baby girl, we will get those French fries, but don't fight me if we aren't at the restaurant soon enough."

I start down the hall to the front of the house where the double staircase is. My hand grazes the carved wood staircase when I hear a noise. *Someone is in my house!*

8

Vassili

M y eyes close for a fraction of a second as I process the past hour. I was convinced that the man in the Maybach being guarded by my dog-faced cousin was my father. Anatoly doesn't exit from hiding without heavy security. Hence, my assumption that Anatoly was in the backseat of the car.

A familiar scent hits me. It's of lemon, fir cones, and black currant. The scent is a favorite of Putin's and my father's. That thought forces my frown to deepen.

I kiss Natasha's soft cheek. "Don't play nice with grandpa," I warn, recalling the first time Anatoly came to my neck of the woods. We were at a daddy-daughter day at the park near our home. She was on a swing when three SUVs pulled up.

Zariah knows nothing about that.

She never will.

We enter the dining room. There's a China cabinet to one side, in the middle is a fortress of a table. Crystal goblets, silver chargers, and other trinkets have made this the perfect throne room. On each side of the lengthy, custom made table, three men stand. My eyes cut to their holstered guns. Then I direct my wrath toward my father. At the park, he was incognito with a red wig, yet wearing one of his usual colorful suits. Today, he swapped the bright blue suit for a canary yellow one, with an even brighter blue silk tie. Enough jewels are on his fingers to have him certified. Fucking idiot.

"Bring her here, bring her here," Anatoly clasps his hands together. "My little Chak-Chak," he says, having given Natasha the nickname. Chak-Chak is a Turkish dessert. Deep-fried and drenched in honey, it's also a staple with Russian tea.

"Cha... Cha!" My daughter trades teams instantly, chubby fists pumping in the air.

"*Moy syn*—my son!" Anatoly snaps at me. "Bring my granddaughter to me. I wasn't invited to her first birthday party. Have some common decency. Let's save the 'you're disappointing me' for later. Unless you're ready to agree with the only proposal on the table?"

"*Nyet.* I'm good at disappointing you. That's the norm for us," I snarl. Though I cuss in front of my child, I place my hand over her ear, the other is trapped against my sweaty ass shirt. She has this habit of picking up words that are said in emotion—or lack thereof. "Have I ever made it seem like I give a fuck about your psychotic requests?"

His hard eyes match my glare, and then they soften while he holds out his hands for Natasha. "Chak-Chak, are you walking yet?"

"A couple of steps." I turn to one of the men. "If those guns go from any of your waistbands, you're all dead."

The man's gaze falls to the floor.

"Pah!" My father scoffs. "Semion is about the only one of these fucks who doesn't care for your threats."

"Good. Make Semion your legacy."

"My nephew?" Anatoly considers the idea with disdain. His lips are set for an argument, but I place Natasha on her own two feet and take her hands. Again, I stop myself from telling her not to play nice. She's pressing off from her knees in an attempt to hurry to the piece of crap of a father of mine.

His praise for my daughter curdles in my ears. Though I cannot recall being so young, I remember my sister, Sasha. Out of all my father's children, Sasha and I had the same mother. Anatoly didn't glance her way much of the time he came over. No matter how hard I tried to make it up to Sasha, she chose the lifestyle my father got rich on. Drugs.

With my support, Natasha takes heavy, shaky steps down the length of the table to her grandfather.

"I like black people," Anatoly's words come out of nowhere. "Can't say this for your wife. Beautiful shape. Dah. Mrs. Resnov has a nice shape. But this girl, my Chak Chak is the perfect color."

My entire body tenses in anger. Anatoly isn't aware as he tugs out of his suit and places his arm next to hers. They're both a golden complexion. "Fuck, I could sunbath for days and not obtain this flawless hue. Girl, you are 24 karat gold."

Natasha laughs at his disgusting comments. My father holds out a velvet box. "Chak Chak, this is for you."

He opens it. The diamond earrings inside are ridiculously large. She'd tumble, attempting to walk with them in her ears. The moment he leaves, those go too.

I sit on the chair next to him and pull out my cell phone. It's almost 2 pm.

"Vassili," my father says my name in a testy tone. Shit, I

assumed he always took great pleasure in saying 'my son' to irritate me.

I toss the phone on the table. "You afraid I'll call America's Most Wanted?"

He's paranoid. Natasha stands in his lap and pulls out his handkerchief in a matter of seconds. Next, she goes for his tie. I smile as he gulps.

"Chak-Chak, too many people want to kill me. Not you, too?" He smiles at her, with a million-dollar row of veneers, Anatoly removes his tie from her tight fists.

"Cha... Cha... Daddy!" She shouts.

This mudak proceeds to gift her with all of his attention. "I have too many kids, sweetheart. Shit, you aren't even my first grandbaby. Doesn't matter Chak-Chak. You are most important. You belong to *moy syn*. You are the princess of the Bratva, yes you are." He laughs.

"She isn't the princess of the fucking Bratva, Anatoly." I sit back in my chair. "What do you want? I have shit to do."

With his tie removed, my father addresses me again. This time, the usual pure anger in his eyes is knocked down a few notches. "You and I have a business to run."

"Oh, you're going legit now? I may need a new manager if Yuri keeps slacking off." I am far from comedic, and my carefree stance slithers beneath his skin.

"How's The Red Door?" He mentions the lounge that I own in honor of my dearly departed sister, Sasha.

"Good."

"I see Resnov Vodka is still the prime seller."

"I have a contract," I grunt. "The family vodka is about the only legacy that I give a fuck about, Anatoly."

"Return my girls to The Red Door."

I shake my head, not even wasting my breath with a response.

"What do you want, Vassili? The last time I came to California, didn't I tell you that there'd be consequences for noncooperation."

My hand slams against the table. The sturdy wood splinters. "You do not threaten me!"

Natasha jolts, her cute little face puckering into a frown. And then she bursts into tears.

The men become tense. Each one easing his hand against the butt of his gun.

"Pull them out, and die," I growl through tensed lips.

"Chak-Chak, your father is a very bull-headed man. He is the blood of my blood. He will get passes, trust me, beautiful. No one in this world will touch a hair of his head or your head. Vassili treats me so . . . in ways that I wouldn't even mention to such delicate little ears. But you and he are my favorite people in the world. I could never hurt the two of you."

"Or my wife," I argue.

"Of course, Chak-Chak, your mother has a free pass too. What sort of man would I be to let harm come to her?"

Our eyes lock. This motherfucker murdered my mother.

"I had nothing to do with it," Anatoly reads my mind. "I loved your mother, Vassili."

Tears burn against my eyes. My knuckles are numb. I glance down at them. They are also ashen gray due to holding them into tight fists. My breaths come short, as I think about all the crap my mother was put through by this man. He made her weak.

I hated her.

I still have him to hate for it.

"Vassili, you removed all the girls from The Red Door. Make your father happy for once and return them," his tone is callous. "You've had ample time. No, you've had more time than necessary. I was sick for a while, so you have had more

59

time than necessary to stop being stubborn. Do it now, before *something* happens."

"Dah, I'm aware of the repercussions of my actions. If we weren't family, I'd be dead. If it makes you feel any better, Malich was the one who handled anything that had a connection to you. He ensured that the cunts were safe, and the rich old fucks kept coming. All the mistrust you have for your baby *brat* is bullshit. Malich plays into the rules where one must do what their parents ask, or their older brother, in your case. But I give respect where respect is given. Somehow, I can't recall a day in my life that I gave a fuck about you."

"Vassili," he breathes heavily, still cooing into Natasha's ear as she cries against this neck. "I tried so very hard with you. In the back of my mind, I knew that you and that other fucking girl were always so much like your mama. But they are both dead now," He says of Sasha and his first wife. "You are *moy syn*," he argues through gritted teeth. Then Anatoly's voice softens again as he adds, "Mine. Do right by me, *moy syn*."

I grab a tuft of my hair. "Sasha. Sasha was her name. *That other fucking girl* was not her name! Do you even recall your own daughter's name?"

"Daughters' names? Hmmm, I don't recollect many of them by name, nyet. Perhaps, that one wasn't mine."

There isn't an empathetic bone in my father's body. I arch an eyebrow and say, "So, I allow you to sex traffic your high-end prostitutes at The Red Door. What's next?"

"You head it, instead of Malich. I don't need my little brother, Vassili. I sure as fuck don't need my nephew. Semion gets a snug wee bullet to the skull when you become king."

"You'd kill your nephew?"

"Dah! Semion covets *your* spot." He stabs my bicep with his index finger. "Contrary to how you see it, all my accomplishments were for the benefit of my first child." He kisses Natasha's head as she snores softly.

"I've been thinking." I stare at him for a beat. "If we took this moment in time and dissected it. Tore it away from the image of the man who had my mother tied to a street sign and had a sign of vulgarities strung around her. If we forgot about the families you've had murdered, the whores you had strung out or gave 'the world to.' What would we have? Anatoly, what kind of man are you without power and fear?"

He rubs Natasha's back gently. The glare he offers warns that my daughter is the only safe person in this house. Blood is slamming through my veins. But I won't fight him. My child is here. There was a day when I would fight my father fist for fist, only to be stopped by multiple guns to my head. In his warped mind, me being his firstborn is my golden ticket to act like an over-privileged American boy. I can play the fool. Cuss him. Fight him. I can portray those Facebook home videos some people think are funny. Those stupid videos tear my fucking heart out because in another world, you respect your elders. But not Anatoly. He'll go toe to toe with me no problem. He'll let me push the limits.

Nobody else can. Malich will suffer. Yuri and Igor will be marked. I continue with, "So what kinda motherfucker are you without the team, huh?" I glare through Anatoly, discerning he had to have sent the email. It would be too coincidental for him to arrive so soon afterward. I'd ask him, but the mudak is a liar. "Who would you be without the Bratva!"

He bestows a loving kiss at the top of Natasha's head. "I'd be the kind of man who still gets shit done."

"I'll think about the bitches, okay?" I lie.

"Returning them to The Red Door?" His eyebrow cocks in hope. When I nod, he asks, "What's to think about? I've lost a mill a week, fucking with you for over a year, Vassili."

I growl, "Then you continue to lose money a little longer." *Until I speak with Malich and we come up with a plan to get rid of you for good.*

"I want out," Malich's response is amplified through the speaker of my car radio. "The moment Zariah kicked my old ass out of The Red Door—"

"It wasn't like that."

"It was," he chuckles for good measure. "She has balls. I love and respect your wife, Vassili. She's like me..." The confidence in his voice fades for a moment. No doubt, my uncle is reflecting on his late wife. "You've got a good girl. Gets shit done. I got the boot from The Red Door. You removed all the illegal crap. Now, I want out. Should've done it years ago."

"Dyadya," I call my uncle in Russian. My hands are tightened on the wheel as I head down the street near Zariah's job. "I can't put you in this situation. I'll sell The Red Door. Besides, the second we opened for business I had nothing to do with the place. I spent millions having it designed as Sasha dreamt." I almost laugh at the thought. "The constructor said the place would be perfect. And then I turned pussy and couldn't step into the place. Shit, you ran the day to day business and the whores until I bucked up enough to venture inside."

"I'm glad that you've been able to deal, Vassili." He huffs. "We've lost very important women in our lives."

"We have." I chew my lip, uncomfortable about the transition in subject. "Zariah made me get rid of them. Clean the place out, ya know? I still don't have much to do with it. That place was my dedication to Sasha, nothing more."

"You'll sell The Red door, Vassili?" He asks in the fatherly disappointment that I learned from him. "All because of Anatoly?"

I glance into the rearview mirror, Natasha is gnawing at her teething ring. "Yeah. Fuck him. I purchased that place in Sasha's memory, but my little sister will live in my heart."

"Vassili, your cousins and I will be okay. I play the part for Anatoly, and I promise you that I have never fucked over my brother. However, he has to understand that when he runs an organization, he either gains loyalty or fear."

I slap down the handle that turns the left blinker on. "Malich, I understand. You always say that there's no ruling with both."

"No, son, there is not. One day his men will turn on him. But the crew who runs his West Coast Operation won't allow him to do anything. We are Resnovs, Vassili. Boss of all bosses or not, your father won't harm any of us unless we have betrayed him. We've done nothing but retire. So what, it leaves a chair open in the big seven. Anatoly owns the big seven."

"But you have a voice."

"Did you hear me? All the mudaks sitting at the table have no say. The table of seven is bullshit, Anatoly rules. Do what you intended, tell the fool no for the umpteenth time. When our father, Anatoly Sr. ruled, only Resnovs had a seat. Now, two of them have been taken by billionaires. Not blood. Not the family! A fucking Italian roach has a seat."

"I know."

"Make him understand that you will not go back on your word. Keep The Red Door, when your glory days in the MMA cage are behind you, you may want to manage it yourself. Don't give it up."

Fuck, am I giving up? "Alright," I reply, sliding into a parking spot at Billingsley Legal.

I nside the building, we are made even further late due to the workers who stop to speak with Natasha. I can't take but five steps before another secretary or assistant says something.

"Oh, did you do her hair?"

"Yup," I reply.

"You are getting good at this."

"Thanks!" I respond once more.

"Natasha, you are the prettiest little girl in the world."

Another one says, "She's spoiled rotten, that's what she is. Pretty little doll."

My glare tracks above the cubicles to the far side of the building, where a man is standing at the door to Zariah's office. From this angle, I can't place his face.

I'm halfway to the room when Samuel comes from his office.

"Vassili, Natasha, some of my most favorite people."

I shake the man's hand, and he takes Natasha from my arms. "We still on for Sunday dinner?"

"Long as my steak is ready." I nod.

"Alright, I'll bring the meats, you bake the cake?"

I chuckle. Samuel is a fan of my Russian cake. It all happened due to Malich, his love of food started a friendly competition. I made Sasha's favorite cake for him.

"Not too loud, Sam. Nobody has to know about our arrangement. But as long as you haven't forgotten about how I like my steak, I got you. Now, this is getting cold" I hold up the lunch that I bought.

"You head on into Zariah's office. I think Natasha has a few more autographs to give out," he grins.

I turn to walk away. Damn, I can recall the day when Samuel Billingsley tried to get my cousin, Igor, to snitch on the rest of my family. Can't believe the same man gave me a chance with someone so important to him. Zariah.

The doorway to Zariah's office is empty.

At the sound of her voice, my pace falters. Her voice is too soft for my liking as she says, "Oh God. This is so good, Tyrese. Almost makes me feel bad for not recalling who you are."

"We have time to catch up," he replies.

"Yeah right, this place is very busy," she responds as I step into the room.

A black man is sitting on the chair across from hers. The mudak is entirely too comfortable in her presence.

9

Zariah

Where the hell did Connie go? The crew had ended up eating at our sushi spot. When Connie texted to let me know, I'd asked her to bring me kakinohazushi. Somewhere in the mix, Vassili texted me thirty minutes late, about how Vadim had run behind schedule with his fighters. Connie dropped off my food, but she had Tyrese with her. She knows I zone out when I'm focused on work. But she shared that she'd left her wallet in the office, so Tyrese bought the damn kakinohazushi for me. Now, he's made himself comfortable, refuses to allow me to pay him back, and is content talking about old times.

My stomach was growling so loudly a minute ago, that I set aside my typing and started to eat. I made a joke about wishing I remembered who Tyrese was to give him the opportunity to cough it up already. But then, out of the corner of my eye, I see my husband. First of all, Vassili has no right to look so damn fine while jealous. Secondly, well, I should be the angry one. Although, I can't while licking the sushi from my fingers.

My face brightens at the sight of him. With Tyrese's back to my husband, he takes that as an invitation to look at me like I've reinvented sex. Little does the attorney know, he's stirred the hornet's nest.

"Vassili, baby," I quickly mention his arrival and place a hand over my mouth. "Oh, you brought my favorite."

I gulp the rest of the sushi down my throat as Tyrese stands abruptly. Damn, my mouth smells like sushi as I rise and step around my desk to hug my husband. His tongue soars down my throat, and he kisses me in ways that make me lose my mind. Vassili's hand steers my lower back, aware my knees are weakening by the second.

As we let go, my gaze narrows at my husband, and then a fake smile plasters on my face. He couldn't fuck with my head like this when we were at the bar in Brazil? He couldn't dance with me? But now he can? Tonight, I'll have words for him!

"This is my husband, Vassili Resnov." I turn to Tyrese, "Vassili, this is the newest attorney at Billingsley Legal, Tyrese Nicks."

The men shake hands. I take the glossy turquoise bag with the words Flour Bakery scrawled on the side. One of my favorite bakeries.

"Nice to meet you, Mr. Resnov. I thought I'd bring your wife lunch, seems she was starving today."

Tyrese's word choice clears my mind of my anger with my husband. I know he didn't! I reply, "I actually asked Connie—"

Vassili gestures toward the door. "Good for you. You can go now."

Tyrese looks incredulous, as my husband dismisses him. He glances toward me.

But Vassili finishes him off with, "Don't ever bring my wife anything else."

"Don't feed your wife after she's *waited* an hour for you?" Tyrese inquires.

Connie must've blabbed about him running late!

Vassili rubs a hand across the bristles at his jaw. "You know who I am? You look smart enough to know, right?"

"I know exactly who you are," Tyrese says, voice dripping in disgust.

"So now I'll ask that you don't even address my wife unless it's business-related. That's a courtesy. Me asking you anything."

Tyrese grits out, "I understand completely."

I offer Tyrese one of those quick grins that warn him to leave the room. He backs up toward the door as Samuel enters with our daughter.

"This is her royal highness, Natasha Resnov," Samuel says. He appears well aware of the tension, but his goofy demeanor permeates the tiny area. "She's a fighter like her father. It took a while for me to gather both of their respect, Tyrese."

"Thanks, Sammy." I take my daughter from his arms. He whispers something to Tyrese that finally revs the man's engine. They leave my office.

Vassili stands toward the window at the far side of my room, arms folded.

"What the hell was that all about?" I ask.

His pitch-black gaze glowers in my direction. "That *mudak* wasn't flirting with you?"

I roll my eyes at the rhetorical question. "He's new."

Vassili bites out, "If the new guy ever flirts with you—"

"What are you going to do, Vassili? Allow his opinion of you, of *our* last name, to be solidified by your choice of actions?"

My husband offers one of his unicorn smiles. Meaning, he only uses a grin when very angry or miraculously happy. "But of course, my beautiful wife. You know from experience that I could give a fuck what most people think of me."

"I appreciate how unpersuadable you are."

"Good. Now, eat your food," he orders, nudging his square jaw to the bag.

"So, what was with the kiss, though?"

"I'm done discussing the matter with you, Zariah." Vassili grabs the bag, and says, "Natasha, you ready for your sparkly cupcake."

"She needs to eat lunch," I tell him.

"The bakery is next door to McDonald's. We stopped for French fries, too. The little bully refused to wait." Vassili steps closer to me, lust consuming that sinfully dark gaze of his. He smiles at Natasha. "Tell mama to be nice to Daddy."

Our daughter begins to pull my hair at that.

"Natasha, don't be a bully like your father."

I place her in the corner where there's an ABC-123 patterned carpet along with toys for her to play with.

Vassili is right behind me when I straighten up.

"The door is open, and Natasha is..."

"Busy," his mouth finds my earlobe and sucks softly against it.

"You were being an asshole. And yes, for some reason that man wanted to play the fool with you. Vassili, were you stuck at Vadim's?" I stare him straight in the eye.

"Oh, your friend brings you lunch, and now you're paranoid? What kind of shit is that, Zariah?" In a snap, Vassili stops arguing to help Natasha right her balance.

I scoff, "My friend?"

"Dah."

My hands go to my hips. "I don't know that man."

Vassili grunts. "Seems like he knows you and was about to take you down a trip to memory lane had I not arrived."

"First of all, Vassili, I didn't even get a chance to correct him, you came in like a barbarian. Second, this is my place of employment."

He waits for a moment, and I know Vassili isn't a fan of clashing with me. Sometimes I have to force him to talk due to him not wanting to be disrespectful. I think Anatoly ruined him for how to deal with a wife. But his hard eyes glare into mine.

He growls, "You are my wife. Act like it."

My lips are bunched together, they begin to twitch in annoyance. Random thoughts bounce throughout my brain. Was he at Vadim's Gym? Am I getting too fat? Or was he with my child somewhere else? Why did the obstetrician say that I'd lose weight while breastfeeding? Hell, I got hungrier!

And now I'm standing before this hoodlum of a husband of mine. Intuition tells me he lied. Love warns that my man would never cheat.

Vassili presses his hand against my cheek. His palm fits along my jaw and he caresses softly. "I never have a problem when men look. You are so fucking beautiful it's to be expected," he says before planting a kiss on my lips. His mouth lingers on mine. "I'm a dick, okay?"

I eat every single word.

"But I don't like that guy. You can tell me later how the two of you know each other. For now, can we eat?"

I murmur, "Yes. Albeit, I don't remember where or how I know him, Vassili,"

"Okay, let's eat before I get really hungry." That deep baritone of his always blows my mind.

My pussy lips jolt, crying for action. I nod and move away from Vassili. Stopped by his hand caressing mine. He pulls, and I follow, pressing my body against his rock hardness. The words are lodged in my throat to say we are still at my office. With the door open to boot, but my mouth waters for him again. This time, the kiss is succulent.

His tongue licks mine, it's purely animalistic. I can't help but imagine it's his cock as my tongue swirls around his.

"I will never let you go," he murmurs in Russian. I remember the first time he said that. He'd annihilated Tiago, and he was searching the crowd for me. I ran around the throng of people, with Taryn's help to catch up to him. I'd cried and made promises. I must've made a monologue of apologies for leaving during his match.

Just like when he'd made the declaration the first time, my heart swells with love. Every ribbon of doubt—my weight, my concern if he has a wandering eye—it all shreds to nothing. All that's left us and the untouchable love I have for him. And the love he consumes me with.

———

Later in the afternoon, I was assigned a new case. The depth of it didn't spare a single moment to seek out Tyrese. He'd said his father and mine worked together. My father's oldest partner on the beat was Ronisha's dad. She and I were friends growing up. So, I've yet to make the connection. During the Sullivan trial, when Samuel put away that crooked cop, nobody in the world existed. It was the first time I felt disgusted at my father. I saw myself in my mentor's custom suit as a top litigator. Justice reigned that day.

Needless to say, the conversation I need to have with Mr. Nicks will have to wait. I'm on the bicycle in our Home gym when my phone rings. It's my mom.

I place the call on speaker. "Hey, I've been waiting for you to check on me."

Her voice isn't its usual happy self. "Well, I had my shows to catch up on."

We've been frick and frack for the last few weeks.

I groan, "Aw, you miss me already? Martin is going to kill me if I trick you into moving back to Los Angeles. Why didn't you FaceTime me, so I can make *faces* at the dysfunctional daytime soaps you love?"

"Humph," my mother replies. For a moment, it feels like I'm carrying the conversation until she asks, "How was your first day back?"

"Mama, no talk of work, it'll slow me down. Besides, I'm on my treadmill now, desperate to undo the last two weeks."

"Not sure if I ate more in Brazil or during Natasha's birthday party." She lingers, "How's Sammy?"

"Sammy who?" I chortle, aware of exactly who my mom is referring to. At the birthday party, my mom and Samuel disappeared for a while.

"Don't play with me, child."

I stop laughing. "Alright, what's with this 'Sammy' business? Vassili's running around calling him Sam like they are from the same gang. And here you go, mom, calling *Samuel*, Sammy. I could've sworn he was my mentor during college. Furthermore—."

"Girl, how is *Sammy*?"

Vassili enters the gym, leaning against the doorframe.

"Guess what, my mom is checking in on Samuel," I mouth as Vassili tells me to hustle. How fast does he want me to peddle? I pay him no attention and address the woman who raised me. "To be honest, Mom, Samuel is well. You saw the man 48 hours or so ago. But let me remind you, during your divorce with dad, you all split friends. Sammy was reverted to previous ownership, meaning Dad has sole custody."

Now I can hear her smiling through the receiver. "Zariah, don't even. I can ask about an old friend. Since the death of his first wife, Sam has gotten married every few years, anyhow. Nobody is *studying* him."

"Studying him." I shake my head at her old-school choice of words. "Hey, tell me about the new guy? You were gone for two weeks, Mom, which is forever for such a new love."

Her voice becomes muffled as she says, "Zariah, the timer went off. I'm making a soufflé, can't let it overbake."

A familiar feeling of worry tightens my shoulders. "Mom—"

The call cuts.

"What's wrong, Zariah?" Vassili asks.

An image of my father yanking his belt from his pants flashes my mind.

He was getting ready to beat... my mother.

"I don't know," I mumble a response to my husband. Breathing heavily, I endeavor not to speak my doubts into existence. Jesus, don't let it be. "I have another mile to do."

"Don't work too hard, girl." His eyes shut in that sexy way that makes my regimen falter.

Vassili exits the room. The conversation I finished with my mother reruns through my mind again. Her tone was a bit lackluster. But what person is happy after returning from vacation?

As a child, I had my job cut out for me in getting her to laugh. When I jokingly mentioned that she and Samuel cannot be friends, she seemed to laugh about it.

After mentioning the mystery man she's dating, she got off the phone with me way too quickly.

I started to dial my older brother, Martin, but quickly think better of it. It's past 10 pm. My mom has late-night TV shows and some faceless boyfriend to keep her company.

However, Martin and his wife are on a tight schedule with their children.

I head out of the gym in search of my husband, to talk over this uneasy feeling. I need Vassili to tell me I'm imagining things or worrying too much. Our bedroom is empty so I call out for him.

"In the kitchen," he replies.

10

Vassili

The conversation between Zariah and her mother is still on my mind. There's too much on my plate to spy on my wife. But when I walked past the gym, my wife had placed Ms. Haskins on speakerphone. The list of crap I need to review with Yuri faded from my mind. Her mother's tone was missing something.

That reminds me, when was the last time I checked on her? Though Zamora was with us for two weeks, I have learned to make it a habit to ensure that everyone my wife loves is safe. With Zamora's frequent travels to see Natasha, I hadn't put much thought into her ongoing protection. Zariah's brother, Martin, is a family man. With a nine-to-five, a wife and three kids to take care of, I suspect he isn't always available for Mrs. Haskins.

While warming my borsch soup on the stove, I pull out my cell phone and dial Yuri.

Instead of hello, he says, "I'm still looking into the email, Vassili. Oh, and Alvarez has sent the contract. What aspects do you want to negotiate? You're not Karo the Champ, so we can't have everything."

"Fuck you too, Yuri. You act like you're being run like a lap dog," I argue. Although I'm about to add more to his plate.

"Did you review the contract? The fight's in Atlanta, mid-July."

"Nyet, I didn't look over that shit. Alvarez can suck these hairy balls, for all I care. He's nobody." I stir the copper pot as the soup begins to simmer.

Yuri sighs. "You say you want to fight. Then you hound me about when, where, how. Shit, Vassili, the venue is enough to offset the bone he's willing to throw you."

"Look, I want you to go to Atlanta."

"We can fax back the contract."

"Nyet! Yuri, listen, this is about Zariah's mom." I grab the remote and turn on the television, which is near the sliding glass door. The low hum of a comedy sitcom sets my nerves at ease. Can't have Zariah overhear what I'm about to say. No need for her to worry. "Yuri, I think she might be getting punched around—"

"Ms. Haskins?"

"Dah, idiot! Zariah only has one mother."

"By who? When?" he growls.

I pull the phone away from my ears. I'm getting fucking investigated through a loudspeaker, here. After my cousin ceases with the dramatics, I say, "Zamora has a boyfriend. I don't know his name yet. But she and Zariah Facetime during every single call except tonight. When we were on vacation, she didn't mention much about the bastard. Now, they were talking, and Zamora blew her off. They're too close for that shit. Something isn't right."

Silence dominates the moment. Then Yuri replies, "Alvarez's camp is gunning for the Center Stage Theater—"

"Why you bring him up now, huh? Yuri, we're talking about Zariah's mother and you bring up that disrespectful mudak."

"Vassili, breathe," he cuts in. "We'll go check out the venue. Center Stage is in Georgia. We also see about Ms. Haskins. Best case scenario, she makes my cookies, we come home. Worst case scenario, you handle the piz'da who's crossing the line with her. I toss out the trash."

My eyebrows pull together. "What the fuck? I gave you an assignment."

"Less than 48 hours ago, my God baby celebrated her first birthday," he drones on. "Her father—which is you, shithead, said we—as in the two of us—"

"Yuri—"

"*We're a team.* So, teammate, should I get the tickets so that *we* can go check on her, or will you?"

I sigh heavily, recalling the whining Yuri did in my office that day. He's right, I need to handle this myself. "Fine. You get the tickets, though."

An evil chuckle crosses over the receiver. My fat cousin asks, "Should I bump him? You dump him?"

"*Nyet!* I'll handle the shit myself. Nobody touches a hair on my loved ones, Yuri."

"That's what I wanna hear, kuzen."

"Baby, what's wrong?" Zariah murmurs from the entrance to the kitchen.

Fuck, what do I tell Zariah? I hate it when she worries.

11

Zariah

Vassili looks up at me, almost as if he didn't hear me enter. From my view of the kitchen, while walking down the hall, he'd been discussing something serious. His brow is furrowed, his sexy lips set into a frown.

"Yuri," he says, tossing his cellphone onto the marble countertop. "He sent me a bullshit contract from Alvarez. He picked the venue for the fight. I've never had a match there. I'm paid pennies. But Yuri believes I can make more than enough money selling my shit there."

A new day is upon us if my husband agrees to the proposal. Vassili talks way too much shit, so I ask, "You're agreeing with the contract?"

"I'll go to Atlanta, check out the scene. See if it's worth signing the papers."

My heart sinks. We just got to a good place. How will we stay there if he leaves so soon? "Aw, can't you virtual tour the venue online? I hate when you go away. We got back from vacation but you're already on the run."

"C'mere," he orders. The sexy thickness of his Russian voice seems to wrap around me from yards away. He says, "I'll have to fuck you so hard you can't think until I return."

"Oh, that defeats the purpose of me staying home and going to work." I grin at him while heading over. "One day, I won't allow you to fuck me into submission. Sex doesn't make everything better."

"Pft! It's either I fuck you brainless or feed you borscht?" he jokes.

"My palate isn't fit for that soup, and you know it." I tease.

He grunts. "I know exactly what your mouth is fit for."

My tongue plays across my bottom lip as I stop before Vassili. I inhale the scent of him. It's perfect, the epitome of masculinity. Fresh woods and patchouli dance into my nostrils. My eyes close as I breathe in more of his strength.

"To your knees, Zariah," he commands. My orbs dance. We're standing in the middle of the kitchen.

I obey his request and kneel in front of him. Vassili's long, venous cock flops out of his blue sweatpants. His dick is king and looks as if it weighs a ton.

"No hands, girl." His hard voice plays somewhere between sinful and sultry. "I bet that mouth of yours is so fucking wet, as wet as that succulent pussy between those thighs."

My body melts. My pink tongue darts out to lick the lengthy curve of him, riding along the wide planes of his dick. When I suck him down my throat, Vassili's groan is like a tiger's deep, low, powerful rumble.

"Mmmm," he groans.

My mouth holds him in a snug fit, slides up and down the entire length of his cock, wetting him even more.

He taunts, "You want to use your hands, don't you?"

I sigh as a response.

"*Nyet*, beautiful, not on me. You can fuck yourself if you'd like."

A trickle of honey flows from my pussy. I bang his cock against my tonsils, in a repetitive motion. My tongue compels his seed to fill my mouth, to slide down my throat. I need his cum to satiate me.

"Zariah, fuck yourself." His command slams through me.

My hand slips into my runner shorts, past the soft hairs of my pussy and right to my swollen lips. When my palm caresses along my clit, my throat moans against the head of his cock. I start to gather a rhythm, my fingers pressing deep inside my ocean, my mouth a second ocean for his dick.

"Stop, Zariah."

My brown eyes rise, glancing past ridges of tattoos on his six-pack, up to his chiseled jaw.

"No," I murmur, taking him further while taking myself further.

"Stop, beautiful. This is about me blowing your mind, Zar." He takes my hand and I arise. "You're sweet, right?"

"I'm so wet..."

"Let me see how sweet you are." Vassili grips my wrist and brings my hands to my mouth. His tongue flicks out, mine does too. I taste the juices that I've made for us, he tastes them as well. Then his mouth meets mine in a kiss. We did this the first night he took my virginity. This is our thing.

"Fuck," he says, "Tastes like water. You ready to go crazy?"

I've hardly bobbed my head once, and Vassili has me over his shoulder. He carries me into the den, where a bear fur rug is in the center of the floor. Vassili lays me down and has me out of the sports bra and shorts in a second.

"Wai... wait..." I try to grab at his mohawk. His head is dodging for the sweetness between my thick thighs before I can remind him that I just finished biking. My left leg gets to jerking as his tongue spears inside of my pussy. His tongue is thick enough to get the job done and zero in on my g-spot.

"Vassili..." I scream, coming all over his tongue. My first orgasm slams through my body, leaving my eyes shut. His tongue continues its onslaught, spearing at my sensitive areas as I ride over a hard wave of desire. A falsetto pierces from my lungs, and I come down from heaven.

He doesn't offer me a moment's reprieve as he licks away at the cum squirting out of me. My skin goosebumps and burns as Vassili rubs a hand up along my waist and to my breast. He's furious in his eating, and my hips have risen off the floor to match the vigor of his tongue. While he snacks greedily on my pussy, he tweaks my nipple. My pussy must taste like the world's best pie because he's working another orgasm to the surface. I can feel it rising from my toes, my leg tenses again. I grab at the fur beneath me and scream aloud.

"Shit, damn—shit, damn, motherfucker," I give a low growl. My body begins to cave into the floor, but Vassili lifts my ass up and continues to dig in. "Shit, da-damn, mother-fucker," I shout again. *Wait a minute, that's a D'Angelo song.*

The crooner was losing his mind with rage in that song, and I'm losing my mind with desire all the same. My fist clamps onto Vassili's wavy brown hair as I slide my hips around. It feels like his chin is pressing against my asshole as he keeps it lifted.

He must need air.

Why exactly did I think of that?

My lungs are burning. I realize that, hell, I'm the one deprived of oxygen.

Vassili eats my pussy until I'm weak. Tears stream down my face, and I have clawed at the bear fur until it's probably missing patches.

"Vassili," I cry, whimpering, sniveling, the works.

"Dah krasivaya," he responds in Russian. I'm beginning to learn. That means "Yes, beautiful."

Vassili climbs up my body and I plant my face along his neck. His face is soaking wet, I grab his jaw and plant a kiss on his lips. My tongue darts out, licking my sex from him.

"Baby, that was so good, I'm gonna cry now. I'm sorry, but I have to cry." I break out into a sob. My husband hates it when I'm drawn to waterworks, and I rarely am. But the dam bursts and tears fall as the glistening, wet lips of my pussy whimper with proof of my craving.

He screwed me seven ways to heaven, and it's over. I sob. This husband of mine. He's murdered for me. He tears men limb from limb. And he loves my body. He cherishes me. How did I deserve this? The tears of joy rattle through me.

"Don't cry," he catches a tear with his mouth, kisses and licks it away.

Vassili places himself between my legs, pressing my ankles over his shoulders. I shiver in anticipation as Vassili lines his cock with my pulsating entrance. He leans down, his face burrowing between my breasts. He blows hard while letting his head wriggle around.

I laugh through the tears. "Fuck me, Vassili," I beg. The wait will be the death of me.

"Your pussy is soaking wet," Vassili growls while gliding his hard cock along my throbbing labia. I arch my hips, ready to aim for my target. Before my pussy can swallow his cock, Vassili's abdominals compress and relax in rapid succession. He offers a boisterous laugh that reminds me who the hell is boss.

"I hate you, Vassili," I reply. I might not be in my right mind, but I'm begging like a 90s R&B singer, he should screw me crazy.... Crazier than I am now.

"You hate me, eh?" Vassili holds his heavy dick. He then

flicks his wrists, and the crown of his cock thumps my clit. "You hate me, girl?"

I hiss, shit that feels good. My hands fist the bear rug. Now, the damn thing probably looks like it could use a couple of bottles of Rogaine.

Vassili's cock slams into me. The muscle stretches my insides. He works his hips back and forth, each drive goes deeper. Tilting my hips as much as I can, I channel my inner yoga and welcome the depth of his cock. Sweat slicks across his muscles as he goes out and back in. My tits shake up and down, and I snatch more fists full of fur while screaming. My throat is becoming raw, and I like the sound of my sultry Beyoncé voice. Or maybe I'm delusional enough to think so. But hell, I like the sound of my voice. I may or may not sound like a strangled cat instead, as Vassili's cock pummels my g-spot.

And… then… Vassili… sits there. His cock living within my wet walls. The rock-hard strength of his shaft is loving the mold he's made. My breaths are ragged, my throat is dead. He starts to rock into me slowly.

The tears have returned. He kisses those away while his cock inches in and inches out. Ten inches in, and ten inches out. My lashes flutter, kissing my cheeks. I'm aware of every second of it. And I die within his arms as he screws me slowly.

When we come together, I'm delirious enough to say, "Baby, get me pregnant…"

"Dah, girl. Let's get you pregnant again." His eruption warms my pussy, filling me all the way up. He kisses me hard on the lips. We chuckle together as his hard muscles sag into my body.

It's almost midnight, way past my bedtime on a weekday. My body is glued to Vassili's as we lay in our sex. Somehow, he ended up on his back, my breasts are against his muscular chest. The Kremlin from Moscow is shaped in a crown on his hard muscles, and my index finger follows the trail of it. The artistry still knocks me out. Although the menacing wolf head atop it still scares me. The lifelike design seems to leap from his skin.

I mumble the Latin words, *"oderint dum metuant."*

Then my finger trails down to his X-rated matryoshka dolls.

"You know what," I murmur, half asleep.

"What?"

"I want all these breasts off your back?"

"What titties?" he responds, thick Russian voice sounding too sexy. The bastard knows what I'm talking about.

I roll off of him. "Um-hmm, you can cover that shit up with my face."

Vassili sniffs. "All you have to do is ask."

I lay on my side. Vassili turns to spoon me now. Once more my eyes close slowly, but I jerk my head awake. When I do, my sight adjusts more. I glance around me at the chocolate brown fur patches on the ground.

"Damn," I pause. What the hell was that? Okay, so maybe I didn't sound like Beyoncé meets Billie Holiday, but instead like RuPaul. Because whoever murdered the dead bear on our floor, couldn't have sounded sexy while doing so.

"What is it?" Vassili's cock begins to stiffen against my ass cheek.

I wiggle my buttocks, and then say, "Besides me sounding like I have balls between my legs, look at the floor."

"Girl, if you had balls between your legs, you'd be dead."

Vassili glances around. "Fuck, between you and Natasha, I can't have shit."

He settles down and I punch him softly. The joke wasn't too far from the truth. "You ready to go to sleep, Zar?"

"Nope. Yuri texted that you guys leave tomorrow. I hate missing you like crazy, so I'll stay awake."

He kisses my forehead. "But you're falling asleep."

"I'm not."

The arched eyebrow he gives is enough to rest his case. I sigh heavily. "Remember when I was eighteen?"

"Shit, I fucking thanked God you weren't jailbait. You were the hottest piece of ass I'd ever laid eyes on."

I pout. He kisses the corners of my lips until they curve into a smile. "Talk to me, Zariah. You never stop thinking."

"I was thinking about all those years I spent giving you a hard time."

"Seven," Vassili cuts in.

"Thanks for the reminder." I offer something of a smirk, but my eyes are getting heavier. "Let's look at those old videos."

"Again?"

I grin. They say the way to a man's heart is food, but Vassili and I are still cultures apart in that regard. So, I know how to motivate, uplift and love my husband. I reply, "Yes, again. The videos from the matches when you were still a cocky asshole."

"You mean when you were cyber-stalking me, girl?"

The playful banter that we delved in during the phone calls while I was in college kicks it up a notch. "Nah, I mean before you had the title that you'll be snatching again soon enough."

He grabs my face and bruises my mouth with a kiss. "This is why you are my wife."

Vassili
Atlanta, Georgia

Z ariah and I stayed up until the sun peeked over the Hollywood Hills. Natasha and I sent her to work with her favorite Dior sunglasses and a most beloved canister of coffee. After picking up Yuri, who has no reservations with wearing a suit in the heat, I dropped off Natasha with Taryn. Then we head to LAX.

Now, it's late afternoon, when the guy at the car dealership escorts us to a supercar. My knucklehead of a cousin squared away everything. I take the keys, and we get into the shiny red Acura NSX.

I glare at the idiot. "Shit, kuzen, God forbid Zamora is being smacked around. How will we look knocking him around and driving away in a $150 thousand-dollar car?"

"First of all, if Zariah's mom is being treated wrong, we're gonna kill the fucker and drop him in a ditch with his car. And yeah, $150 'kay.' Should we have upgraded?" Yuri asks. His ugly mug is set in a smirk.

"*Nyet.* This is good. I need speed." I rev the engine. The rental car representative gives a fist pump. Fucking idiot. I can't open this bitch up, not in this area. I sure as fuck don't need a cheerleader to get 'er wet. The purr is perfect. I head to the exit, saying, "When I need to think, I'm on my Harley. Seeing that there's no way in hell that your fat, ugly ass is fitting on the back of one, this is how we roll."

"Speaking of ugly mudaks. Did you narrow the list down?" he asks.

I stop at the final checkpoint and hand over the rental car agreement for it to be stamped. "Narrow what, Yuri? There's only Anatoly or Maxwell who'd send that email. Why?"

"Dah, why?" he parrots. This is exactly the reason that I don't work with people. I delegate shit. Let my cousin tell it, he's been butt hurt and we have to be a 'team.'

I grab the stamped paperwork, hand it to Yuri, and make a smooth getaway. "My dad wants The Red Door. And that mudak will do anything to get it. Maxwell, man, I don't know. She tried to invite him to Natasha's birthday. The bitch didn't even come to see his first grandchild by his only daughter. Of course, that mudak would gain satisfaction from locking me in jail, but why now?"

"Dah, it doesn't connect—doesn't make sense, Vassili. Zariah's father waiting this long? Brings new meaning to trying to catch you off guard." He pauses for a beat as if he's becoming uncomfortable. I glare at Yuri and he adds, "Okay, okay! The timing is right for your father. I can see Anatoly pushing you into a corner for defying him, but he'd make a request."

A sea of yellow cabs mixes with various Lyft and Uber drivers while we all navigate toward the airport exit. I breathe heavily. Is this idiot listening to anything I've said? "Anatoly made a request."

Yuri eyes me in curiosity.

"The Red Door, fuck, keep up."

At the stoplight, I GPS the location to FTNT (Fight Nite) Radio Station. It's a local subsidiary of the Ultimate Fighting Championship (UFC). With talk of an impending match between myself and Alvarez. Although I'll make the mudak sweat before I sign that contract, FTNT has invited me for the afternoon.

Yuri licks at his fat chops saying, "Maybe we should eat something before we—"

"*Nyet*," I cut him off, following the navigation app. "We're late enough as it is. Tell me something . . ."

"Something," Yuri barks back, annoyed over a lack of food.

"How do you manage me, yet are unaware of various timeframes of the shit that you've scheduled?"

"I can't think when hungry," my cousin grumbles.

An hour later, we're in the break room of FTNT. Long tables are stationed throughout, with more food than even my cousin can consume. With fingers shining with chicken grease, Yuri pats my back. "You are my favorite."

I shake my head.

"Eat," he says in Russian.

"I'm going on in a few minutes, and I had a shake for breakfast. Got to have my mind clear. You know these piz'das love asking about old shit."

"Do them like you did Alex Brown." He mentions one of the most famous television sports commentators. It never fails. Alex comes at me with something that Yuri or I told the producer was not to be discussed.

They all do it.

I'll be asked about Gotti if there's enough time.

They'll ask, *'How do you feel about having your belt snatched away by The Legion? Why didn't you tap out?'*

Yeah, dumb shit like that. *I can do this.*

A young Japanese woman with a microphone in her ear and a clipboard in hand pops her head int to the breakroom. She asks, "How're the sliders?"

With his cunt full of food, Yuri winks.

The mention of the tiny cheeseburgers got us in here. Not sure how I'm going to get Yuri out unless he eats it all while I'm on the radio. He traded in and up for barbecue wings and tacos.

"Good," I reply to her since Yuri is polishing off more food and is unable to speak.

"We're ready for you, Karo." She grins at me.

I head to the door. Yuri washes the food down with a coke. "I'm getting nervous," he says.

I flip him the bird and head out. The reverse psychology he attempted crashes and burns. But I take a deep breath and head into the studio.

Through the glass walls, I see that the media room has enough contraptions to keep Natasha busy for days. Before we enter, I'm introduced to the radio personality, Lizelle "Black Zombie" Jackson. He's Atlanta born and bred, and at age 40, this is his new normal, cauliflower ears and all.

"Killer Karo, I've waited too long to have you in the building. I've been a fan of every match."

I nod my head. "Last time I saw you, you were taking down the War Machine."

"You saw that?" His voice grows heavy with surprise.

"Saw it live."

"Bruh, it was him or me."

"Close match." Shit, I'm warming up. They like when you say more. I'm not there yet.

"Yes, sir, close match. It takes guts not to tap out to any

old submission hold. Most of these youngbloods will..." he *taps* the table, "soon as you touch them."

I chuckle at that.

"Look, I'm not one of those motherfuckers that spring shit up, but can I ask about Gotti? You've probably explained it a thousand times before. But my fans want to hear it from your mouth. Will you give me that?"

"No problem." I respect his gumption. Lay it on the table from the start. I prefer that to a weasel popping in without asking.

He explains the dynamics of the show, the length of time we chat, commercial time and that its satellite radio. No censorship. It seems like only a few minutes have passed when the Black Zombie introduces my arrival.

"What up, ATL? Every time we talk, it seems I'm introducing someone great. But truly, truly, I tell you, we have greatness in the building. None other than Vassili Killer Karo Resnov. So, hit those chat buttons. Call in. Leave us a question. I promise to give you all the *deets* on Karo, past, present, and future."

We chat for a while about my younger years. Surprisingly, Black Zombie has my stats down.

"Karo's looking at me like I'm a creeper or something. He didn't know I'm a true fan. I've been representing long before Juggernaut was put to sleep. That ankle-lock submissive on The Hauser—still the talk of the town. He had a big mouth, you shut that shit down and tore into that leg!"

"I remember that." Still not many words, but fuck it, I like this guy.

"The beef you two had during promotions was priceless. You're one of the few youngbloods who doesn't talk shit without backing it up."

"I had my days."

"Shit, you have 25 TKOs, 10 subs and 2 losses. I only have

one problem with that, Karo." He pauses for effect. "What took you so long to get with the submissions? Those TKOs under your belt had folks shitting bricks, but the subs! Man, the submissions! Oh, look here, Arnold from Decatur, he's agreeing with me. When you started getting into submissions, the world...it was a more beautiful place."

I laugh with him. "I was a hothead back in the day. I always thought power was in here." I punch my fist into my left palm.

"Karo, buddy, they can't see you. But I'm telling y'all, there's some serious bromance going on here. The question screen is lighting up like no other time before. There's no way in hell we can take them all." He pauses to read one.

I take the lead. "Do you all want to know where I'll be fighting soon?"

"Shit, yeah. Half these calls are about you taking down Alvarez, and this is his hometown. I'll have him on the show in a week, hope he isn't listening now." The Black Zombie chuckles again.

"I might be fighting him," I say, not all that interested. "I'm ready for Karsoff."

"Yesss, I see where your head is at. Karsoff is a few steps away. We need you to get that belt back. Karsoff, if you're listening, I bet Karo can put you to bed by—"

"Damn, put him to bed? That's a little bit much."

"Then lay it all out, Karo. How will you take down Karsoff?"

"He has a big mouth, but I shouldn't. Should I..." I joke.

"TKO? Come on, Karo, you're better than this."

We laugh like two motherfuckers drunk off Resnov Water.

"Then I'll hit him with a triangle choke."

"Old school?" he says, processing it slowly. "Simple. Classic. You might want to bash his head in, KO 'em as your old

MO. He'll be studying all the ways to get out of the triangle choke. Although, it will shut his mouth real good…"

A fter the show, The Black Zombie and I chat for a while longer. I get his address to send him some of my beloved vodka, and Yuri takes the keys so we can head to Ms. Haskins' home. I glance through my phone. Zariah has texted me nonstop throughout the broadcasting.

She's sent me the following texts:

"Aw, my baby is playing nice for the first time!"

"Black Zombie is right, that ankle lock was gangster."

"He should be your hype man. I swear he was auditioning to be one of your hype men."

Then her last text message isn't induced with happiness, but sad emojis. She'd sent, "I miss you already…"

After a shake of my head, I call her up. My wife answers promptly.

"Beautiful, I'll be home late tonight. You still sleepy?"

She yawns on key. "Yes, all day. But that won't stop me from waiting up for you."

"Don't wait up, girl. I'll wake you."

"I bet you will. Get to the airport with plenty of time, Vassili."

"I love you, Zariah." Yuri parrots my words. I turn away from my childish cousin, and my voice lowers as I reply, "*Nyet*. I love you more, *krasivaya*."

I hang up. Yuri makes kissy faces and I wave him off. "That's how you are with Taryn," *In your case, you shouldn't be…*

The housing track that Zamora Haskins lives on is full of summertime action. Kids roam big front yards getting into some good old-fashioned summer trouble.

A mixed-race boy, wide shoulders, running a scrimmage. He stiff-arms everyone on the opposite team and makes a touchdown.

"Yuri, I've gotta fucking have myself a son, soon," I grumble, considering Zariah's recent agreement to get pregnant for me again.

"Maybe you only have a girl?" He reaches over to flick my ear, but I catch his hand, twisting it swiftly. Yuri gasps, "I'm driving, piz'da!"

"Who's the cunt now?" I let his hand go in enough time for him to switch gears and turn the corner.

He parks in front of a tan home with slate stone. Having only visited on a few occasions, I'm sure Zamora's cooking kept him from his usual forgetfulness.

Ms. Haskins opens the front door with sunglasses on. Who wears sunglasses in the house? It's hotter than my home, St. Petersburg, will ever be. But she could've slipped the shades on while stepping out.

Instantly, I'm floored at the idea that a man placed his hands on my wife's mother. I put my hand on the roof of the passenger door and get out of the car.

"Boys, I didn't think you'd have time before your return flight." She hugs us and invites us in. "Yuri, your cookies—"

"Oh, Ms. Haskins. You didn't!" He's somewhere between 350lbs and six-foot-three yet his voice dips. Yuri becomes a pock-faced kid as we head to the kitchen.

Zamora walks faster than a rookie's knees lock up after a busted nose. Too anxious to stop. She removes mittens from the drawer and opens the wall oven. Back to us, she asks, "Isn't your flight home any moment now?"

"A little later," Yuri offers. "Allow me," he adds, taking the mittens from her. Shit, we Russians can be nice when it behooves us. We sure as fuck will figure out why Zariah's mother is flighty and shrugging off people. She's one of the most genuine people I know—and I can only count the rest on one hand.

At a loss as to what to do, Zamora Haskins still hasn't removed the sunglasses from her eyes, yet continues to chatter. "I wish Zariah had come with you all. I know we came back from vacation, but I have missed time with my baby girl."

"Can you do me a favor?" I finally speak.

"What is it, Vassili? Why aren't you guys eating these cookies?" She asks, picking up a cup towel to wrench around her fingers. "Sheesh, you aren't even mentioning healthy eating when I make the peanut butter cookies."

"Please." I gesture to the shades. "Remove those."

Her head tilts somewhat. Zamora touches the shades as if she forgot they were on. "These?" she squeezes.

"Please, I'm worried about you," I reply, wishing to God I could look her in the eye, so she understands I'm real.

"Worried?" Zamora waves a hand. "You are a good man, Vassili. That's all that I ask."

"I will continue to be a good man."

Yuri places the cookies on a marble block on the counter. The day his fat ass doesn't eat any food in his wake, an apocalypse has dawned. Zamora knows that. Her gaze slides back from me to Yuri.

"What's the name of the guy?" he asks.

"He didn't mean anything by it." Her tone is hardly audible. She turns away from us, passing the time by removing a spatula.

"Ms. Haskins," I speak up.

"You-you've started calling me Zamora, Vassili." She

purses her lips. Embarrassment creeps up her throat as she leans back against the counter. "Will you tell Zariah?"

"If it happens again. But we need his name. Let me see your face if you don't mind," my hard voice is as soft as it's ever been. An image of my mother begs to take me under, but I stare at Zamora. I can see my wife through her. And we all know, I'd kill for my wife.

"Zar will be disappointed. The day the two of you married, I-I stopped considering Maxwell. Stopped praying that he'd change for me." Ms. Haskins' lips bunch together as she gingerly removes the shades.

Fuck, she isn't sporting a typical shiner. Her eye is swollen completely shut. I rub a hand over my jaw.

With a grunt, Yuri's face goes to the ceiling. He strides away for a moment, huffs and then comes back. I'm shocked still. Though I've witnessed my father and his goons beat my mother and sister a thousand times, this kills me every time. This world is fucked.

Voice barely audible, she speaks to the ground, "He got angry. First, when I went to Brazil. Then I forgot to tell him I'd be in California the weekend after for cutie pie. He thought we weren't serious—*I* wasn't serious enough about us. Like I had been traveling with someone— another man."

God, if there isn't something in me that wants to hug this woman and tell her 'thank you' for striving as long as she did. She took punches to keep her children from growing up in a broken home.

I blink and realize that Zamora Haskins-Washington is not my mother.

But fuck it, she birthed the love of my life. I have too much respect and too much to thank her for anyway. Though I can't hug her because I'm not a hugger. I speak through tensed lips, "We won't tell Zariah. What is the man's name, please?"

"Matthew Overstreet."

Mr. Overstreet works at the Commerce Trade Center. The woman in the lobby said he always leaves his office around 6 pm. A quick check of his Facebook account indicates that he hits Crunch Time Gym at 6:45 pm, only to leave an hour and a half later. He's a man of routine and loves to catch the female trainers in his selfies. A regular old douche bag is what he is.

It's 8:15 pm, and I have to hand it to my cousin. With his assistance, I'm seated in the back of Matthew's car, hands clenched tight. Yuri is in our rental, parked a few rows away. I think about my mother. She gave up on Sasha and me, leaving us with one of Anatoly's women. But earlier today, I recalled the time she had more than herself to care for. She'd taken up sanctuary in a nunnery when I was a tot. Most of the time, I keep the woman who birthed me from my mind. Why not? She gave up. But I begin to fixate on the past. Darkness surrounds me and life in Russia pulls me under...

The lights flash as Matthew hits the alarm button. My stone sculpted outline is lit up and instantly drowned back in darkness. He slides into the front seat and doesn't seem to recall that he left the radio on. It's not now.

He shuts the door, and his finger is poised for the 'push to start' when I speak. "Don't."

Matthew's shaky hand yanks away from the button. He grabs for his keys to hit the alarm. I snatch them first. Stiff as a board, he leans back against the driver's seat, eyes closed. His breaths become ragged as I settle into the middle seat in the back again.

"Go ahead, Mr. Overstreet. Turn around. You're thinking I will rob and not kill you if you don't see me."

He lifts somewhat and tugs out his wallet, tossing it over his shoulder in my general direction. Without so much as moving a muscle, I listen as he stutters, "There's at least four-four hun-hun... hundred. I... I can take you to the bank."

"Money is the least of my concerns."

"Okay." He shakes out.

"Turn around, Mr. Overstreet."

"Nnnoooo," he replies.

"I'm here because you touched the hair on the head of someone I love. Have a good look into my eyes. Know my motherfucking face, because if you ever see me again—" I cut myself off. I'm not Yuri, shooting them, bagging them, and tossing them ain't my thing.

I bark, "Turn the fuck around!"

"I'm trying!" His stiff neck cranes. Moments pass by as he believes that the lapse in time will result in me having a change of heart. When he makes eye contact, my glower pierces through his. The bitch can't seem to choose an eye to connect with.

"You like to hit women, Mr. Overstreet?"

"No!" The word expels from his mouth without so much as a stutter. "I love Zamora, I'd never hit—"

"You're lying to me. Isn't it the universal norm that people hate liars?" Damn, I sound like my wife, "universal norm." "Have you seen me before?"

His eyes close, then he nods. "Yes, sir. You're a fighter."

"You piss yourself?" I ask. "C'mon, I smell fear from my opponents in the cage. I can smell piss, too."

"I'm sorry."

"You are sorry."

My fist slams into his face. My knuckles crush against bone. His forehead will always, and forever be indented in that precise spot.

I get out of the car, and zig-zag around the cars to the lane Yuri's parked in. The driver's side window zips down.

"What the fuck you doing, kuzen? We can't leave the body," his voice lowers.

"He's alive."

"Should I?" He starts to open the door.

"No," I shake my head. "He won't hurt a fly in the future. I'm sure of it."

"But that mudak touched your mother in law, Vassili," Yuri replies through gritted teeth. "You're a fucking Resnov, put him down!"

Ignoring him, I reply, "Now, they have matching eyes. Or in his case, his face is—"

BEEP. BEEP. BEEP!

My narrowed eyes turn toward the Chrysler. That fool is slamming a hand down on the steering wheel.

"Oh, should I manage the situation?" Yuri snarls the sarcastic line that I'm usually telling him. Then he goes off in Russian about "getting it over with."

"I'll handle it!" I cross back to where Matthew is parked.

Through the rolled-up window, his eye that isn't swelling widens. He slams his hand down onto the steering wheel again. I try the door. It's locked.

"Open up," I order.

He sounds less like a pussy when shouting, "Fuck you!"

Seriously, does he believe a door will double as his savior?

My fist slams through the window, glass shatters down around my feet. Matthew ducks as even more shards spray toward his face.

A woman who so happens to be walking by with earphones, jumps. Must've noticed me from her peripheral.

"Don't mind us. He beats women," I tell her.

With wide eyes, she jogs off to her car.

Matthew dives for the passenger seat. I reach through, grip his muscle shirt and yank him through the window.

"You wanna act like a bitch, huh?" With my left hand snatching the collar of his ultra-tight shirt, I yank him toward me.

There's no way Matthew's gonna run from this ass beating. My right fist sprays like bullets against his face. My target is crushing his skull in where I had smashed his forehead before. Then I jab at his neck and ribs. Matthew slams against the trunk of his car. He's not as heavy as before. I realize I'd been holding his entire weight.

"What happened to all those personal training sessions?" I pause. My left fist clenches his shirt. His legs do a two-step before me. "Save yourself, Mr. Overstreet! Fight me, dude. I'm a few inches taller than you. Fight me!"

He tries to speak, blood splashes from his mouth. "I'm sorry…."

"Fuck you and your apologies." I let Matthew go. His feet clop like a horse, noodle legs hardly able to sustain him. I hit him with a right, then a left elbow that sends him back in the other direction. Then I finish him off with another right. Instantly, an image pulls me under.

"Don't look, my child," my mother shouted. Men walked past, they spat at her and called her the names that were strapped around her neck.

"Shluyukha—Whore!"

"Piz'da—Cunt!"

My eyes were glued to her pale white face. I hadn't seen her since she ran off on Sasha and me. Though I was a kid, I never felt so small. I stared at her, my face devoid of any sort of emotion. My father stood next to me, a freshly rolled cigarette in his hand.

Anatoly kneeled so that we were the same height. "She left you, Vassili."

"You beat her, Anatoly! Look at these people. They laugh at a

Resnov! Who laughs at a Resnov, huh?" I argued with him. Not a single hair on my chin and I shouted at my father. "You let them beat her!"

"I didn't beat that bitch," he puffed air in my face. "She's no Resnov. Just the first woman to have a child for me."

"Let her down, now!" I hollered. The people along the street laughed. His men cackled as I pushed at my father. I was a skinny motherfucker, and yet my mind didn't make the connection that I couldn't put him down. That I couldn't kill my father.

I started toward her. My fingertips grazed the straps binding her to the streetlight. Anatoly grabbed my shoulder and pushed me to the ground.

He glared down at me. "I said, she's no fucking Resnov."

"But she's my mother."

"Vassili, what happened to 'fuck her?' She left you, didn't she?"

My ears burned in shame. Yeah, I said it. A bruised ego rots the mind, makes you forget.

"Just go," My mother said, her face was too carved and disfigured to smile, but I felt it. She wasn't mad at me. I'd forgotten about her first attempt to get away with Sasha and me, a few years back.

Back on my feet, my arm swung out. Anatoly clasped my small fists, then tossed me to the ground again. Pain slammed through me as he kicks my ribs. Then his team jumps in, kicking me in the back.

"You hit your father over this cunt?" Anatoly finished his statement with another kick. I rolled into a tiny ball, with the sound of my mother screaming for them to stop.

A siren is screaming. Had to have been for a while, because my eardrums ring. The top of my head is being pushed down like protocol requires when being tossed in the back of a squad car.

"What the fuck are you doing to my kuzen!" I can hear Yuri shout from behind me.

With the handcuffs behind my back, I'm cranking my

neck much like Matthew did a few minutes ago. Through the rearview mirror, Yuri can be seen as resisting arrest. It takes four cops to get him down to the ground. He fights, arguing that Mr. Overstreet, who's on the asphalt nearby and hasn't tried to get up, is at fault.

13

Zariah
Earlier in the evening...

After work, I fight traffic to Taryn's house to pick up Natasha. Vassili and I don't believe in childcare while our daughter is unable to articulate her feelings. Taryn's father is in government and with a Somali model for a mother, she has it made. Natasha's godmother spends her days shopping and is a godsend in times like these.

I stop at the gates where a hut houses a security detail. Aware of my car, the guard opens the gates while waving me through.

Taryn lives in the pool house behind her parents' mansion. Hopefully, she and Yuri marry one day, so after years of hoeing, he can make an honest woman of her.

The front doors of the mansion open, and I veer to the left to get around a humongous cement fountain. It's Taryn's mother, who rarely is ever home. The model is at least half a foot taller than her husband. They make an odd pair. His tiny eyes peer straight through you. She's ultra-slim like Taryn, and her looks blow her husband away.

"Hi, Mrs. Takahashi." I start to get out of the car.

"Hello, Zariah." She grins. "Taryn is in the house with Natasha. Come on in."

Mrs. Takahashi offers one of those 'loose' hugs. The kind glamorous women offer, so as not to ruin their Italian silk dresses or smudge their perfect makeup. Looking at Mrs. Takahashi reminds me to hold my head much higher, and to work these stilettos.

"How is your mother? Your father?"

How is my father? Hell, somebody tell me. Damn, Mrs. Takahashi and I haven't crossed paths in years. When I was younger, realizing that my father had a crush on her was a shock to me. I mean, dad and I share the same rich dark skin. I love the skin I live in. But my mother is as light as they come, and the women who came after! You can toss cooking grease on them and kick them out of a safari in Africa; there'll be no frying. I didn't think Maxwell could look at someone of our color. Mrs. Takahashi has us beat with beautiful jet-black skin. One time, Mrs. Takahashi wore a silk dress, much like she is wearing now. Her tits played a game every time she strutted from hip to hip. It made me see *red* when my mother didn't backhand his ass across the room like he used to do with her—for some trivial reason.

"My mom is well, happy," I smile.

"And your dad? I'm never on the same continent for more than a week or two. I miss those barbecues."

"Tsk, my father is operating an entire police station while I do me." I place my hand on my hip as Mrs. Takahashi stops.

"Hmmm, Maxwell ran the police station on Grand Avenue before becoming Chief." Mrs. Takahashi smiles. "I take it Maxwell isn't playing nice. Does what you're saying have something to do with that delectable man you married?

I owe you a wedding gift and a baby shower gift . . . and I would assume a first birthday gift too."

I wave a hand. She owes Taryn a sweet sixteen gift and more. Mrs. Takahashi is like one of those good friends where no matter how much time passes when you come together, she can read you like an A-B-C Book.

I reply, "Yup, Dad and I are estranged. My father believes that I settled..." *Fell and am slumming it, rock bottom.*

Her lips set into a line for a moment. "Fathers want the best for their daughters. I defied mine and married a Jap—shhh, can't say that out loud. My father spat those words when I did not return home to marry the man of his choosing. There's nothing like a father's love. At times, it's overwhelming."

My eyebrows rise. That's the understatement of the century.

Mrs. Takahashi waves her slender manicured fingers. "Maxwell will get over himself. Now, come in. We have had so much fun with Natasha."

We pass a foyer. Vibrant pink designer bags make the black-and-white checkered tile virtually invisible.

"Goodness," I reply as she tells me to watch my step. "Sounds like you just got my baby's first birthday covered."

"You know me, shopping with a medium is so much better than sending gifts," she purrs.

I can hear my daughter's happy banter. "Daddddaaaa, Daddaaa, momma, Fry!"

"She can eat," Mrs. Takahashi says as we enter their grand kitchen.

Taryn is zapping a frozen corn dog in the microwave while Natasha sits on a highchair. "Girl, this baby wants French fries. I ate the first corn dog because she kept turning those fat cheeks to me."

"That's how she rolls. Can I trouble you for a few Cheetos

or cheerios?" I grin. "Vassili did his best to get Natasha interested in his raw fruit smoothies. She acted a plum fool one
day because someone I know bought her McDonald's. Now,
she's a junk-food eating monster."

"Look at me like that, if you want, Zar." Taryn bites her
lip. "I'll continue to blame McDonald's on my cuddles."

"Your cuddles?" Mrs. Takahashi asks while heading
toward the door to the wine cellar.

"His name is Yuri Resnov." I squeeze in. "Your daughter is
in love." My smile warns that I hope they're in love. In high
school, I had to remember more than one of Taryn's
boyfriends' names from one date night to the next.

"Oh, another Resnov. Hold that thought." Mrs. Takahashi
opens the door and disappears down the stairs.

"So, are you in love?" I corner Taryn as she grabs another
tiny, plastic plate for Natasha. My hand on my hip doesn't
intimidate her one second. She skirts past me, opens the
door to the refrigerator, which looks like the rest of the
walnut wood shelves. Taryn grabs condiments out before
pulling the hotdog from the microwave.

"How many times will you ask me that?" she finally
inquires.

"Until you tell the truth."

"Yuri isn't the type of man to fall in love with, Zariah," she
murmurs. Without glancing my way, she places her index
finger over the breading of the hotdog to make sure it isn't
too hot.

"How can you say that? You see what Vassili and I have?" I
gasp. "You encouraged me to run after him during the match
in Brazil! Taryn, you and Yuri are magnetic."

Mrs. Takahashi comes from the cellar with a bottle.
"Pinot Noir. And I've seen what Zariah has with her
husband. It's is pure hotness, needs to be on the cover of a

magazine. Can that be said about my daughter and 'Mr. Cuddles?'"

"Mom," Taryn huffs while placing the plate in front of Natasha, who promptly pushes it away. "Please, sweetie pie, eat it," she coaxes, holding up the corndog. My child playfully paws it away. Had it been me, Natasha would have slapped the damn thing across the room.

Taryn's mother and I wait for her response. She's always been overly confident when finagling a few men at a time. She has a habit of bragging about the men wrapped around her finger. Instead of doing so, Taryn opens the refrigerator, retrieves a string cheese for Natasha. Then she makes a beeline to another cabinet and grabs the stim of three wine glasses.

"What's wrong, Taryn?" I ask.

"Yes, do share," her mother adds. "If you care enough to give the man a nickname, Cuddles, then you must like him. Although, I can't say that I'll ever be attracted to someone who's... cuddly as in a lot of muscle?"

"Mom, you don't understand. Heck, when this heifa says Resnov, that doesn't even ring a bell, does it?" Taryn offers a pathetic laugh while heading to a table with plush, studded chairs.

"No, can't say that it does." Mrs. Takahashi uncorks the bottle as I sit down. She's drop-dead gorgeous and oblivious.

"Their family has been known to dabble in ... mafia stuff," I speak up. Taking my drink, I down a good, long sip.

"Zariah, they *are* the Russian mafia. They're the fucking Bratva!" Taryn gulps the wine down until the glass is no longer stained blood red.

Mrs. Takahashi shrugs. "When I was younger, I fooled around with a Kenyan drug lord. Might not have been a good thing to do in retrospect, but dangerous sex is...daring, passionate."

"Vassili isn't with that." I stumble into the conversation. Why did I speak up? Her mother is glamorizing a lifestyle that I don't condone. So, I sit confidently in my beliefs.

Taryn glances at me.

"Well," I start, "is there something I should know?"

"No, Zar. Yuri says that his father has slowly cut down on assignments. Malich no longer controls the San Pedro port. But your husband is the son of," she makes an elaborate gesture. "Girl, your husband is in it for life, no matter how much he busies himself with MMA."

I huff. "You believe that?"

"I do."

"So then why do you continue to fuck with Yuri?" Oops, I forgot that her mother was sitting here. She doesn't say a word, just waits for a response as well.

We receive a lethargic shrug. Taryn pours more wine into her glass. "I can't stop. Yuri treats me like a queen. His cock is monstrous."

"Ohhhh," Mrs. Takahashi claps her hands.

I roll my eyes and ask, "When you feel—cock aside—that life is too much, what will you do? How could you string him along?"

Can't stop my brain from diverting to lawyer mode. Removing my feelings from the equation, I glance her directly in the eye. "What about Yuri's feelings?"

"Yuri would never hurt me. When we connect, the world stops, and he isn't participating in any illegal activities. Shit, I got that from you, Zariah. It's a job and a half for him to assist Vassili in securing matches, Karo merchandise and everything regarding the MMA world. But there will come a day when Yuri and I can't be together. And you ask if I love him. Nope, I can't do that to myself."

With a lump in my throat, I finish off my drink. I'd asked her about Yuri's feelings, and she chose not to share. I try to

107

focus on the smooth taste. Damn, Vassili never ceases to remind me of how I overthink. The dynamics of my relationship with him seem similar to Yuri and Taryn's. Heck, she implicated that I'm in a worse predicament. I watch the red liquid fill my glass while ruminating over the time I assumed Vassili was Malich's son. I wished to God he wasn't. The joke was on me. I fell in love with danger.

"Okay, Taryn, I can't fathom how easy it is for you to play with your own heart. Nevertheless, if you don't love him, you don't love him."

"Stop being so closed-minded, damn," Taryn says. "My parents are in an open relationship. They dole out their time to whomever they please. We're good at not allowing our heart to become involved. Don't judge me, Zar."

I stop myself from squirming in my seat. Mrs. Takahashi is too close for me to give off any social cues. "Taryn, my only endeavor is keeping you from breaking your own damn heart. No, Honorable Judge Resnov here. You're right about one thing, though. Vassili would kill me if I considered adding another man to the equation. I'd only be obliged to do the same if the tables were turned. We are jealous people."

"You're like your father," Mrs. Takahashi says. "There's nothing wrong with that."

I all but scoff. Like hell can I be compared to my father. Instead of acknowledging and redirecting Taryn or her mother, I share what I'm certain of. "My heart isn't set up to be played. So, I married Vassili through good times and bad times."

"The two of you are too young and in love to know a thing about bad times, not yet." The model shakes her head.

I beg to differ. This past year has been hell. "Well, I may not have the ability to predict the future. Regardless of the cards stacked against us, I'll be damned if I spoke vows into the universe about my love for Vassili in vain. Shotgun Vegas-style wedding or not, I'll snatch him up myself if need be."

Taryn starts to chuckle. "Heifa, you need to be in somebody's courtroom, with all of that arguing. Are you pregnant?"

My glass perches along my lip. Am I? "No, I can't be pregnant."

"You two aren't screwing?" Mrs. Takahashi asks, causing me to sputter on my wine.

My mother and I have always had a good relationship. When Dad had a crisis at the LAPD, Mom and I hit the road on the weekends. And my older brother, Martin, inundated himself in high school sports, so he was only there when we needed him. But it was nothing like this level of openness. Taryn and her mom wait on bated breath.

"We are definitely screwing," I respond with a giddy little chuckle. I should've declined the second glass of Pinot Noir since I can hardly drink my husband's family's liquor. Thinking about him, I calculate that it's going on 8 pm in Atlanta right now. So, I text him a quick reminder about his late flight tonight…

14

Vassili

"Can I have my phone call, *now?*" I ask the guard as he places me into the community cell. The scent of dirty balls and breath clogs the crowded area. To one side of me is a man wearing too much eyeshadow, another dude who smells like he bathed in rum, and my cousin. The processing took a few hours. Each time I asked, those mudaks acted like I spoke the words in a foreign language.

The guard locks the gate without so much as offering me a glance and heads toward the security door.

"Who? Vassili, who the fuck will you call?" Yuri asks from behind me.

I let go of the bars and turn around with a snarl. For a man who's familiar with the backseat of police cruisers, the cops had their job cut out for them. Shit, this motherfucker is the reason they treated us with extra force.

My death glare must not penetrate. Yuri continues to taunt me with, "Who, Vassili, huh? Who the fuck are we gonna call? My dad wants to be out of the game. He can't make demands without collateral. Igor is sick as usual. This mission isn't for you know who." He mutters my father's name beneath his breath as if I've ever been in a predicament that Anatoly fixed. There'll never come a day. He finishes with, "You gonna call Zariah? How about she chews you a new asshole? Ha! We sure as hell aren't in our area to make demands."

Rubbing the back of my neck, I take a seat on the cement slab. "We'll be out soon."

He stands in front of me, still flapping his jaws with, "Our return flight leaves at 11 pm, Vassili."

"You, get the fuck out of here with all that arguing," I roar. "If I say we're leaving soon, we are. I need to make a call."

Air swooshes past my nose as Yuri slaps a hand toward my face. Although deadly with a gun, my cousin is no fighter. Despite being older, Yuri turns into the pesky little brother I never knew I wanted when we bump heads. I toss a stiff finger at him. "Do it again, you'll be on a gurney like that motherfucker we left."

"Oh yeah?" He glares down at me.

I stand to my full height, chest puffed out, lips sneered. Yuri is as menacing, in his coal gray suit and shiny shoes. The crowded cell is divided in half as the guys smell a fight coming on. We toe around each other, sizing each other up as if this is our first fight.

"I'm fucking tired of you calling the shots, Vassili," he grits.

"Shut your cunt. Do something, then!" I'll allow him to toss the first punch. Then I'll bash his face in!

My cousin goes for a cross hook. Too bad there's a faint

glint in his eye. It reads exactly what he'd intended to do. My hand catches his fist, and then I smack it down.

His stance is all wrong as he issues a sloppy uppercut. The hit is thwarted by my forearm. I laugh as my cousin slides his shoe between my Nikes, tripping me up.

The readymade crowd cheers as Yuri's heavy body lunges toward mine. I counter the takedown with a knee to his jewels. The cheers are followed by heckling. Fuck them, I wanted him to stop with the pussy monologue.

"Fu—" Yuri stops breathing, grabbing at his balls.

"See, I was waiting for you to shut up, kuzen."

He lowers himself, bullrushes me with his head spearing toward my abdomen. Like a wave, the tight-knit group of guys moves to the opposite side of the cell. My hands gather into a tight fist above my head. I pound against his spine as mine slams against the cement wall.

"Fuck," I gasp, hardly able to get the word out.

Yuri starts pounding against my lungs. Shit, I've taught this fucker too much while he watches my practices and matches. I reach beneath and grab his neck, spinning him around. When Yuri's ass hits the ground, his eyes are wide with shock. I have him in a triangle chokehold, the one I promised to Karsoff for his mouth. Well, my cousin's mouth is even more annoying. I watch his face tremble. His lips gloss with spittle and he gasps for air.

CLANK. CLANK. CLANK.

A baton grates along the bars. The noise aggravates my ears, so I let go of my cousin. He falls face-first on the ground.

"Hey, you boneheads, break it up or no calls," the guard says.

I hold my palms out, as innocent as they come.

"Resnov," he shouts, "Which one of you fucks is Resnov?"

"Right here," I nod, holding my side, as my cousin croaks.

112

"Well, who wants to make their call first?" He glances between us, the pathetic pair that we are.

"By all means," Yuri wheezes out at me.

The electronic bars slide open. I determine whose more than capable hands will get us out of the mess that I've made...

15

Zariah

Fog surrounds my brain. Yet, I feel like I'm clinging to something entirely too soft to be my husband's frame. The scent fusing into my nostrils is faint. Although it sends another moan roaming along my throat. Vassili's musk surrounds me. The thought hits me that the scent of him is a day old, and I rouse myself awake.

"Vassili," I grumble, pushing away his pillow. My eyes begin to adjust to early morning as I mope. "Why didn't you wake me up when you got home last—"

I sit up. His side of the bed is empty. The digital clock reads 4:10 am. Where the hell is my husband? I reach for my cell phone and the charger that I could've sworn was connected to it. The cord slips between the bed and the nightstand. Damn, I didn't plug my phone in all the way last night.

I press the home button on the iPhone. It has no juice. My attempt is in vain. While sticking my hand between our custom-made bedpost, I bump my temple on the edge of the nightstand.

"Zar, wake up, girl." I can hear my husband's usual response within my psyche. It's too early for a macchiato, and he should be here.

Leaning down, my fingertips feel for the charger, and I finally clasp it. Sitting back up, I connect it to my cell phone.

The brightness of the white screen burns my retinas. For a fraction of a second, the burgeoning bump on my temple no longer exists. I start listening to a stream of voicemails. There's one from 9 pm from an Atlanta area code. Since the number isn't familiar, I skip it and click on my mother's message. What was she calling me for after 2 am?

"The boys missed their flight, honey, don't worry." Her indication has the opposite effect.

There's a voicemail promptly after hers from Vassili's phone number. I listen as he confirms the *alibi* my mom previously offered. "Uh, beautiful, we will stay the night at your ma's. We... couldn't get back in enough time."

Hmmm, his thick Russian accent is mixed with the 'got my hand caught in the cookie jar' tone. The entire scenario further sets my intuition at work. I click on the oldest message from 10 pm.

"Sweetheart, I need you to call me at this number." Vassili seems to be treading water. "Soon as you can, girl, call me."

Due to him not utilizing his cell phone to "call me," I dial the strange number. When I hear a greeting about the 'county jail' my heart flops in my chest. What the hell is going on?

I dial Vassili.

The call transfers straight to voicemail.

"Boy, call me when you get this," I say through gritted teeth. "Are you in jail?"

Damn it, I'm so rattled that I'm acting like my mother from when I was a senior in high school. She'd leave elaborate voicemails with questions and seemed hell-bent on an answer. "Call me." I get the words out again and mash the END call button.

Next, I dial my mother's number. It's a little after 7 am. If she doesn't answer, my fury will be unleashed.

Mom answers at the last second, in a cheery tone, "Good morning, honey. What are you doing up so early?"

The usual background soundtrack of pots and pans clanking around settles me for a moment. My mom is safe and at home. But what more can I expect, she's a creature of habit. "Mom, where is Vassili? Is he there or is he in jail?'

"He and Yuri spent the night. They missed their flight. I have more than enough room. You received my message, right?"

My Spidey senses are blazing. She disregarded my statement about jail. Nobody lets something like 'so how are you doing, did you just get out of jail?' slip from the conversation. It's a statement that you correct to clear your name. At least, I believe so. Instead of demanding answers, I inquire, "How did they miss their flight?"

"Okay, Maxwell Washington *Junior*, what's with the questions? You should be sound asleep. They're still asleep. I'm making breakfast. If you've completed your interrogation and would like to talk to me or provide a message for him, I don't mind..."

"Mommy, I am going to ask you one more time," I assert myself, in a respectable tone. "Did Vassili take a trip to the jailhouse, lose his phone there, get robbed?" As I speak the words, they sound all wrong. I can't visualize my husband as a victim of a crime, let alone imagine a viable robbery scenario. "Was he in jail anytime last night?"

The sounds of banging pots and pans continue. "Hmmm, let me think back."

"Momma!"

"I bailed them out. It's not like my alimony checks couldn't cushion the blow, but Yuri transferred the money back into my account. It was nothing, honey, nothing at all."

I grumble and gripe for a moment. Damn it, my mother is covering for my husband's antics. She bailed them out.

Is Taryn right about Vassili's undeniable connection to his family business?

Did he and Yuri ...

What the heck have they been up to?

"Oh god, did they..." My throat is constricted, which is a saving grace because *Nancy Grace* has nothing on me. When it comes to taking names and asking questions, I reign. I begin to hyperventilate. Can I have this conversation over the phone? It implies that my husband is part of a criminal organization. I press my head back against the bedframe and sigh heavily.

"Zariah, stop over-analyzing. Child, I can hear your mind churning a thousand miles away. All is well."

I scoff. "My mother bailed my husband out of jail. This is some bullshit. Mom, forgive me for cussing with you."

Shaking my head, I contemplate the conversation that I had with Taryn and her mother. There was no such thing as censorship with regard to their mother-daughter relationship. "I can't believe this."

"Honey, breathe."

"Oh, trust me, if I'm capable of communicating, then I'm more than proficient at breathing." I grip the phone in my hand and grumble. "You tell that man to call me when he wakes up. I have a bone to pick with him."

"Zariah—"

"No, there's a couch with his name on it if he wants to go gallivanting around ATL! Shit, he's in the doghouse. Love you, Mama." I hurry to end the call as my imagination begins to take me under.

Through thick and thin... good or bad... I have to lead with my heart, and Vassili owns it. My breaths seize up at that thought. He's my eternity, no matter what...

Natasha is grumpy all day. I consult with Samuel after telling him that I need the day off. There's a man whose perception of my last name 'Resnov' needs correcting and here I am, calling off work.

Samuel said he had friends in the department and would look into why Vassili and Yuri went to jail. Yes, I'm aware that the public database will allow me access to whatever shenanigans they've been up to. But hearing the story from the horse's mouth is my aim. And then, with Sammy's assistance, we will fix whatever foolishness those two have caused.

When I arrive at LAX, I don't resemble the respectable black girl my parents raised. I'm in yoga pants and a camisole, holding Natasha. She's dressed to the nines courtesy of Mrs. Takahashi. Taryn's mother bought Natasha more clothing than she could wear before growing out of them. So, we are a pair. She's positioned on my hip. From outside looking in, I could be the nanny as we're stationed at the bottom of the escalator. A lousy nanny at that because my frown is set.

He trends on social media during a match. But today, he's being slammed for fighting an unarmed man. That much I gathered from the Facebook newsfeeds on my cell phone. I told Samuel that his hands and feet are registered, and he broke the bad news earlier. Vassili will have to return to Atlanta to speak with a judge next Tuesday. For fighting.

Heated blood courses through my veins. I plan to listen to his story, and then I am going to rip him apart for being so stupid. There is no amount of foolishness in the world that can cause a man to need to use his hands on another. Unless someone disrespects my mama, I handle my shit in a civilized manner.

"Natasha, I'm going to talk to Daddy until he is sick and tired of my voice. Okay, cutie pie?"

She smiles at me, all because I mentioned her father's name. Little traitor.

I add, "Daddy's in trouble."

"Daddy," she giggles.

"Trouble." I accentuate the word, through tensed lips. With the imaginary 'angry black woman' stamp on my forehead, people have steered clear of me. In the crowded terminal, the anger resonating from my body pales as I feel *him*. Vassili is here. My gaze ascends the escalator, and there he is.

The chocolatey waves of his mohawk caress ever so softly against his brutal dark eyes. He looks like the badass he was painted as. And he's wearing the same jeans and shirt he wore when leaving yesterday morning. Our eyes connect as the escalator brings him closer to me. My lips twitch with how harshly they are set. He looks happy to see me. Shit, he also looks like sex on a stick. A sexy tree that I wouldn't mind climbing . . . *keep your anger. He's in trouble. Don't give in, Zar, don't do it!*

"Daddy!" Arms open wide, Natasha tries to lunge from my arms. In her glee at seeing her father, the danger goes over her head. I grip at Natasha's knees in an attempt to save her. Vassili is at our side in seconds, scooping her up before she can fall.

"Girl, you are not ready to jump yet." His ropey, strong arms grip her tightly. She kisses his cheek as he tells her how much he missed her in Russian.

Yuri is behind this beautiful pair that melts my heart. When I see him, my eyes narrow harder.

"Hello." I eye the two cousins.

Aware of the storm that's brewing inside of me, Yuri nods subtly.

"Zar, don't look like that." Vassili's sexy voice tempts me to forgive him as he kisses Natasha's cheek. She settles her arms around his neck. He reaches out to kiss me as well—

On the heels of my tennis shoes, I turn around without offering him a word.

Fifteen minutes later, we have walked through the car garage. Vassili has attempted every other minute to rouse a 'friendly' conversation out of me.

"You want me to drive?" he asks, once we're a few yards away from my car.

"Do you want to explain why you beat up Matthew Overstreet? I'm not familiar with that name. Explain that to me!"

"She doesn't know?" Yuri grunts.

Vassili gives him a look.

I wag a stiff finger at the both of them and ask, "Oh, you two are trading signals now? Yuri, talk to me, buddy. What kind of fun did the two of you have last night?"

"Zariah," Vassili's voice booms against my chest cavity. His tone startles Natasha into a frown which brings an onset of tears. He kisses her cheek, mumbles something about 'chalk chalk' that makes her smile. "It was not like that. I will talk to you about it later. That's a promise."

Yuri gives him a look.

"You want to tell me, Yuri, go ahead." I fold my arms.

My husband passes our child like a bag of potatoes to his cousin. He gets in my face, "I'm not fucking talking to you right now. You gave me the cold shoulder, Zariah. Allow me to mention, there'd be hell to pay if the situation were reversed. You'd have a problem with me ignoring you, but I won't dish the same shit you served. We will have this chat later."

"No, we can have it now," I counter.

"Nyet!" He takes my arm and escorts me to the passenger seat. Yuri straps Natasha into her car seat before sitting on the opposite side of her.

"What possessed you to fight the man, Vassili?" I ask once Vassili navigates the freeway for a time.

"Girl, I tried to have a conversation with you, you refused. Now, you will wait."

"*Boy*, you might have jeopardized your career. How am I the only one making logical sense? So, what the hell's next, Vassili, since you might have sent your ass to jail for fighting a civilian. You can't fight a common citizen off the streets!"

He gives me a stiff shoulder.

"Will you follow in your father's footsteps?" I argue. It was a low, way below the belt comment, but Vassili understands the type of woman I am. At least, I assumed he knew that I want better for him. When you love someone, disappointment is a hard pill to swallow.

And I know he isn't like his father, but Vassili has jeopardized his career and love... the MMA world... for fighting. So I must be a bitch.

16

Vassili

"My father?" I spit the question while rubbing at the stubble along my jaw. I had less than three hours of sleep last night. When Zamora bailed us out, I once again promised that I wouldn't mention Overstreet to her daughter. Now, I'm in a fucking predicament.

Then my wife compared me to that piz'da? I ask, "You believe so little of me, Zariah?"

"I apologize." Her shoulders rise and fall slowly. "Toss me a few facts, baby. Make me believe otherwise, so we can get you out of this mess you've made."

"Uh, Zariah," Yuri speaks up from the backseat. "We didn't do shit. That douchebag provoked us."

"Did he now?" She scooches around in her seat, voice dangerously content. I almost tell my cousin not to speak. Anything he says is incriminating. My wife has this built-in lie detector test, and I'm still stuck on her fucking statement about my father.

Instead of letting Yuri taste his foot, I throw the ball in

her court. "You'd compare me to that motherfucker? You think I'm like my father?"

"Don't yell at me." Her chin juts out. "I'm trying to help you."

"Tell me, Zariah," my hands tighten around the steering wheel in disgust, "how the fuck am I like my dad?"

She's silent for a moment.

"Huh!" My bark sends her shoulders jolting. "First of all, you're good at keeping secrets. How long did you allow me to believe Malich was your father?"

I grunt and turn toward the road. Fuck, she has me there. "What else?"

"You're acting like a heathen, fighting people. Can we go back a few minutes ago? Let's chat this out, Vassili, please."

I shake my head. My father has people to kill people. And my wife is throwing elbows at me for a measly altercation? "Girl, I'm a professional fighter, so come with it. Come harder. How the fuck am I like Anatoly?"

She snaps, "You—"

"You guys!" Yuri's voice rises. "The daughter that the two of you had *together* looks like she's about to cry now. Can you knock it off for a while?"

We're back to silence.

Later on, I spent hours getting Natasha to fall asleep. Every time I sang the Russian ABCs, which is usually her favorite, she'd fall into a fitful sleep, only to awaken.

"You worried Daddy's gonna leave?" I ask, rubbing her back. My daughter smiles up at me with her few teeth. Only one of her eyes closes. It's a further reminder that getting out of the nursery without her being in a deep slumber, might be the hardest thing I've ever had to do.

"Should we start on our story? The one about the princess and her ogre of a father?" I ask. She gives a sleepy little coo. Since Natasha started cutting teeth, I shared super exaggerated stories with her just to hear her laughter. While I'm adding dragons to the story, I hear a doorbell ring. My stomach rumbles. Good. I heard Zariah making a call to Taiwan Chang's, one of our favorite takeout spots, when I was bathing Natasha.

Thirty minutes later, I tiptoe to the door of the nursery. I consider washing the day off but head downstairs instead. Zariah is in the den, seated in my leather chair. She's got her legs folded under her sexy ass. Her freshly showered dark brown thighs look creamy in a pajama shirt. There's a carton of chow mien in her hand. She's eating it with chopsticks and offering me an angry stare. I head to the kitchen, pick up the brown paper bag from the island. It's empty.

Really?

From the open kitchen/den floor plan, Zariah grumbles. "Don't be so dramatic, Vassili. Yours is sitting in the oven. Although, I considered getting your least favorite."

I grab my food, and instead of going near my wife, I sit at the table. We eat in an ocean of silence.

I'm finishing up when Zariah heads into the kitchen with her empty container. Though I made a promise to Zamora, I'll try to explain my rationale for bashing Matthew's face to her daughter. He's an asshole should suffice...

"You ready to chat, Zar?"

"Are you and Yuri done with the deception?"

I scoff. "Are you fucking kidding me? Deception? Counselor, that's left field. You know it."

"Then you'll tell me everything? Vassili, you have my heart. I'm scared, okay? I can't be without you."

"You're mine, Zariah. I love you." My tone is hard, raw, confident.

"What possessed you to beat some man on the street within an inch of his life?"

Longing sparks in her eyes as her hands plant on her wide hips. She must notice the slight hesitation on my face because Zariah returns to her spot. She clicks on the DVR list, choosing a Lifetime Movie. One of those man-bashing ones where the husband listens to everyone but his wife. I fucking hate those movies.

I can't tell her that the mudak whose skull I crushed was beating on her mother, so I head upstairs for a shower.

***

A few minutes have passed, moisture plumes around me and hot water slams down from the showerhead.

"Will you turn down the heat?" Zariah asks, standing wide-legged, arms folded.

She's watching the water glide over my chest. My cock rises at the sight of her in that long t-shirt that swallows her curves. I fist my cock in my hand.

She licks her lips. "I'm still angry with you."

"Good for you." My wrist glides slowly. I imagine her lips sliding over my shaft. No, her pussy or that virgin ass, skimming up and down my cock.

She gulps. I turn down the water temperature, and the shirt goes over Zariah's head. She starts for her short-panties, the ones that cling to her ass and leaves the bottom of those thick cheeks out. I love those fucking undies more than when she wears a thong. I grasp her hand and pull her inside before she can remove those.

Water waves up her thick weave. She caresses my cheek, and I glance down at her.

"Vassili, should I be mad with you? I'm sorry for earlier,"

her voice dips. "I didn't mean to add your dad to the equation. But should I be angry?"

I plant a trail of love against her gratifying lips. Then I kneel, my mouth touching her flat stomach and trailing down to the top of her panties. The panties are soaking wet. I bet it has nothing on her soaking pussy though. I move around to bite the back of her ass where it falls out of the bottom of her panty shorts.

The rain shower masks much of her moan. Zariah places her hands against the glass wall for support. With effort, I peel the material off one hip at a time. With a shaded, lustful gaze, I admire all that ass in my face. I slap one cheek and then palm the dark meat in my tan hand.

I groan, "Fuck, you are thick in all the right places."

Then I rise. I can feel her heart slam into her throat. I turn Zariah around.

"You still mad, girl?" My hand smacks and cups her pulsating lips. My fingers delve into silk curls, seeking out her clit. Her pussy lips tighten and contract.

I press fully against her, dominating her soft body. Her nipples are hard against my chest. "You wet or are you mad, Zar?"

"Both."

I nip and then murmur in her ear, "I like that."

Once again, I press her up against the wall. My chest now to her back. Her hips rise, her ass thrusts back, spearing my cock against her left ass cheek. Her angered tension fades for a moment as she yelps. The attitude she has causes me to chuckle. I clamp a hand along her neck, and command, "Tilt that ass more, Zar."

Her hips curve, her ass rises. I bend down again, getting a good look at the angle of her butt.

"Tilt more or I'm gonna have to fuck that ass, sweetheart. Angry as you are, you're still scared of it." I grunt in laughter.

Her eyes flash at me. From the side profile, I run my hand over her buttocks and then my thumb stretches out in search of her pussy. She's afraid of me screwing that tiny little hole. My thumb finds her wet, sopping pussy with ease. I stand back up. My hand once again claims the back of her neck.

The side of her face is pressed to the glass. I kiss her lips and ask, "You ready for me to fuck you?"

"Fuck me, baby!"

My cock is harder than titanium as my legs take on a wide stance. I clutch the back of her neck and glide in. My dick is swallowed into her throbbing cunt. Her breasts slam against the glass as I fill her entire pussy.

She's angry. I can feel that shit way down in my bones. I grip her neck and drive my cock into her pussy, letting her ass cheeks slam against my dick.

My other hand swats against her ass so hard that Zariah almost straightens.

"Keep the motherfucking position," I growl. She has a bone to pick with me. Fuck that, me too. She compared me to my father. My dick slams into her, balls deep.

17

Zariah

The water pours down on us in torrents. My nipples slap against the cool glass wall with each thrust. I'm on my tippy toes, as Vassili screws me from the back. The angle of his cock slaughters my walls. My pussy releases mini orgasms with each driving force. I can't even count how many times he's taken me to heaven while battering me with his dick.

Mmmm, I love that pain.

"I'm beating the fuck out this gorgeous pussy, Zar."

"This pussy is yours, Daddy," I gasp, my lips against the glass. It's pure greed that has me leveraging myself to slam back against him. "Fuck me."

"Shit," he grunts. "I'm breaking this pussy."

I scamper to clasp the walls, wanting to pull my hair out. He's screwing so deep in my stomach, that my future walk will forever be changed.

"Harder," I beg. Each thrust clears my mind of all the red

flags. He's dangerous. Everything about him is dangerous except his promises.

His swat along my hip brings stars to my eyes and death to any thoughts of him being like his father. A sharp breath escapes my mouth as he flogs the same spot. The hurt catches fire from the center point of my pussy and expands outward. The instant it reaches my hair follicles and toes, my mind goes numb. And I beg for more hurt.

"Shit, Vassili, fuck." I once again feel like a drunken woman, steadying herself on weak legs and tippy toes.

The way he screws my insides sends me to another galaxy. It's enough to clear him of a thousand misgivings. I reach between my body and the glass wall to fuck with my clit. My fingers work the shit out of it. I'm still angry. The pain becomes my haven.

With strong arms that have beaten many of his opponents, Vassili turns me around. He's screwed the tension right out of me. My legs go around his hips, as he buries his dick deep inside me. Our hearts implode against each other's chests, creating a drumming symphony.

"I don't give a fuck how angry you are, Zariah," he whispers in my ear. Vassili's cock burrows deep in my juices as he growls, "You belong to me."

I reach my arms around him, pulling the Russian stone-god to me and kiss him hard. "I belong to you," I solidify his claim while our tongues dance together.

His cock drives inside of me one last time. His warm seed is so strong that it erupts deep inside my pussy. I cling to him, neither one of us is ready to let go.

M y cell phone alarm awakens me. The clock we use is on Vassili's side of the bed because he's always up at the crack of dawn for a run.

"Zariah, baby, turn it off," Vassili kisses my lips.

I'm still submerged in a contented shade of black. My eyes are closed, not ready to open yet.

"Hmmm," I grin blindly, feeling my husband looking at me.

"It's Saturday, sweetheart. What's with the reminder?"

The reminder? Oh, yeah, dread seeps into my heart. I open my eyes, reach over and turn off my cell phone. I groan, "We have to meet with Sammy before he leaves for a seminar this afternoon."

"We? I thought he was cooking us dinner tomorrow evening? Sunday dinners are his thing."

"He is, but I can't wait until then, Vassili. We need to go over your case."

There's a hint of hesitation in Vassili's demeanor. Then he scoops me up and plants me on his waist. "Didn't I tell you not to worry?"

While straddling him, I offer a faint smile. "You did. But I can't stop, Vassili. I love you."

A vein pulsates in the side of Vassili's neck. Doesn't he know that this is the wrong time to bump heads?

We're at Samuel's Venice Beach home. The beach surrounds us in a 90-degree angle. The furniture is perfect for a man who doesn't have tiny terrors ready to stamp a train of dirty fingerprints everywhere.

We've come so far, the three of us. Instead of judging

130

Vassili, Samuel sits on a recliner between the two love seats Vassili and I have claimed.

My legs are crossed, my foot rattling with irritation. Samuel attempts to rationalize with him. "The more we are aware of now, the more we're able to defend you."

Duh! Sammy's voice is too friendly. He's offering my husband a choice, one that he doesn't have. I will help regardless of the nonsense going through Vassili's mind.

"Vassili, you have two lawyers here ready to build a titanium case for you." I sit forward in my seat. "I love you, let me help you."

"Girl, I won't have you as my attorney." His chuckle is contrite. "I said that years ago. End of discussion."

"Why? Because I'm not seasoned? Sammy is, talk to him." I gesture.

"Nyet. Zariah, I believe in you," he sighs. Rubbing the chain-link tattoo on his forearm, he turns to my mentor. "Sam, this meeting ... I don't need it. I'm going to handle the situation myself. Come Tuesday morning, I'll be dressed in a suit and will speak to the judge myself. Zariah and I'll see you for dinner tomorrow. She's wasting your time."

"Are you sure?" Samuel asks.

"He's not," I butt in.

"Judge McKinley is a hard ass," Samuel tries. "My connections will not be of any use without your side of the story."

Again, I speak up. "Yes, his side of the story. I'm sure you told my mom why she had to bail you out of jail, Vassili."

His lips bunch into a frown.

"Well, if he won't give it, then my mom will." I snatch up my leather purse.

My husband is cussing in Russian underneath his breath. Then he addresses me, palms out in a truce. "Zariah, c'mon, beautiful, stop the madness. Do you want to get your mother into this mess?"

"Zamora?" Samuel arches an eyebrow. "What does Mora have to do with it?"

"Hello, Mom," I place her on speaker. "I need you to tell me what happened the night Vassili and Yuri were arrested."

Her voice rings loud, clear, although hesitant. "Tsk, honey, they didn't do anything wrong."

"Mom, please explain it to me." Hot tears begin to slither down my cheeks. Intuition attempts to seep into my bones, but I'm not ready for it. Not ready for a truth that involves my mom.

Samuel's got a hawk-gaze on the phone, awaiting her response.

Vassili's eyes warm with concern before he leans his head back and takes a breath. His dark as sin eyes glower, causing me to feel hot coils against my skin.

"Ms. Haskins," he cuts in. "You don't know anything."

Samuel glances around in consideration. The intuition regarding my mom fades, as I realize my husband's comment was leading! Totally leading. Heck, he sounds like a Russian mobster, prepared to murder a potential witness.

"Honey, are you crying?" My mom asks.

"Yes, mom. My husband is in more trouble than he realizes. Vassili, you aren't as invincible as you think. Think about Natasha. This is a crucial time in her life to be gone." An image of him behind bars pops up on an imaginary projector before me, whisking away the deep blue sea. His love has me drowning. "Someone tell me something!"

"Okay," My mom speaks up.

"It's nothing," Vassili says as she admits to knowing Matthew Overstreet.

The muscles in my abdomen knead, twisting rapidly. Intuition returns with a vengeance. It's a dread I know all too well.

Voice tiny I ask, "Is he the man you've been dating?"

"Yes, honey. We were dating for a year."

"That's a rather long time without introductions, Mom. You know how I am, queen of interrogations. Twenty-one questions an all." I scoff, more anxious than I let on.

My husband shakes his head at me.

But I still ask the question I already know the answer to. "Does he… does he hurt you, mom?"

A heavy silence ensues. All the nightmares from my childhood come roaring back until Samuel speaks, "Mora, love, does he—"

"*Sammy?* What are you doing there?" The embarrassment in my mother's voice rings into my ears….

The community park near our home is an upgrade from when I was growing up. I'm not mentioning the switch from seesaws to a sandbox. I also grew up in a well-to-do area of Los Angeles. But our park is child-developmentally friendly.

I'm halfheartedly pushing Natasha in a swing, with an extensive seatbelt contraption. These rich mothers can never be too safe. Who am I kidding? I've seen more au pairs than bio moms at the park. My mind is inundated with other things.

"I'm awful, aren't I?" I ask Vassili as my mother's story twines in my ear. She told the story about her relationship with Matthew Overstreet to save Vassili. Her heart breaking into the receiver while I sat, overwhelmed with guilt. Mom didn't want Samuel listening to every word.

If she could only see his face.

Giving Natasha another lackluster push, I ask again, "Vassili, answer me. Am I awful?"

"You are," Vassili says, grabbing Natasha's feet. She's

angled with her frizzy hair blowing in the wind. "Now, move. Our baby is a stunt double."

"Dang, tell me how you really feel," I grumble taking a few paces back.

"You're in trouble, no discussion needed. You'll pay later," his voice is ominously sexy. And I'd like to see myself pay later if I didn't feel like a jackass. In the next instant, the frown is expunged from his face, a smile in its stead. As Vassili lifts Natasha's feet higher, she's damn near upside down. Then he says, "Swoosh."

"Daddy!" she giggles before being flipped back. I have to move further as Natasha soars higher than I've ever attempted.

"Vassili!" I shout a warning, which lands on deaf ears.

Natasha vaults toward him, fat fists waving around like a war machine. Natasha swings back and forth a few times. Then Vassili catches her legs and repeats, sending her higher into the universe.

"She needs a helmet," I grumble.

"*Nyet,* our daughter loves it."

Vassili plants me on the kitchen counter after we've double-teamed our daughter. We fed, bathed and put Natasha to sleep.

"I need a shot of Hennessey," I groan.

The sexy laugh that comes from deep in my husband's abdominals makes my body wet. He places his thick waist between my thighs and pulls off his shirt.

"*Shit,* Vassili, I'm asking for a pity party. Which means you have the tools at your disposal to get me drunk. This is a once in a lifetime opportunity."

"Okay," he nods. My hands barely have a chance to caress

the eight pack of his as he starts to back away. He pauses, then in a sarcastic voice inquires, "Oh, can I get your drink, your highness?"

"Humph, you're still being an asshole, aren't you? Earlier, my only thought was saving you from joining the Aryan nation in jail—"

"What the fuck?" His thick eyebrow rises.

"Hello, you're white. There's only one place for you in the pen. So that's my excuse for setting up my mom. I feel like middle school. There was this one time when Ronisha, you remember her?"

"Of course, Zar."

"Tsk, my mind is frazzled. There was this one time when Ronisha got me on the party line—a phone call with random kids. Needless to say, I was too much of a 'white girl' for most of the people on the call. I blindsided my mom with Samuel's presence. Now, I need copious amounts of liquor to help me forget. Which, might I add, can be how I repay you." I bite my lip as my hand slides over the smooth ridges. Then I let my index finger glide over the KILLER KARO tattoo, which is spread across his chest.

He growls, "Zar, you think you are allowed to state how your punishment will play out?"

"I'm offering you the grand opportunity to get me drunk as fuck. Vassili, be calculating and ambitious."

He moves back into my area, brushes a kiss along my neck. "When I give you an order, you have to start listening."

"Yeah, you told me not to have the meeting with Samuel. I'm wrong. Can admitting my faults be punishment enough?" Heat pricks at my eye ducts. The hurt in my mother's voice while explaining her relation with Overstreet was tangible. Although I expect it didn't exceed the pain she must've felt after knowing Samuel listened. She was in *another* abusive relationship.

Vassili presses his lips to mine. His kiss encourages me not to start crying. He then says, "I'm your husband, Zariah. You must trust that whatever action I choose is in the best interest of our family."

"Wait," I grab out for him as he pulls away again.

"No using me like a piece of ass." He goes to the refrigerator and pulls out the vodka.

"Oh no, I want some brown persuasion. That stuff will have me acting a fool."

"Maybe I want you ready to be committed, Zariah. The crazier you are, the easier it is for me to get to certain parts of your body, i.e. your true punishment." He opens up the Resnov Water and gestures for me to tip my chin. The vodka splashes into my mouth. A small bit trickles down my chin and neck. He licks that up. My pussy starts to rain like the vodka that was dripping down my neck.

"What sort..." I shake my head to help ease the burn. "Shit, no more. Now, what crazy stuff are you considering?"

"The kind of shit that requires me to get you good and drunk." We chuckle as he pours more in my mouth, this time, I don't swallow. He places his mouth over mines and drinks.

"So, where you headed?" I inquire, feeling my reaction time fade by the second. Damn, I only had about a shot and a half.

He grunts. "You want me in that tight, wet pussy, don't you?"

My head bobs up and down slowly. "Yessss..."

"I want to," he begins, voice slow, deliberate and powerful, "fuck your ass." Vassili takes the bottle to the head and then he hands it over.

"You ready for me to screw your tight ass, girl?"

"Nyet," I giggle, tipsy already knocking at my door. I sip from the bottle. Liquid fire slams down my throat, inside my chest. Vassili tips the bottom of it, and I end up guzzling down more than I anticipated.

He orders, "Take off your clothes."

I press on my palms, intending to jump down, but the ground sways. I chuckle.

"*Nyet*, don't get down, Zar," he tells me while brushing my lips with a kiss. Vassili places my hands over my blouse.

I slowly start undoing the buttons.

"Damn, girl, you'll be forever." He grips the silk material and pulls, buttons go popping everywhere.

I glance around at the buttons scattered across the marble flooring and gasp. "So it's like that? This is my favorite blouse!"

Vassili unbuckles my pants and gathers my panties with it, sliding them together down my hips. My ass is now on the cold marble slab. He's still in his army fatigues.

"Take yours off, too," I pout.

"In due time." He grabs the bottle, offering me more. I turn my head and he asks, "What happened to you getting drunk?"

"Boy, I am drunk!" I slur.

He pours the vodka along my chest. "One day I'm going to cum all over your tits and make you lick them off."

My voice is small, heavy with desire, "You can now."

"Nah, I've got other things up my sleeve."

"Oh, I re-remember. You wa-want me to be a bad girl," I slur. I grip the chocolate waves of his mohawk as Vassili licks the vodka from one of my tits. It takes ages for me to realize that my fingers won't be gripping the marble countertop. He applies pressure to one of my nipples, I moan. My hands press backward, as I lean back for him. I pour more vodka onto my body. The cool liquid rushes over my breast, into my belly button, drenches down my pussy and mingles with my wetness.

As I groan with delight, Vassili licks up every trail the vodka makes.

"Can you stand?" he asks.

Dang it, but I giggle, again. Vassili holds out a hand. I take it and move at a snail's pace until my left foot touches the ground and then my right.

"Turn around," he commands. "Hands against the counter."

Feeling my body mellow even more, I'm quick to do his bidding. My palms go to the marble ledge. My lower back begins to arch. Wet liquid shoots down my lower back and between my ass cheeks.

"Mmmm," I purr.

Vassili bends over and licks me down below. His tongue prods against my asshole.

"Shit, that feels good," I murmur. I rock my hips back as he eats my ass out. Then he slaps the inside of my thigh, forcing my stance wider. His tongue nudges my pussy as his fingers work their way into my ass. Again, my ass is begging for his penetration. I work my hips until more of his fingers slip into my hole.

"Oh, so you want me in this ass?" The drum of his voice is delectable.

"Yeah, Vassili," I cry out. "Keep fucking my ass."

"I'm not fucking you yet." He removes his finger, and then his tongue slides up my pussy to my asshole before he gets up. Vassili stands right behind me. The sound of him taking his belt off is titillating to my ears.

"Fuck me, baby," I tell him.

He pushes his pants off with the heel of his barefoot, kicks them away. His belt is still in his hand. Vassili swats my ass with it. Pain shoots through me, and I'm so ready for him to replace it with a pain that I have never felt before. His cock.

Vassili enters my pussy from behind. My mind starts to catch up. It's on the tip of my tongue to beg him to fuck my ass. Screw me with his big, white cock.

"Girl, you are fucking wet for me," He marvels. "You should see my cock."

"Can I taste it?"

"Nyet, I have other things for you to do."

I whimper at his refusal. Vassili continues to screw me, my back arching perfectly as he grips my ponytail. "Keep wetting my cock with that thick, sweet pussy, girl. You got that pussy sloppy, gushy, all for me."

I force my hips back, meeting him thrust for thrust. Until he pulls out. His cock slides up my labia and to my ass. I gyrate, gliding his hardness across my tiny hole. "Vassili... don't stop."

His cock nestles against my butt.

"Girl, you should see how beautiful your ass is." Vassili smacks a cheek before he rubs the pain away. "Now, drink that vodka."

I reach over, grab it, and guzzle it down.

Then my hands grip the ledge. He must've put some sort of gel on his cock because the glorious crown is cool against my ass. He works his cock head into my ass.

"Shhhhhit, Vassili," I growl. It hurts so good, I love it.

18

Vassili

Her asshole is puckered and tight. In the past, I've fit four of my fingers into that tiny little hole and loved how her pussy came on my cock. That's what I'll do now. My cock moves back down from her ass. I bang inside of her wetness again and again. Zariah works her ass back against me, slamming my cock till it sinks deeper and deeper into her pussy. My balls slap against her sweetness. Jaw tensed, I fight not to explode inside of her miracle pussy.

I lean back on my calves. Cock at attention. Zariah turns her head as I slam the belt down on her hip.

"Fuck, Vassili!" She glares.

Again, the belt swats around the same spot. Her eyes spark with fire, this is a pain she has to take. Once more, the pinnacle of my manhood brushes against the tight entrance of her ass. It's so fucking beautiful. My cream-colored cock is nestled between her dark-chocolate tits. I can see cum squirting from her pussy and down her legs. Damn, I want to lap it up like a dog. But now is not the time. I lean against my calves once more. Next, I let the head of my dick slither across her swollen clit.

"Shit!" Zariah screams. "Fuck me, baby. You can screw me. You can fuck my ass," she growls. "Just fuck me."

My lips spread into a smile. Her excitement is contagious. Zariah wriggles her ass back against me.

"Hold still." I grab a bottle of lubrication from the table that she hadn't noticed me pull from my pocket. Like hell am I going in my wife's ass without any extra protection. She isn't one of the bitches that I used to fuck with. Despite her eagerness, there's an art to stretching her tight hole.

"Vassili," she whimpers.

While I lather my heavy, hard cock with lube, I give her pussy another jolt. My thumb's loving the tightness of her asshole now. My thumb and finger work against the firmness of the inside ring of her ass. My cock is a piston in her ultra-wet valley. She bucks like the most gorgeous Arabian horse and rides out another orgasm. An ocean of her sweetness rushes along my cock as Zariah comes harder. My toes tuck underneath and clench. The tension abets me in my desire not to explode inside of her because tonight I'm headed into her ass.

She moans and groans and sags something fierce against the marble counter.

Damn, my dick is sloshing inside of her cunt now. My lubed up fingers continue to widen her out while she recovers from that hard orgasm.

"Baby, I want it..." she feigns as my fingers tweak and stretch her hole.

My cock slides in and out of her channel as I entice her with this response, "Dah. I know you want this cock in your ass, beautiful. I'll give you that now." I slip my cock from her pussy, picking up the lube again. I coat my already soaking piece.

My slick cum-coated cock lodges at the puckering of her thick, round ass.

My hands skim over the side of her hip and up her tiny waist. Now, she's silent, no more begging, but this gorgeous body of hers speaks volumes. She's ready. She trusts that I'll fuck her good in the ass and that I'll do my best to love her without hurting her. The crude mushroom-shaped head of my cock kisses ever so softly against her asshole. I slowly push my way in.

"Mmmm, Vassili."

"Don't tense up, Zariah. I promise you'll love this. Just breathe, my beautiful wife."

The whimpering transforms into a heavy sigh as my cock inches inside and past her tight entrance. Fuck, what a heavenly fit. I make leeway and then give her time to breathe.

"Mmmm, Vassili, I love you…" she breathes the words.

"I love you, more."

For every inch I take inside of her ass, I caress ever so softly at her lower back. I listen to her body. About three inches of my cock screws her ass now. She's too beautiful to force it. I reach beneath her hip to rub softly against that tiny, little bulb of hers. The action of me working her clit sends her pussy lips to shiver.

I pull out of her ass, this was enough for now, and slide into her pussy. This time, I fuck Zariah until she bucks back, and I cum deep inside her.

Monday morning, I stand in the bathroom. I grab the waves of my hair, wet after a fresh shower.

"Time to get rid of you my old friend," I give a cocky grin, determined to be the image of a pristine 'white' boy.

Fuck, this is for Zariah. Nobody in this world can force

me to change my image. But for her, I'll play the part tomorrow. She was worried about me being locked up. I grab the clippers and plug it in, ready to look like a brand-new man… Well, a *new enough* man.

Come tomorrow, I'll have a freshly shaven face and a suit covering my tats. I'm almost content with this decision until I see my name in lights.

On the 30-inch flat-screen TV across from the sink, MMA Sportscaster Alex Brown mentions my name. "Anaconda Alvarez has pulled out of the contract with Vassili Killer Karo Resnov."

What the fuck? How did Alvarez pull out of a contract that I had yet to sign? Yuri and I never got around to the convention center in Atlanta. That piz'da is a fucking liar. I grab the remote and turn up the television.

"This news has come amid Karo's recent assault of an unarmed man," Alex says. His face is sneered into a judgmental frown. "Karo, if you're watching, call in. I'm confident your fans are interested as to why you'd beat up an innocent man."

"Yeah, well fuck you." I flip the bird at the TV screen as he continues to bash my name. Then I grab the hair at the front of my head and buzz it off. I recall the last time I was interviewed by Alex, that bitch was riding my cock, raving about my latest fight. And I promised him that Juggernaut would fall in less than—what, eight seconds? I think it was eight seconds. The crowd used to be my bitch. Now to hear from him that neither Alvarez nor Karsoff want to fight me due to my current legal matters? He can suck a diseased cunt!

"Boy, are you in there grumbling and griping?" Zariah calls out from the bed.

Fuck, I register that I was mumbling.

"Go back to bed, Zar."

"Humph, I'm glad you are aware that I still have an hour

before I need to dress to go into the office. Thanks for turning up the television as well."

"Girl, go back to bed." I buzz off another piece, my brown waves fall into the sink. With a frown, I nod at myself. Wait, need to get rid of the frown as well. Samuel, Zariah and I finished the discussion about how to get myself and Yuri out of the heat. Samuel had our cases transferred to a judge who has zero-tolerance for domestic violence. The clean look will solidify that. Yuri isn't much for tattoos Basically, I'm the one who needs to cover up and fly straight.

"Baby," Zariah calls out once again, this time her voice seems preoccupied.

"*Dah?*" I take a warm towel and rub it over my buzzed head.

"C'mere, now," she orders.

When I enter the bedroom, Zariah is sitting against pillows in the bed. Her cellphone is in a horizontal position. She's listening to some dude whose cussing makes me look like a saint instead of a sinner.

"Girl, what are you listening to?" I ask as I hear my name.

"It's a short clip of you from the other day..." She smiles as her eyes land on me. "Oh, lawd, what is going on? What happened to my thug?"

I rub a hand over my head, again. "I knew you secretly craved a simpleton."

"You aren't even capable of sounding like one." Her eyes are full of life as she gestures for me to come closer. I climb into bed on top of her.

With her eyes sparkling playfully, Zariah speaks in a tone filled with mock fear. "Can I-can I touch it?"

"You sound scared," I say as she laughs again.

Her lips softly plant onto mine. Her tongue comes out, and she licks before nibbling on my lip. At the sound of more cussing and joking, my eyebrow rises.

"Oops, I had it on repeat," she shares. "Rodney is funny as hell. When I'm at work and need to de-stress, I'll click on his Facebook page."

Zariah digs around for the discarded cell phone and I cuddle next to her. She adds, "He has this habit of assessing the craziness going on in his world. You made the cut."

She clicks onto a YouTube video. A black man is on the right side of a split-screen. He's sitting in a chair, in what could be a home office. On the opposite side of the screen is a fuzzy video from the night I beat down Matthew. Whoever took the footage didn't catch me in the backseat. The camera starts rolling with Matthew honking his horn.

"My wife is too brilliant for this mudak," I grumble kissing Zariah.

While chuckling, she pushes me away. "Hey, I finally know what mudak means. Google tells me everything. And it would behoove you to share this post on all your social media. Rodney is as good as free PR for your bully brand."

In the background, Rodney can hardly speak for laughing. "His forehead is lodged *way* into the back of his throat. I don't know if he was incapable of driving away. But I'd be damned if I'm going to create a scene after somebody punches the breaks off me! Wait a minute though!"

I glare at the screen, the only part of Rodney that's visible is his teeth as he continues to laugh.

"I don't do comedy, Zar," I mumble, settling next to her.

On the opposite side of Rodney's screen, I'm back in the picture, having returned to Overstreet's car.

The comedian exaggerates, "Karo, seriously? You beat the man into next week. Why come back and serve him with another beat down? I just learned that the victim's name is Overstreet. Needs to have it changed to *Street!* Had him blending in with the pavement. Wait, wait, look—"

Rodney pauses from all the dramatics as I watch myself

pick up Matthew from the ground. Somehow the comedian has added sound effects to the fight. Every hit seems to SPLAT, POP or CRUNCH.

I squeeze my arms around Zariah's midriff. "You listen to this bullshit?"

She stifles another bout of laughter. "It's funny. Matthew Overstreet deserved it. Wish I was there."

"Like you'd have been good with me trying to knock his head off?"

"Humph, you *did* knock his head off! Under the circumstances, I might have run up, kicked him and ducked out of the way."

"No need to run, I got you anytime you need to let off steam."

"Oh, so we should hit the streets, knocking people's block off whenever we're stressed?" She can hardly kiss me for grinning now.

J udge Styles is supposed to be a softy, or at least Sam said so. He pulled a favor by switching her out with Judge McKinley.

But when I take my seat next to him and Zariah, looking fit for a fucking J. Crew suit listing, Styles goes off. She mentions how I have a higher level of accountability as a fighter.

My voice is tapered, "In my defense—"

"Don't speak," Samuel says under his breath.

Imaginary horns pop out from her blond hair. Ironically, she's sitting in front of the great seal of Georgia. Wisdom. Justice. Moderation. My ass.

Styles jumps on me with, "This is *my* courtroom, Mr. Resnov. It's my time to shine, not yours. I saw the video of you wiping the *streets* with Mr. Overstreet. The DA is ready to lock you up for using such tactical strategies on him."

Fuck, this could be pure comedy. She has that mudak, Rodney, beat with her reference to '*street.*' Her facial expressions aren't as fanatical as Rodney's, which is what seals the deal. But instead of this being a stand-up comedy, Styles continues to carve me a new one.

"Mr. Resnov, you are a weapon. Your hands, your feet, your body! Now, Mr. Resnov, what do you have to say for yourself?"

Shit, I would say that I didn't kick the motherfucker, but do I get to speak? Zariah nudges me in the side.

"Oh," I begin, fixated on my thick Russian accent. "I would like to say that Mr. Overstreet deserved every single hit. As you can see in the video, I did not kick him, your honor. I didn't use a takedown, none of that. I used my hands —like everyone else is more than capable of using during a fight." Fuck, this isn't helping.

"Your Honor," Zariah speaks up, "May I be allowed to approach the bench?"

"Would that be a waste of my time?" Styles inquires, ice-blue gaze still glaring through me. Then she turns her attention to my lawyers. "Billingsley, Washington, I respect you. Nevertheless, I'm baffled. How will you convince me that Mr. Resnov is not a threat to society?"

I try not to grit my teeth as the judge called Zariah the wrong last name. If it were my turn to speak, I'd let her ass know that, too!

"Yes, your honor," Zariah holds up photos. "I believe these photos are relevant to the case."

· · ·

Judge Styles gestures toward her bailiff. The beefy fucker eyes me. My 'good' boy persona slips for a second as I frown at him. He takes the photos from Zariah and heads to the judge.

Seconds later, Judge Styles gasps at the sight of what she sees.

"Ms. Washington, these are some very despicable photos. Please state the name of the person in these photos for the record."

"They're photos of Zamora Haskins Washington, my mother." Zariah's voice breaks. "My mother is—was dating Mr. Overstreet, Your Honor. As you can see, there are many bruises inflicted on her person, which were all at the hands of Mr. Overstreet. Each photo is time-stamped below."

A moment passes before the judge's pursed lips loosen as she glances at me and then at Zariah.

"And where is your mother, Ms. Washington?"

Zariah turns. "She is here, your honor."

"This court will take a temporary recess." Styles slams down her gavel. The sound rings out throughout the cherry wood walls of the courtroom. Styles gestures toward the District Attorney and then to us. Samuel and Zariah start to rise when I do, but they tell me to sit down.

For a half-hour, I've twiddled my thumbs like an idiot. When the hearing is resumed, Samuel beckons for Yuri. My cousin's case was scheduled separately from mine, due to his resisting arrest.

Zariah sits next to me. I reach over, caress a few strands of hair behind her ear.

"Baby," I whisper to her. "Tell me something."

"Shhh," is all she will say while squeezing my hand beneath the table.

I sit back, bite my tongue like a lapdog, with no orders. Styles drones on and on about how I must be held to a higher standard.

It's either I tap it out or go off. Not that I expected special treatment, but Zamora didn't need to add herself to the equation. I fucking did this, poured out her life of abuse for Zariah to see, Sammy to see, the whole damn courtroom to see. Regardless, any person, man or woman, should want to retaliate. You don't go around smacking people—unless you're me, of course, and in a cage. If I tune into Judge Styles, I'm liable to tell her something she doesn't want to hear.

"Vassili, baby, respond," Zariah murmurs.

My eyebrows knit together as Yuri nods, "Yes, ma'am—uh your honor, of course."

"This is the good old state of Georgia, Mr. Resnov, and Mr. Resnov. We don't have vigilantes around here, so I suggest the two of you return to California post haste."

What? So, I am free? I nod my thanks, standing up as Zariah, Sam and Yuri do. I whisper to my wife, "What the fuck happened here? She's been riding me hard."

"You are too easy to read, Vassili. All that 'I'll handle it myself.' Boy, bye! You pissed of Styles, but we fixed it." Zariah hugs me tightly. "We are a team, Vassili. Next time, keep me in the loop, so we don't have to wait until the last possible second to *team* up."

Damn, so Zariah held off before garnering sympathy from the judge. Her look tells me it served me right.

I growl in her ear, "You're in trouble when we get home."

"Better be the kind of trouble I like."

We all head out of the courtroom and down the corridor to the exit. I hold Zariah's hand and fall back a few paces to align myself with her mother, who hasn't said a word this entire time.

"Thank you," I tell Ms. Haskins. Placing my arm around her shoulder, I give her one of the many hugs my mother missed out on. Zamora's as humble as my mother had been in the past, offering a soft smile before waving off my show of gratitude.

"You're my son now, Vassili, and I love you."

"Aw mom," Zariah is teary-eyed.

Yuri is opening the door. I hardly get a chance to tell the woman who birthed the love of my life that I love her as well. A microphone is shoved into my face. Yuri is at my left, and Zariah is to my right.

There's a mass of reporters, some are held at bay by a few police officers in an attempt to keep the peace. Even more have caught up with me, asking their questions all at the same time. I tune into the closest one.

The reporter says, ".... Alvarez, Karsoff, The Jedi...they're all interested in offering you a shot in the octagon, Karo. Your fans around the nation are elated that you've sought justice for your mother-in-law."

That's right, mudak! I want to call out the sports commentator, Alex Brown. That bitch tried to drag me through the wringer, but none of my fans had anything negative to say. A few of them tweeted that Overstreet had to have deserved it.

Jaw held high, I respond, "I'm thankful for the fans who stuck with me even though they saw me painted in a negative light. I want everyone to know I don't condone bullying. Never have, never will."

"How will you handle bullies in and out of the cage, Karo?"

"I can't predict the future," I shrug.

"Who's first on your list to defeat?" The reporter asks, as more recorders head toward me.

"Who will you fight next?"

"Killer Karo is going after the best," Yuri says.

"Karsoff," I reply. My face doesn't even spread into a smile. But inside, I'm elated like a kid at New Years, the most popular holiday in my homeland. Alvarez is beneath him, Jedi is a bottom feeder, and neither one of those mudaks would win in the cage with me. As Yuri bitched, I have to work my way up. I'll start from the middle because my belt will be within my grasp sooner rather than later.

"Mrs. Resnov," the reporter turns to my wife. "We're also told you were of assistance during the court proceedings, acting as both Mr. Resnov's attorneys. Is that true?"

"Yes, I and attorney Samuel Billingsley were available. Due to the special circumstances of the case, the guys pretty much pulled through without us."

"Will Matthew Overstreet be charged, and what will those charges be?"

"Sorry, I cannot comment on an open investigation." Zariah's grin is enough ammunition to know that Overstreet isn't getting off scot-free.

"Thank you, the two of you are a winning team." He nods.

Zariah squeezes my hand again. "See, baby, keep me in the loop and you'll never go wrong..."

19

Zariah

Despite my elation that I won't be living the single-mama life, the feeling of shame surrounds me. I unknowingly dragged Samuel into this mess. My mentor and my mother don't fool me, they've had feelings for each other for a while now. Deep ones. Knowing my mom, Samuel's inclusion hurts her more than anything that asshole dished out. She has this way of hiding things from people and I don't just mean the bruises. She hides the hurt from the ones she loves, and I'm no fool. My mom loves *him*. Their case is a Catch-22. Her southern belle charm won't allow her to sully her reputation by pursuing her ex-husband's best friend.

Sunglasses mask much of my mother's humiliation, yet her glance is to the ground. Her lips are in a hard line. Mom broke out of that bout of melancholy when Vassili thanked her. One would swear she's never received much acknowledgment from the male species. Now, she's as quiet as ever as Samuel drives us in a rented Escalade.

"Can we at least have lunch before the Judge wants us out

of Georgia?" Yuri asks, having commandeered the front passenger seat.

"Mora, what do you suggest?" Samuel asks, glancing through the rearview mirror.

She shrugs. "Anywhere is fine."

Damn, I thought I'd never see the day again when her tone of voice hardly reaches above a whisper.

"C'mon," he cajoles her. "This is your hometown, Mora. You know where all the good eats are." His eyes are the perfect mixture of playful and hopeful.

Since I have the middle seat in the back, I offer my mom a tiny elbow nudge.

She speaks up. "What are you in the mood for?"

"Anything." Yuri sounds like a kid. "I'll die if I don't eat soon."

"Fat fuck." Vassili shakes his head and then apologizes for cussing in front of my mother.

"Humph," she says. "We know good and well, Vassili, that you cuss like a sailor. Now, I can recommend barbecue chicken, upscale Italian, French, and—"

"Ribs." Yuri makes the call for everyone.

———

We end up in this hole in the wall joint; where canned soda pop is served with your meal or you can pay a quarter for a Styrofoam cup. But with an "A" grade, and a to die for homemade barbecue sauce, I cannot complain.

When I come out of the bathroom, Vassili and Yuri are pushing two tables together. Samuel is at the station where my mother is grabbing napkins and forks. He appears to be talking to her, but her level of interaction is uninspiring. One day, they're going to force my hand, and I'll desperately shout for them to 'just do it.' Just get together.

I stop myself from heading over to them. First, I have no idea what to say. Second, my mom is a pro with the cold shoulder. So, I'm about as helpful as a public defender on the first day of the job.

A burst of air comes from the door as it's opened. Martin enters the eatery, his eyes scanning over the tiny dining area. His eyes target my mother. Shit, none of us told my brother anything about the hearing. I would expect the head of HR had other things to do this weekend than dabble in social media or the news.

Scampering to my feet, I hurry toward the entrance before he can confront my mother about her lack of judgment. We're half masked by a life-sized pink piggy, standing on its hind legs in an apron.

"Hey, Zariah, we need to talk to Mom, now." He pulls off his prescription glasses, pinches the bridge of his nose. He's about to walk off when I plant myself in front of him again.

"I understand where you're coming from, big brother. Now is not the time. Sammy's here, we're all hanging out for lunch—"

He cuts in, "I heard that our mother was being..."

"I know." I try to calm him from crying. When I blink, the day Martin had enough of our father flashes before my eyes. With a tear stricken gaze, my brother fought for our mom. "Listen, I invited you to lunch so we could all get together while I'm in town. I didn't uh . . . mention—"

"The court hearing! I don't recall that, because I heard it all over the radio on the ride here."

"Alright, Martin." I chew my lip. "I wanted to share the news with you in person. Nevertheless, now is not the time. Not in front of friends."

"What should I do, Zariah?" He turns his wrath on me. "Pretend to be oblivious! I'm sure in the eyes of most people watching the news, a professional fighter going off half-cocked was the reason this made national coverage. The domestic violence is not that important to them, but that asshole hurt our mom. We can't allow her to keep screwing with—"

"Martin, I'm not saying pretend to be oblivious. And look," I nudge my chin to our mother and Samuel. She's slowly beginning to blossom. "Sammy's a good guy. Would be nice to have someone like that for mom."

"Samuel is married to a different woman, every two years or so."

"Well, Mom and I have this theory that he's still heart-broken over his first wife's death. Remember?" *But it would be nice if they gave it a shot.* I huff, since Martin has no interest in talking about a love connection. "You know what, last week when Mom asked me about him, I made the same statement. Maybe he hasn't found the right woman."

Martin scoffs. "The right woman is his ex-best friend's *ex-wife*? Zar, you stayed with dad when they divorced. You don't know what mom needs, I do."

Mom begged me to stay with Dad. I've never mentioned her reasoning, so I clamp my mouth shut.

"Zariah, baby." Vassili heads over to us. "You are hogging your brother all to yourself." He wraps an arm around me, instantly pacifying the tension in my shoulders. "How you doing, *brat?*"

They shake hands. Maxwell replies, "Not too well, man. I owe you for what you did to that asshole. Zariah and I need some sort of intervention with our mother. She's too old to be a punching bag."

"I see." Vassili nods. "Your mother is such a beautiful woman. How about you have that chat with her at another time, though. She's sitting with an old friend, and this is sort of a celebration. But, I promise you, the day won't end before you two have that talk with your mother."

I breathe easy as Martin nods. The three of us head to the tables. It isn't until we all have a basket of ribs—well Yuri has two—that my mom eases back into her fun-loving self. She sets aside a rib that has been utterly demolished, not a trace of meat is left. She asks, "Who's this Karsoff that my son is going to put a can of whoop-ass on?"

"Mom, 'can of whoop-ass?' What do you know about Stone Cold Steve Austin?" I chuckle.

"What do *you* know?" Vassili feigns jealousy, kissing and nibbling my jaw.

"No, Stone Cold didn't coin that term. It was Chuck Norris," Yuri says. "Had to be him. I watched his movies and shows. When Malich would be angry that I wasn't studying, I'd tell my pop that Chuck taught me enough English."

Our entire table is rowdy and laughing now—except for Martin. My brother can be so uptight, sometimes his reactions are long overdue, too! I had called him with a hunch after I returned to California. He said mom was alright. Now, he's ready to start an intervention as he chews his food in silence.

"Wait, wait," Samuel speaks up. "Popeye made that statement. It had to be Popeye who said, 'can of whoop-ass.' That's from back in my day."

My mother is teary-eyed with laughter, and I hold my sides. Martin almost chokes on a glass of sweet tea before he caves and lets a good chuckle take over. Damn it, but I wish I was capable of refuting Sammy. I can't stop laughing to debate with him. Popeye was a television cartoon and couldn't have possibly said those words.

L ife's good. I've taken the rest of the week off work to attend Vassili's training practice. Media swarms the bikeway, ready for him to officially announce his fight with Karsoff. My man is going to break the German fighter's head off, and I'm ready for it.

We're in the middle of Vadim's gym. Some of the other fighters are crowding around the cage. I have to hold Natasha on my hip, or she will attempt to run to the fence. Our one-year-old is stubborn enough to forgo perfecting her walk so that she can try to run.

"What song are you coming out to?" One of the fighters shouts.

Vassili stands on the canvass dripping wet with sweat. Dammit, if I wasn't holding our child, I'd be as hot and bothered. My husband gestures to me. I come closer to the cage and look up at him. He takes Natasha from me.

"Yuck, you're so sweaty," I tell him.

"Tell the DJ to play Trace Adkins, *Whoop a Man's Ass*."

"Huh?" I bite my lip. The singer doesn't sound familiar. Lord knows I've had it up to my eyebrows with underground rap music, foreign and domestic.

"Trace Adkins," Vassili tells me.

I head over to the DJ who is stationed where the free-standing weights usually are. She has purple hair that's shaved off on the left side, displaying a skull tattoo. She offers a bewildered look when I mention the singer.

She pulls out her iPhone and starts searching for the song. "Got it."

"Thanks." I head back toward the cage area, and my pace stops. I turn back to the DJ, and she shrugs her shoulders at the sound of a guitar. A man belts out country lyrics. Trace Adkins croons about having to whoop a man's ass sometimes.

"Oh no." I shake my head and shout over the music, "Hell, no Vassili! You are better than this!"

"Kuzen, I like this song, that mudak is gonna underestimate you, with this bullshit. You got to…" Yuri sequences his wording to shout the chores with Trace Adkins, "whoop a man's ass sometimes."

The DJ shouts through the speakers. "Vassili, you've gotta let me remix this. Still can't have you going out like that."

When Vassili steps down from the stage with Natasha, she has her hands over her ears.

"Oh, I thought she was a ruffian like you," I say before kissing my husband's lips. "Though I'm not a fan of country music, I can see you whooping some ass to this song. Boy, you love making a statement, don't you?"

He lifts an eyebrow as his only response. Cocky bastard.

2 0

Vassili

On Monday morning, Natasha and I take a trip to my uncle Malich's home. She's in the playroom with Igor's younger children while I sit with my two cousins in the kitchen. Every time Yuri passes the bottle, I smack the back of Igor's head.

"Kuzen, you cannot have any," I warn him through gritted teeth. "Let your pops go a day without taking care of your grown-ass!"

"Just a little taste," Igor says. The diabetic lucked out with a father who loves to cook. Malich enables him, then saves his fat ass.

"Ask again, and I'm going to punch you into that wall," I grit out.

"*Nyet, brat,* you don't need any of this," Yuri says, pouring himself another shot.

My wrath lands on him, dark gaze and lit with anger. "This is your big brother, Yuri. Don't wait until I correct his ass to step the fuck up. Okay?"

"Man, he'll do what he wants in spite of what we say, Vassili. You can beat him to a bloody pulp—"

"Hey," Igor cuts in. "I don't need any of you piz'das speaking for me."

"Who you calling a cunt!" I bark.

With a softer voice, Igor asks, "Are we playing cards or what?"

"Nobody said we were playing cards, man." Yuri huffs. "It's time to head down to the pier, right? It's Monday, Igor. How am I more aware of your schedule than you are?"

Malich sets plates in front of us. "He's not going to San Pedro. No one is."

"Dad, what do you mean?" Yuri unclasps the top button of his suit. "Every third Monday, Igor goes. If he's sick, then I go."

Malich slams a hand onto the table.

"We're out, Yuri. You haven't had to assist with a shipment in months. Guess what, Igor still makes himself sick. Shit, son, you were out a long time ago. Managing our champ here," Malich says, patting my shoulder, "is job enough."

"Did you tell Anatoly?" Yuri asks.

"We stopped receiving his shipments last month. Albeit, there's no telling him. My big *brat*—brother—thinks that he can bully us into it. Anatoly is wrong. Our lack of response should've gotten through that thick skull of his by now."

"Nobody told me shit." Yuri pushes his food away. "I have things to do. I could use the extra funds. What about the art dealings? I've handled those requests every quarter."

Our family has an artist. One of my half-sisters can free-hand the Mona Lisa with her eyes closed. It seems my father is capable of investing time in his children when they have a select skill that benefits him. We have a connection at Smithsonian and receive an inventory of new shipments. With

Yuri's assistance, my sister replaces the originals with her knockoffs. He, then, places the originals on the black market.

Yuri huffs again. "I need money."

Malich puts his fork down. "What's wrong, son? I cannot see the two of you going broke anytime soon. The matches. The Killer Karo clothing and memorabilia. The sports water. Your commercials still play, Vassili?"

"*Dah!*" I nod.

"What's with you, Yuri? Have I raised you to be greedy?"

"*Nyet*, father." He rubs a hand over his face.

"What the fuck is wrong with you then?" I ask. My cousin's anxiousness unsettles my bones.

"I'm proposing to Taryn. Is that okay with you?" he argues.

"Fuck, yeah. That doesn't have anything to do with me. You sure, though?" I glare him straight in the eye. They're inseparable when we double date. He's even more of an idiot than I thought for even considering settling down with someone like Taryn.

"What do you mean, *am I sure?*"

I put up a hand, not one for arguing. *Make your own mistakes with that bitch,* my face says it all.

"I'm proud of you, my son," Malich tells him. "Ready to make an honest woman out of your girl. When I decided to remove myself from my brother's grasps, it wasn't with the heavy heart I had expected. Your mother pleaded with me over a thousand times to cut ties with Anatoly before she died. He had taken over after your grandfather died, and I couldn't see myself leaving such a hot head to rule the Bratva."

"It's all about respect, not force," I mumble in agreement.

Malich nods. "*Dah!* It is. That numbskull is unpredictable. Anatoly would've been dead a month as the boss, without someone to smooth the waters for him. Too slimy," his eyes apologize to me for talking about my father. I shrug. "I've always told my sons, you too, Vassili, to never have regrets. I didn't pull out soon enough. Regrets like that stick to your heart, never go away."

"You were trying to save Sasha." I wolf down my food, momentarily strangled by emotion.

"Yes, me and your aunt continued to support Anatoly after Sasha was born because we saw the way he treated your mother. He was rapidly changing. He needed us in America. We saw that as a prime opportunity to take Sasha. If only he'd let us raise the girl."

"But my piz'da of a father wouldn't allow it." I frown.

"So yes, we will always have a few regrets. Striving for a better future isn't one of them. Not removing myself from the fold soon thereafter will always weight heavy on my mind. Now, Yuri, you are a millionaire. I am, of course, wealthy enough with the money I have made helping Anatoly build his empire over the years. But with that being said, what type of ring do you want to purchase this girl?" Although Malich is cushioning the truth with a joke, I feel that he isn't too keen on Yuri settling down with Taryn. The bitch is a gold digger, plain and simple. Telling Yuri the truth won't help at all. Some people cannot be told. They have to see it for themselves. It's not a good idea for him to drop money hand over fist as I did with Zariah. Instead, he needs to simmer the fuck down and evaluate exactly how unworthy she is.

"I want a ring made, like Vassili."

I bite my fist. *This isn't gonna work well for you, brat.*

"And you love this girl?" Malich inquires. Something in his voice is desperate for his idiot son to see the light. Every once in a while, Yuri gets pussy whipped. Torn the fuck down over some sour cunt.

"Is the bitch worth it?" Igor asks, plain and simple.

Yuri growls, already on the defense.

"Don't speak like that," Mikhail growls, entering the kitchen.

"What, brat?" Igor cocks a brow. "Our baby brother wants to propose."

Mikhail runs a hand through his dark hair, eyebrow raised. "Sounds like you're not too keen on her, Igor. Albeit, you're not marrying her. Yuri, brat, take her to church."

Yeah, and watch the bitch burn. I stop my thoughts. Mikhail is the voice of wisdom when he speaks. The watered-down version of Malich's wisdom. Although Taryn isn't half bad, she's not marriageable material. So, half-ass advice won't cut it.

"We love each other," he says.

"Then take her to church, brat." Mikhail regards the rest of us with a grunt and retreats from the kitchen.

"Uncle," I switch gears. "I need your help with something. Yuri and I have been trying to handle an issue for about a week. Shit got in the way."

Sliding my cell phone from my pocket, I mention the email. Malich comes around the island, placing on his prescription glasses. He then takes my phone to read the email about Frank Gaspar.

"Who is this little shit?" he asks, glancing through the photos of the decomposing body.

"A rookie cop," Yuri says. "I don't recall Anatoly ever wanting us to put anybody on the beat on payroll. Only Detectives and higher-ups. Have you heard of him?"

"Frank Gaspar? *Nyet.* Never." He places down the phone. "But we will know everything there is to know about him by the end of the day. You killed him?"

"Vassili punched him around a little, I did the deed." Yuri sniffs.

163

"He looks like a nobody. I'm assuming this email implies that somebody wants to make something out of nothing?"

We nod.

Malich sighs heavily. "You think your father did this to rattle you? We aren't picking up his shipment. He went ahead and sent it anyway. Hmmm, he'd be mad at me, not you, though, Vassili."

"Then it's Zariah's father!" Yuri slaps a hand onto the table. "How many times have I offered to put him down? I can take it easy on him, too."

"You're still having trouble with Zar's pops?" Malich's eyes widen in surprise. "We're all family now. What's going on there?"

My shoulders lift a little. "Zariah and Maxwell aren't on speaking terms. He hates me as much as I hate him. Zariah sent him a birthday party invite but the mudak didn't come."

"Jesus," Malich says. "That beautiful baby and her gorgeous mother don't deserve the silent treatment. He'd miss a grandbaby's first birthday because he hates you? That's bullshit. Shit like this makes my blood pressure increase. I'll make the call, figure out who this Gaspar is. See if he works for Anatoly or Washington. We'll go from there."

Later in the day, Malich is in the state-of-the-art kitchen again. The aroma of his famous meatball mozzarella soup wafts throughout the room. Months after we got married, that very soup set Zariah's nerves at ease when she met with the majority of my family. He picks up a plate of Russian bread and comes to sit down next to me.

"Uncle, you cook like we're celebrating a holiday," I say.

Zariah, who arrived after work, sits next to Igor's wife,

Anna. The women hold their conversation. Anna smacks Igor's hand as he reaches for a pelmeni—a Russian dumpling.

"You've had enough," she reprimands him, and then she's instantly back to laughing and chatting with Zariah. One of Igor's oldest daughters sneaks another pelmeni to Natasha, and the rest of the family is crowded around.

"So, uncle, any update?" I ask. He offered to cook dinner this evening because Frank Gaspar shouldn't be discussed over the phone.

He nods. "I got a response while grabbing that last plate. You want to finish eating or talk?"

"Talk," I reply. I have a month to make weight for my match with Karsoff. Camp week is hell with a French fry loving daughter and a wife who had no problems cheating on me with Fatburgers.

Yuri rises when we do. My wife hardly pays me any attention as she and Anna have switched subjects to some sort of a new facial wash.

We head away from the loud house and out onto the patio. Yuri leans against a column, and I pace the area while glaring at the turquoise lap pool.

"Okay, so for starters, Frank Gaspar isn't named Frank Gaspar. And he's not a cop," Malich says, sitting at the patio table.

I stop pacing. "Who was he?"

"An actor, a nobody. That automatically clears Washington." Malich drums his fingers on the table. "Knowing that crooked mudak, he'd have his own come after you. Not leave a trail by hiring an actor to pretend to be a cop. The real Frank Gaspar is on the force. Not in Los Angeles where it would be easy for Washington to send someone after you. The real Gaspar is alive and breathing and working at a precinct in Fontana."

Yuri and I exchange glances. He rubs the back of his neck,

and determines, "We had a few matches in Fontana, back in the day. Vassili is too big these days for that area. But who the fuck would still be angry with you, brat? What have you been up to?"

I shake my head. "I haven't been to Fontana, since firing that slimy ass promoter. Shit, the last time I was there, you were, too."

"Oh! The promoter who skimmed off the top, the bottom and the middle?" Yuri chuckles.

"You two done chatting it out?" Malich asks.

"*Dah*," I grunt as Yuri sits across from his dad.

"Good, because I'm aware of who did it. Danushka. So, either your father was desperate to scare you, or she's parted ways with him."

My body is drained as I sink into the chair to my cousin's left. Danushka. That bitch. Eyes closed, my father's motto runs through my mind. *Can't have a daughter without a son.* There was a time where the mudak forgot about me because he had babies popping up all over Russia. But Danushka is his second born. Just a few days younger than me. Shit, my father always jokingly said, if he had a girl first, he'd break her neck and start over. No matter how badly my father treated Danushka as a child, her tenacity was astounding. She worked her way up in the Bratva, snatched assignments from others. All she desired was recognition from our father. Shit, she thought my sister and I would disappear after my mother got the guts to run off with us.

"You aren't sure if she's working for Anatoly?" I finally ask.

"We've seen her in action. In the past, I'd heard about your father asking for a political figure in Italy to be dealt with, for example. Prior to a member being appointed to the task, the guy or girl is dead. Danushka then left her mark on the body."

"Dah, that cunt loves to catch my father's eye when he least expects it," I scoff. "What the fuck does that bitch want with me?"

"There isn't a shadow of a doubt in anyone's mind, Vassili, your father still wants you to be his successor. That's why Danushka is fucking with you."

My hands slam against the patio table with so much force that Yuri has to push back in his chair to get out of the way. The table is flung across the grass. It leaves tracks of mud and grass in its wake and slams into the pool.

I catch my breath as the table sinks to the bottom of the water.

"I am not fucking with the Bratva! Anatoly needs to get it through his head, Malich. I refuse."

"Nephew, take it easy," Malich's voice is tempered. "Blowing a gasket will not stop your father or change his beliefs. You are his firstborn. Good as royalty in his mind."

"Where the fuck is this cunt? Where is my half-sister?" My wild eyes rove back and forth from the two of them.

"Nobody knows," Yuri says, kneading the back of his neck.

I growl, unable to speak for a moment. "I'd call Anatoly and ask him what the hell is going on, but that motherfucker is incapable of a straight response."

Again, I start pacing over the cement slab. My fists swoosh out before me as I punch, cross, jab into the air. "You think he sent her?"

"Would be better that he had," Malich says. "She's a wild card. So if he sent her to screw with your mind—like she's clearly doing—then he would have her on a leash. If she's acting of her own accord..."

My voice booms, "I don't want her around my wife and kid."

"Have you told Zariah about her?" Yuri asks.

"Fuck yeah, I showed Zariah a photo, everything. She knows to stay away from Danushka…"

21

Zariah

Only a few months have passed since I met Danushka Molotov and we've connected in such a short time. We crossed paths on one of the lowest days in our lives. We were two melancholic wives in the alcohol section of Whole Foods.

At the time, my husband was pissing me off. I couldn't fathom how he'd want to return to the cage after a torn patella. I'd tortured myself with YouTube videos of the worst MMA fights to ever occur. Fighters broke their legs and had their skulls cracked. That was the worse time in my marriage with Vassili. I was so very afraid of him returning to the cage.

Danny was dealing with her demons about marrying a fellow Russian. We talked for a few moments. It sparked the start of a relationship that I needed. I have Taryn who isn't married, and I suspect may never settle down as long as she still has her looks. Where I'm from, too many friends are a bad thing, and so I didn't have any married friends until I met Danny.

Obviously, she has the same first name as Danushka Resnov. My husband's forehead vein pops out each time he reminds me to steer clear of his sister. I've done my due diligence. Background checks and everything. His sister looks like the Terminator. Pale. Brown hair. Big nose and muscular. Danushka Molotov is platinum blond, lithe, tan.

In my car, I shuffle to work within LA traffic, when an incoming call interrupts Tye Tribbett's latest CD. Starting my day without praise and worship is something I wouldn't wish upon my worst enemy. I'm a mess and three quarters without a sane mind! But I stop singing along and press the touchscreen to accept her call.

"Danny? I saw your text late last night. Are you back in town?" I gush into the phone.

"Yes. And I'm hijacking you at noon today for lunch."

"Ha, that's fine. So, did you get the house?"

"We did. As you know, my husband and I traded in Bel Air for Italy for a few months. Our new home is in escrow now. We're vetting potential caretakers for our home here."

"Humph, look no further, I don't mind moving into your home while you're away." I joke. Danny's husband has a hand in the steel industry and international banking. Aside from how busy he is, their home in Bel Air could entertain a person for a year. From grand courtyards to a theater, and bowling alley, the mansion has it all.

"Alright, I'll pencil you in for an interview," Danny joshes. "Horace is conducting background checks and all. But I want to invite you to Italy."

"Girl, I told Vassili that we have to take a trip to Apulia one day soon. I'm so happy that you guys are working out," I say, traveling down the street. Billingsley Legal is a few blocks ahead.

"I wouldn't mind having friends over for a week or so. Horace could spare at least a week to entertain. I have you to thank for that, Zariah. I wasn't much of a talker in our marriage, before."

"That's what marriage is about. To compromise, you have to talk it out."

"My family is different. We are old school Russians, and I've had such a negative mentality. I knew that if I married someone from my culture, it wouldn't work out. *Russian men*," she says in her thick accent. "But I fell in love with one. And here we are, Horace and I are working out."

Turning the wheel, I navigate around the Hot Chili's drive-thru line, across from the law firm. Idiots sure know how to *act* when it comes to good food.

"Alright, Danny, I'm heading into work. What time and where should we meet for lunch?" I maneuver around the tail end of an illegally positioned car.

"I've learned to cook. At least I attempted to. Horace and I took a class. If you are feeling courageous enough to try one of my new recipes, meet me at my place at noon? We can always go out instead, my treat."

"I'll meet you at your place." I swoop into a spot.

A t Billingsley Legal, I seek out Tyrese Nicks. He exuded the wrong kind of vibes when we crossed paths last week. From his eating me with his eyes to the distaste he had for my last name. Also, what's up with the mysterious history we have?

Vassili cornered him in my office. My husband's actions are fresh enough for the incident to have occurred yesterday. Due to my husband's recent acts of aggression which sent us to Atlanta, I had no time to correct Mr. Nicks. Until he has chosen to promote or move on to other endeavors, we have to work together in common accord.

The firm is built on the foundation of family, and he's the new fish.

I find him in his office, typing away. No mementos on the wall or his desk. Nothing to jog my memory of how we know each other.

"Good morning," I assert myself at the door.

The typing stops. His gaze drags over me from head to toe and back again. My dress accentuates my curves, stops mid-calf and is fashioned with a thin cardigan. High heel peep-toe booties and bangles finish off my ensemble. Those dimples of his are resurrected as he grins and says, "Come in."

Well, entering his office isn't necessary for what I need to get across. But I oblige and take a seat across from him. I ask, "So how are you liking the new job?"

"Pays the bills." Flippant fucker. As if I can't tell his navy-blue suit doesn't hug his muscles in a way that screams it was made specifically for him. He comes from a good black family, and I am not aware of that due to any sort of knowledge of him. Except for the diplomas peeking from a cardboard box.

Tyrese offers a half-smile. I don't match that. "I'm learning how to sympathize with people, Zariah. My previous professor suggested that I give a damn about people before I become..."

"This big bad wolf?" I cock a brow.

He nods. "This place serves two purposes. I learn to communicate with quote-unquote victims before I move along to DA."

I can appreciate a man with confidence, but he made our clients seem like *nobodies*. I say, "What better way to do it than with the ex-Chef Deputy District Attorney and working with a demographic that needs people to give a damn. That's a winning combination."

"Precisely. Is that still your plan as well?"

Tyrese's inquiry offers the perfect opportunity to insert me.

"No, my original plan would've caused me to burn out before I made enough money to give a damn. So my father once worked with yours? And apparently, I know you?" I cross my legs, lean forward and await his response. Usually, it makes a man choke when I'm too forward.

"Damn, woman, you truly are an attorney. We either lie or bite. That hurt." He offers a killer smile. "You don't remember me, whatsoever?"

He asks questions for my questions. My lips set into a line. This is a man's world, but baby, I play well. "Do you have a problem with my husband? Or my last name in general?"

Tyrese rubs his clean-shaven face. I can't stand a man whose face looks like a babies' ass. "This conversation is headed exactly where I anticipated. Zariah, I'm astounded by your choice in a husband."

"Elaborate," I grit out. My brain whirls. I can't fathom why I'm having this idiotic conversation with a man who has no relevance in my marriage. But I'll let him build his case. And then I'll be the lawyer, hell, I'll play executioner on his ass. I see my father through his gaze. So judgmental.

"You always wanted to get the bad guy when you were a kid, then you married him."

Who the hell is this man and why does he believe he knows me?

Tyrese's desk phone rings on key. The motherfucker has the last word as he picks up the headset. He offers a greeting into the receiver.

"Put whomever you're speaking to on hold," I order.

"Excuse me for a second." Tyrese places a hand over the receiver. "We can finish this conversation later. How about lunch—"

AMARIE AVANT

"Now!" My index finger slams onto the mute button. "Let's start with an apology? Oh, I forgot. You're learning to be apologetic while working with victims of spousal abuse and *whatnot*." I huff. "Oh, and while we're on the record, damn it, I apologize that you were *forgettable* when we were teens. I'm making that assessment based on how old you look, mid-twenties like myself. So, with that said, I'm going to be apologetic enough to forget you're a misjudge of character. My marriage has nothing to do with you. If I were to become a defense attorney, whomever I'm set to prosecute will encounter the same *Mrs. Resnov* as the next person! While you concluded that I lost my fucking mind and married a hoodlum, I'll grant you that assessment. Mr. Nicks, we do not know each other; therefore, I have yet to do an assessment as well. Meaning your beliefs about me are invalid."

"Zariah, I'm not trying to be a dick—"

"That concludes this conversation. Have a blessed day." See, Tye Tribbett and the gospel choir have assisted me with starting the morning on the right foot.

W ith a humongous knife in her hand, Danushka slices and dices like a small-town butcher. She has a thin yoga body. I assumed our lunch would consist of all veggies, as evidenced by her cutting more cucumbers and zucchini for the salad on the counter. But it's almost 1 pm, and I'm nursing an expensive glass of wine, with a name that I cannot pronounce. I lean my elbows on a marble counter while sitting in a kitchen so grand that I must poise my pinkie finger. The aroma in the oven is to die for.

"Almost ready?" I ask. "Danny, that lasagna has my stomach rumbling."

"Let's see," Danny mumbles, peeking inside of the oven. She grumbles in Russian, turns up the temperature on the wall oven, and then tosses her mittens on the counter.

"Maybe I should've taken you to lunch instead?" She gives a wry smile while heading back to the chair across from me.

"No worries, here. I could lose a few pounds," I say, comfortably seated in the plush chair. On a buttery cracker, I've constructed the perfect tiny sausage and aged-cheese slices. These damn things are good.

"I did learn to cook. Horace, too. Nonetheless, we always had the chef there to instruct us." She chuckles. "Because of you, I've stopped frowning. Life is good, you know?"

Unsure how to respond, I pause a moment before saying, "I am happy for you."

"My favorite line used to be *Russian Men, pah!*" She makes a face at that. "I can't believe Horace swept me off my feet. I can't believe we are a year into our marriage. It's crazy."

"What's crazy, in retrospect is how you and I were raised." I shake my head in thought.

"Yes!" She agrees. "Zar, you were destined to marry some anal-retentive businessman. I should be with … someone, not Russian. Our parents almost ruined us for the good guys that were already there to sweep us off our feet."

A smile perches at the edges of my mouth. By way of parents, it would've just been my father who set the foundation for me to focus on a different life. I have seven miserable years of toeing the line and not taking the plunge. While we wait for the lasagna, Danushka and I stroll down memory lane as I share about how Vassili and I met. Of course, I nix the Sergio aspect. A half-hour later, the conversation shifts again. We've quickly become old friends who can delve into and out of chats.

"Oh goodness. I dated a football player once. My family expected him to be uneducated and…" she leans back in her chair. "And I didn't care how the guy treated me as long as he…"

"Wasn't Russian?" I ask, tasting the crisp smooth wine.

"Yup. This is why I love you, Zar. Not only do you finish my sentences. But we both married men we couldn't fathom spending the rest of our lives with."

"We stepped out on faith and it paid off." I agree with her wholeheartedly. My soul is settled having a friend like Danushka who, unlike Taryn, fights for something good. In my past, I never saw myself with a knight in shining armor. Maxwell Washington, my father, is who I can thank for that. I never knew marriage was about unity until I met Vassili and we became a team.

L ater on, Danny and I are stuffed. The recipe to the lasagna she made is in my leather purse as she walks me past a marble fountain to her front door.

"I am considering the housewarming in Italy," Danushka says. "We have yet to meet each other's husbands. Vacation makes for a good double date, right?"

I nod my head in agreement. Too many times in the past Vassili was out of town to promote an upcoming match or her husband was away on business. Hugging her, I reply, "We can always set aside everything for some 'us' time. Italy sounds like a perfect enough place for it."

22

Vassili
Las Vegas, One Month Later…

This morning, I read my Bible to Natasha, yet anxiety tornadoes through my soul. The thump of music against the cement walls signifies that the second match is now beginning. I finish my prayer, kiss the cross around my neck and stand up.

Fight, Vassili. Get in fight mode. God has blessed you...

A thousand times I've contemplated faith. Now's the time to focus on my capabilities not fixate on bullshit. But before I can mentally offer the same credo again, I ask, "No news on Danushka?"

"Not now, Vassili," Vadim grumbles. "You've prayed, let's warm-up. Nestor."

"I'm hot as fuck," I tell him. I address my uncle, Malich, who's sitting on the bench with Yuri and Nestor, with the lockers behind them.

My arms swoosh out as I complete rapid punching

combinations. I'm burning up inside, and I'm consumed with what the fuck my sister has been up to. Why email me?

"*Dyadya?*" I nudge my chin to my uncle. Nestor settles back down.

"Not yet," Malich says. My uncle isn't much for traveling, and I'm ruining one of the select few times he attends my matches with talk of Danushka.

He gets up, walks over and places his hands on my shoulders. "You have a belt with your name on it, Vassili. Get it back. The best thing Danushka has going for herself is getting into your head."

Vadim takes over with, "Do you want Karsoff there as well? Fucking with your mind?"

My glare tracks across both of them. They know the answer is 'no.' My little half-sister hasn't reached out since dropping the bomb that she knew of Frank Gaspar's death. Although there isn't a stream of dead bodies everywhere I walk, her motivation has unleashed the beast in me. What is her reasoning?

"Nestor," I cock my head to him. He jumps up. Time to spar.

I keep my head down. A blinding light shines down on me as I head toward the cage. A camera crew is in front of me, tracking backward. The music is funneled into my ears with the buds that I'm wearing. Though I can't see a foot before me, the muffled sound of screaming tells me that not a single seat in the place is empty.

"Karo..." The crowd's chant pierces through the rap music I'm listening to.

I stop at the cutman, feeling like a caged tiger in my skin

as he applies Vaseline. Then I'm climbing up the stairs, and once into the octagon, I flip three times and land on my side of the canvas. I miss being the favorite, the last man out, to assess my opponent as he stands here, stalking the cage. Now, here I am, the announcer is running stats for the German as he comes out.

Forever passes before the opening bells ring. Karsoff steps forward to touch gloves. I gesture for him to get the fuck back to his side. This is not a game. I'm hungry for blood, for a weak pulse.

We crash into each other. Like those fucking punching boxer toys I wished for but never got as a child. Karsoff and I toss bricks for fists. Then my left fist zeros straight for his nose. The German stumbles backward. I press forward, taking the right jab to my chin with a sneer on my face. That mudak gets confident until my right hook strikes, sliding across his jaw. That one single hit shakes Karsoff to the core. In slow motion, he goes down, with my machine-gun fists spraying across his face every step of the way to the canvas.

"Put the pressure on 'em!" Nestor shouts from my corner.

This was too easy...

I grapple over him. Karsoff begins to turn over. Instead of protecting himself or fighting back, he grasps at the canvas as if he wants to get up and run. With this position, I loop my leg around him. My bicep zips around his neck, and I choke him back to me, into a triangle chokehold.

Karsoff reaches a hand around, punching my ear. The pounding causes my ear to ring. I let up, stand and shake my head. He's left in a vulnerable position. As I reach down, Karsoff's leg swipes out. He issues a rapid succession of turtle kicks. I glare at this bitch, jumping to defend myself from his right foot.

I step back, my glare telling him to get up. I'm going to

bring this cunt back down. So far, he's tried to run and did a shitty job defending himself when I stood up. A few 'boos' break through the chanting crowd. I gesture for him to get up, because tonight, I feel like entertaining.

Karsoff rises. He's back to his cocky self. This mudak was afraid of the takedown. As we go back to tossing punches, the bell signals the end of the first round. I glare at my opponent one last time before moving toward my corner.

"You good?" Vadim asks.

"Good, Good."

"Your knee—"

"I'm fucking good, Vadim. Knee, body. All of that. Good." I snatch the water he hands over. "*Spasibo*," I grunt out my thanks in Russian. Cool liquid quenches my thirst as I toss the water back. Then I crunch the paper cup and flick it over my shoulder.

At the commentator table, two casters are chatting it up.

"The ferocity in which Karo came into the cage woke me up just now."

"Me too. Almost forgot there were a few matches before this, and we aren't even at the main event."

"Karo looks better than he ever has in his entire career. And c'mon let's face it. We can count on two fingers the time Karo didn't rise to the occasion. He's one of the toughest fighters in the circuit."

"Karsoff looks more mature in the ring tonight as well, Johnny. After the first takedown, he came back smoothly. What he had going for him is matching Karo's pace, and not flying off the handle."

"Karsoff has made an excellent recovery, and he may be the current favorite, but I'm going against the grain. The moment Karsoff hit the canvass, he was a scared animal. If Karo can get another takedown, I predict vengeance will play out."

"That's right, Johnny," I mumble to myself. I'm going to serve Karsoff the beatdown of his life.

The bell chimes. Time for round two. This time, when I take my opponent down, his ass won't be getting back up.

2 3

Zariah

My heart lodges into my throat. Damn, I prayed that Karsoff would be a punk. Okay, maybe not "prayed in Jesus name" per se. Although my fingers were crossed, and I wished with all my might. Vassili and Karsoff go toe-to-toe, trading bomb for bomb like the first round was a warmup. Announcers are calling out predictions and last-minute ideas. The masses around me scream loud enough for my eardrums to vibrate.

Granted, I do my best to keep the confidence for Vassili's sake. There may never come a day when I watch a match without squirming in my seat. His fight with Juggernaut last year ended so soon, I didn't even get the chance to become a 'nervous nelly.'

Natasha stands in my lap, jumping all over my legs. In a shimmery purple dress, with a ribbon in her curly hair, she makes for the perfect cheerleader for her father. Her fat fists pound the air as Vassili does a cartwheel kick that lands on Karsoff's ear. My husband is showing his ass now! All these signature moves I learned to put my mind in this invincible superhero mode. I snatch up some of our daughter's energy.

"Kill 'em, Karo!" I scream so loudly that Natasha glances back at me. Her pupils drag up and down my frame. This child of mine glares at me like: *no she didn't!*

"Sorry, baby." I chuckle, rubbing her ears. Is this child mine? This girl with her dramatic sense of humor?

"Give 'er here," Yuri says, seated to my left. The instant I hand Natasha over to him, I'm out of my chair screaming and performing gymnastics moves. I can't do the third round —damn, I'm not doing much. But I can't stomach one.

"Kill, Kill!" The vocal cords in my throat strain. *Jesus, give my baby some David versus Goliath strength! A shot and drop 'em!*

There are seconds left. My eyes dart from the two of them, going brick for brick. Finally, a missile of a right-hand lands against Karsoff's nose and a mean uppercut drops him.

He bounces up.

"Stay down, motherfucker!" I growl.

From my peripheral, Yuri glances at me much like he did when I went into labor in Kentucky. Vassili stands there as Karsoff seems to forget where they are. He popped up like a jack-in-the-box. Now, his legs are buckling like a newborn calf. Karsoff stumbles into the cage, his fingers grip onto the wiring. Vassili slams a looping right hook into the side of Karsoff's head.

For a split second, it appears the fighter recollected exactly where he was and what he was doing. His hands clenched into fists as he hit the canvass.

Vassili goes in for the kill. He slaughters Karsoff with follow-up strikes and lets his fists rain down on him. Luckily, his enemy turtles up, and the referee tosses himself into the mix.

Vassili backs up and allows Karsoff to be rescued. My husband pounds a fist against his chest. His barbaric antics send an earthquake of spasms in the walls of my pussy. I'm so wet for him right now.

After a long cheer, the referee stands next to Vassili as the fight stats are announced. While Karsoff is receiving a whiff of a scent that while rousing him, the referee grips Vassili's fist and holds it up.

My husband is declared the winner.

Then the commentator steps up, with a microphone in hand. "This is two fights in a row now. You've come in and been very dominant. Karo, what's been the difference?"

My husband's muscular frame is drenched in sweat. "I'm thankful to be here. God keeps my hands up. With faith, there's only one way I'm going."

"You made a fadeaway overhand that caught Karsoff's temple early on. Then you gave the fans more entertainment and Karsoff a chance to redeem himself. This is one of the most entertaining matches of the season..."

"Aw, baby." My lips caress a kiss on Vassili's eyebrow which has seven stitches. He returned to the hotel room with Yuri. I expected them to go out and celebrate. That was the plan if Natasha dozed off. The alternative is painting the town as a family.

I give him the once-over. He's wearing Nike flip-flops. I can't recall a day when his left big toe ever survived a fight. The damn thing is always broken. When I start to hug him, he grimaces.

"I'm sorry, baby," I moan. Next, I reprimand him with, "Why don't you ever say you're hurt?"

"Nyet, I'm not hurt. I'm . . ." Vassili mentions something along the lines of being invincible.

Yuri's gaze is searing through us. I step back from Vassili, guilt clinging to me. The poor guy was watching us with longing in his eyes. Unaware of my feelings, Vassili pulls me into a bear hug with gritted teeth.

"Just one rib," he growls, squeezing the breath out of me.

"Boy, why don't you ever say anything? I don't have x-ray vision." I softly press against his chest. "And I hate when you hurt."

He caresses my cheek. "If my wife wants a hug, fuck it, that's what she gets."

"Humph! Broken ribs and all?"

"One rib, girl."

He lets me go and heads to the bedroom, where a Disney movie is playing loudly on the Pay Per View channel. Natasha loves to sing to the music.

"I'll be back after a quick shower."

"Okay," I smile and then address Yuri. "I'm sure Natasha will fall asleep in the stroller soon. You guys can go hit the club."

"You look beautiful, Zariah. *Nyet*, I'm not feeling the club scene. What were your plans?" He asks.

"Well, if Natasha chose to party the night away, we were going to head to the dolphin exhibit at The Mirage," I begin. Due to how forlorn he's looked this weekend, I add, "Would you like to tag along?"

"Of course, more time with my Chak-Chak."

"Chalk what?" My eyebrow crinkles.

"Chak-Chak. Vassili calls her that sometimes. But *dah*, I'll definitely come. Malich doesn't gamble, it's no fun alone. There's nothing else for me to do," he pouts. "Taryn is sick so..."

"Taryn is sick?" I repeat, having spoken with her earlier yesterday. She was bragging about a date with a New York banker. The guy had sent her a first-class ticket to meet him in Milan. Feeling sorry for the big guy, I wave a hand and keep the manipulation on rotation with, "Oh, yeah, she is cramping."

"She told me she had a stomachache," Yuri's eyes shade in thought.

"Which is it, girl?" Vassili's tone is curved as if he's testing me.

Where the heck did he come from? I turn around. He is definitely in a defensive stance. With his shirt off, jagged muscles, a bandage around his hard abdomen and a hard glare. Vassili asks, "Cramping or a stomachache?"

"It's the same thing, Vassili," I cut my husband a look. Then offer Yuri a reassuring smile. Taryn is fucked up. And Yuri is a Resnov. I'm sure killing the messenger works for a big guy like him. Clearing my throat, I add, "Um, I'm going to help the big bully shower. Yuri, if you hear Natasha become restless, check in."

With a small nod, Yuri settles down on the couch. He sits, wide-legged and fingers steepled in thought.

Vassili stands at the door to the bedroom as I enter.

"Congratulations, Zariah, you could've saved his life," Vassili tells me.

"How?" I scoff.

"He wants to marry the bitch."

"Oh, God." Shit, my poker face is for the courtroom. We move past the television, which is across from the bed where Natasha is watching a Disney movie. There's a scattering of pillows on the floor around the bed to stop her from falling. Although, our daughter is a pro at the pull-up and can shimmy down a rope if necessary.

With Natasha safe, I shake my head then add, "Marriage with her is a bad idea."

"Ya think? Fuck yeah, it's an awful idea. This is the first time Yuri has dated a female for longer than a few months. He cares about that bitch, and evidently, she doesn't share his feelings. You should've said something."

I head to the luxurious bathroom. "Yuri's your cousin, why me?"

"It's easier when it comes from a girl, shit, I don't know. I've never been fucking cheated on." Vassili closes the bathroom door behind him. Crap, I'm locked in with him. My husband never argues or debates with me. First of all, he says a man should not argue period. It's for women. Sexist much. Secondly, he's afraid of confrontation—or he was before he had a broken patella. I won the fights by default. Meaning he'd be quiet until he was calm enough to chat. On occasion, Vassili uses his forearm conditioning thingamajig to get under my skin while I try to carry on a debate with him.

Right now, I'm not in the mood to defend Taryn, argue or chat. Because battle wounds are sexy.

I try to conclude my opposing argument with another tender kiss on his lips. Then I murmur, "Vassili, you'll never be cheated on. I love you with all of me. Also, the consensus is that either one of us would murder the other due to infidelity. Let's get out of their business."

His frown deepens. "So, my cousin loses out on tens of thousands of dollars on a wedding ring for that bitch, fuck that! You go tell him that his bitch is a *bitch*."

My hand goes to my hip. "Vassili, if you don't stop calling my friend—"

He corners me against the counter, his hands slamming down on either side of the edge. "What are you going to do?"

My fingers brush ever so softly against the "K" in KILLER across his left pectoral. My voice is silky as sex. "Vassili, may I suck your cock?"

"*Nyet! ... Dah!*" He growls and then nudges his head to the floor. I sink to my knees. Vassili leans back against the counter. The sound of his belt unbuckling and his zipper moving titillatingly slow sends a rush of saliva into my mouth.

I gulp it down, imagining his seed. Vassili fists his cock, running his large hand over his extremely long, thick erection. His dick belongs all over me. In my mouth, between my breasts, pounding my pussy, and he might not even have to get me drunk enough for some anal action.

My fighter looks ruggedly sexy. His bruises enhance how strong he is. I'm imagining him slaughtering my pussy as hard as he slaughtered Karsoff. Kill the cat. He hits his cockhead playfully against my cheek. "You wanna suck daddy's cock?"

"I want to suck daddy's cock. I want daddy's cum in my mouth. All over me..." Shit, did I say that? I'm hypnotized by the way his hand works his cock. Wish it were me.

My husband's eyes glint gorgeous obsidian and his mouth pitches into a cocky grin. "Okay."

Vassili stops fisting his dick and I throw my lips onto it with eagerness. My mouth is warm and wet against his hot, slick, titanium rod. I toss it back down my throat and attempt to gulp the head of him with my tonsils.

I glance up at him.

"Fuck, keep your eyes on me, Zar," he commands. "You my good girl?"

I hum the perfect response against his crown.

"*Nyet*, Zariah, you're my bad bitch tonight."

My eyes stay trained on him as his cock pounds my brains with each swish of my neck.

"I can cum all over your face?"

I nod.

He grips my ponytail, and I choke his cock deep into my throat.

"Fuck yourself, Zar. If you want me to nut all over you, fuck yourself."

My neck action keeps my head bobbing up and down. Like I'm going for an apple in a water-filled barrel, the tip of his dick slams my tonsils. I reach down over my skin-tight dress and grab my tit. My body is hot, my pussy is aching.

"Fuck that pussy, girl. Once you cum all over your fingers, I'll cum all over your face."

"Mmmm." I moan. I'm in love with the taste of his dick. It takes me a while. From tweaking my nipples to roaming my hand along my abdomen.

Vassili reaches down, growls at the pain from his rib and helps me pull my tight dress up over my hips. I press my thong to my side, shove his cock back into my mouth and three of my fingers into my treasure. The release of feeling something inside of me has me momentarily satiated.

"Suck harder, or I won't cum, Zar."

My tongue swirls around his head, and then to the back of my throat, he goes.

"You wet?"

I do my best to nod while sucking his cock like it's solid gold.

Vassili commands, "Bitch, work that pussy."

My fingers move rapidly. His hand twines in my hair, pumping me up and down. My lips glide over his cock at a rapid pace. A flash of ecstasy masks my face when rain drenches down my fingers. His seed sprints into my mouth. He pulls out. I'm masturbating the long orgasm out of me as his warm cum shoots across my lips. I lock my mouth open, to catch as much as I can, and continue screwing myself. Thick globs of cum mask my cheeks and lips. With a glance into the mirror, the walls of my pussy throb. I've never looked so sexy in my life.

I rub my index finger along my chin, around my fingers and drag the rest of his cream to my lips and lick my mouth clean. Vassili is staring at me like he wants to screw me now. Again…

Vassili holds out a hand, helping me up. I start to kiss him. He turns away.

"Okay…" My eyes water instantly. Why won't he kiss me?

"*Nyet, nyet.*" Vassili groans, he kisses my mouth hard, then rough, then tender. He feasts on my lips. "I'm sorry, Zariah."

"What? Vassili, did the doctor give you any pain meds?" I place a hand on my hip. The momentary lurch of my heart has ended, now I'm concerned. He's usually knocked out after norcos. But what's up with his ever-changing attitude?

"I shouldn't have called you a bitch."

"We're married, Vassili. We were having raunchy porno fun." I scoff. He seems consumed by anger at himself. Disappointment? I grin. "If you call me that while we are arguing I'll chop your balls off." Really, I'll try.

"I won't call you it ever again."

Natasha starts crying. The credits for the Disney movie are running.

I sigh heavily. "Vassili…"

He steps inside of the elongated shower and turns it on. No matter how much I want to resolve things, this discussion is over. Vassili is further away from me than he's ever been before. Even during those seven years that I denied him, we were still tethered to each other.

24

Vassili

"You're looking for me?" Her unforgettable voice is weighted down with envy and strife. I prefer it over the sound of me calling my wife a bitch. *What the fuck was I thinking?*

Zariah had asked me to come all over her. That's something I've done to cunts who've asked.

But my wife?

I shouldn't have wanted to fuck her ass! I shouldn't have called her a Bitch. That shit was running through my brain in rapid succession. On repeat, prior to answering my phone.

I head into the upstairs office, although it's just Natasha and I. She's playing in her playpen for now. My hands clutch at my phone as I speak in a gritted whisper, "Danushka, fuck yeah, I've been looking for you. Where are you at?"

"How cute. Is my big brother requesting a sibling date?"

"Why did you email me?"

Fuzzy silence comes through the line. After a few moments, my sister says, "To determine your level of connections. In your assumptions, it was either Anatoly or Washington, right?"

The bitch is playing the power card. I bark, "What the fuck do you know about Washington?"

"Lots. He is easier to persuade than you've been going about. However, Vassili, you never played nice in the sandbox."

I listen for any signs of familiarity. Rushing water. People in the background? Drilling wells! Something! It's silent on her end.

"Vassili. Or Karo. Which do you prefer?"

"I'd prefer you forgot my name entirely." I settle down into my custom leather chair.

"How can I forget the beloved of our father? Everyone loves you. You're a legacy. There's no forgetting about you."

"*Dah?* And there are few people in this world that I love. Like my wife and daughter. You're aware of them. And whatever is up your sleeve better have nothing to do with them." My Russian accent thickens with each word. Imagining her pulse dip, I threaten, "You got that! Or I choke the life out of you with my fucking hands."

"You know what, Vassili? Only you could get away with murder. The choice words. Let another one of our brothers or sisters make pointed threats, I believe our dad would give the order. Bang. Bang."

Grunting, I toss back, "*Your* father, not mine."

"Stop it with the reverse psychology already, Anatoly loves you in spite of…"

"Everything Little Danushka does for praise?" I smile. She may have won the match by tossing out her awareness of Maxwell Washington, but I win the war. Our father's love is all she's ever wanted.

Too bad, in this instance, I'd rather let her win.

Win her father's love. Followed by her leaving me the fuck alone.

"Correct, Vassili. None of my endeavors matter," her voice almost breaks.

"What do you want?" There isn't a single sympathetic bone in my body for this bitch. Her mother ratted mine out the last time my mother attempted to flee my father.

"This is what I want. To keep you on your toes, big brother. For now, that is." The call goes dead.

I'm left sitting with my hands bound into fists. Danushka is a hard woman to catch up with. The real kicker is not knowing her game plan. What is her motivation...

25

Zariah

Having returned to work after an extended weekend in Vegas, nothing much is on my plate. The case I'm currently handling deals with the Versa family will. Edgar Versa, the owner of a line of upscale home improvement business, died. Death and rich offspring segued into a lengthy argument. Sarah Versa is my client, and Edgar's granddaughter was the black sheep of the family. A party hardy, pill-popping, alcohol guzzling, toss a grand each night for fun type of girl. Until her parents cut her off. Edgar's bout with cancer sobered her up. Sarah cared for her grand-father. Now, her mother believes she tampered with said will.

Sarah does have much to gain. And with her parents sticking it to her, Billingsley Legal was all she could afford. But the real kicker is, nobody, but Sarah gave a damn about Edgar until he gave up the ghost.

My mission is to gather evidence of his frame of mind

while altering the will. The timing has become a red flag, due to him having it reconstructed a few months prior to his death. I'm scanning statements from Versa's doctors and nurses, recounting his last days when Lynetta pops her head inside of the door.

"Mrs. Resnov, we have a mother who just arrived with her children." She chews her gum impatiently. "She's saying if she goes away, she might not come back… She received your card from that nonprofit, *The People's Love*. Tyrese is trying to handle it but she's asking for you."

Oh, Tyrese is it? Over half a year has passed since I became her boss. I'm referred to by my last name while the newbie is Tyrese?

"Okay," my eyebrow furrows. It's a quarter past five and the front door should've already been locked. All the attorneys work on rotation in the evening and our secretaries assist with lock-up. Clearly, Lynetta has her shoes geared toward the back exit. It's summer, the nights are long, but why work overtime?

While reviewing the last note from the man's doctor, I mumble, "Leave the keys. I'll place the alarm on my way out."

"Alright, you may want Ty to stay," she advises as I glance up. "Just for safety reasons. I'm leaving the keys on my desk. I have to get to the childcare center in a few."

Um-hmm, she has until 6:30 pm and lives a few blocks down the road. I start to wonder what she means by safety reasons. Growing up in Los Angeles, I know certain streets not to venture onto. Or is she referring to the woman and her kids?

"Thanks," I call out while logging off my computer. I slide into my cardigan and exchange the house shoes that have kept me comfy all afternoon for my high heels.

A woman with a Hispanic accent continues to ask for me

as I walk around the cubicles. A voice that I assume belongs to Tyrese, offers to help her.

"No, no, I talk to Zariah. Just Zariah, *por favor*," she begs. As I near the bend to the front door, there's stifled crying.

"That's not a good idea, Mrs. Noriega. Please bring your children to my office, and I'd be glad to assist you."

"No," she replies.

My eyebrows crinkled. If the woman insists on receiving help from myself why would Tyrese attempt to intervene? The doorbells chime. My first line of vision is Tyrese taking a deep breath while placing his hands into his suit pants. His back is to me. The mother and children are gone.

"Mr. Nicks, why wouldn't you escort Mrs. Noriega and her children to my office if she was so insistent?" I snap. "What happened to empathizing with clients—learning to have a heart? This was a prime opportunity."

Under his breath, he mumbles about having a heart. I haven't seen the man's dimples since I chewed him up and spit him out. But after the bout of grumbling, he smiles at me. "Mrs. Resnov, it'd be better if she received assistance from—"

I put up a hand, my expression is enough to get him to shut up. I stalk out the door into the evening summer heat. Headed to the bus stop is a woman, who cannot be more than five feet tall with two children clinging to either side of her. The children's sobs are muffled by their mother's hips. My pace falters a few empty parking lot rows away as the sun gleams down onto what I assume is a neck brace.

"Mrs. Noriega," I call out while hustling over to her.

She turns around, eyes swallowed up by shiners and glossed with tears. The contraption I assumed was a neck brace is some sort of anchor, wired to her jaw. I stop myself from grimacing at the anguish she must feel when speaking.

"Are you . . ." She begins, every word labored.

Extending my hand, I politely cut her off, so that she's not forced to endure the pain. "I am Zariah Resnov, nice to meet you."

Intuition slams into me. Tyrese's attempt to score the case was on account of whoever caused Felicidad so much pain. My mind instantly goes to my family. Vassili would snatch me out of the workplace and slap an apron on me for the rest of my employable life. He doesn't want me defending cases like this.

"Felicidad Noriega," her thin lips move with restriction.

"And you are?" I hold my hand out to the oldest. Her son is about ten. A black line of grim is embedded under his fingernails, and his soiled clothing sticks to him.

"Juan," he replies, dark eyes shining up at me. I smile as he offers my hand a hearty shake.

Felicidad's daughter has her face burrowed into her voluptuous hip. I place the girl to be around five at most.

"My sister is Rosemary, she doesn't speak."

"Are you guys hungry? I'm starving."

"No, no," Felicidad has difficulty shaking her head.

"Yes," Juan replies at the same time.

Rosemary peeks at me. They're all hungry.

"Well, Felicidad, Hot Chili's across the way might be a great place for us all to talk."

"That's a great idea," Tyrese speaks from behind me. "The chili cheeseburger has your name on it, Juan."

"Oh yeah!" The boy agrees enthusiastically.

I glance back at him as he catches up to us.

Felicidad bites her lip. "Uh... I don't know, it might be too expensive."

Tyrese is finally at my side, he places a friendly arm around my shoulder. His hand clasps around my elbow to hold me into position. With his opposite hand, he gestures toward the pedestrian walk. As the family starts before us, he whispers into my ear, "You think I'm a jackass. Fine. There's no way in hell I'm leaving you with them."

I grind my teeth and glower at him. "Remove your arm, Mr. Nicks."

Tyrese squeezes my arm a little, before holding me firmly. "Her husband is one of the top dogs of the Loco Dios gang. Nothing you say or do will get rid of me. Call that my good deed for today, if you'd prefer, but I won't budge on this."

In the late 90s, my father was the leader of the gang unit. He was in charge of cleaning the streets, and he did. The Loco Dios were rid of each of their highest-ranking members. Nobody is still aware of how, but like with many gangs, what goes down must come up. By the next year, illegal residents and other younger members flooded into the spots designated for the 'top dogs.'

We walk across the street, and I'm hesitant for the first time. Each of my domestic violence cases in the past has given women a voice. Helping them seems like I'm paying penance for not serving my father the smackdown he deserved. But the Loco Dios Gang? Natasha's my priority now. And Vassili is the boss.

Rosemary peeks over at me from her mother's arm. My heart swells at the notion of how I *will* help keep her safe.

While pressing the pedestrian button, I wonder if the Noriegas are here illegally. Felicidad's speech was scattered. Though, Juan seems like he has a very strong head on his shoulders. He met my eyes and introduced himself in perfect English.

Well, at least we are in a predominantly black neighborhood. So, I can't see any cholos, Loco Dios or not, attempting to start anything.

There's a strong oil frying scent coming from Hot Chili's

as we enter. The restaurant has a seating area with old dusty red vinyl booths. With no servers to bus tables, we all glance up at the backlit menu on the wall.

Juan opts for the chilly cheese hamburger Tyrese recommended.

Tyrese subtly convinces Rosemary to try what he and Juan are going to eat in a kiddie combo version. I saddle up to Felicidad and say, "I've been eating way too much. I'm going to check out the chicken salad. You're welcome to anything on the menu."

It's a quarter to seven when we return to the law firm. True to form, Tyrese has not made any moves to leave me to lock up. I settle Rosemary in the toy area, in my office, across from the table.

"Juan, I don't have too many toys for a boy your age—"

"Toys," he shrieks, not an ounce of testosterone in his tone. "I am too old for toys."

Felicidad glances back and forth from us in an attempt to comprehend our conversation.

Rosemary is predominantly Spanish speaking like her mother. With hand movements and other gestures, the five-year-old caught on at the fast-food joint. So, I try out my high school Spanish. My voice hesitant and each word slips out in hesitance as I ask if she'd like to play with the toys.

Her mother offers the most humble, beautiful smile I've ever seen, as she appreciates my attempts.

Rosemary unwinds her arm from around Felicidad's waist and then takes tiny steps to the toy chest. Something of interest must catch her eyes because she zips the last few yards and hunkers down to play.

"Juan, I have a Nintendo Switch somewhere around here,"

I begin, sitting down and opening my file cabinet. "And a whole lot of new games for you— "

"No, thanks. I know everything you want to ask," Juan assures. "I have to help my mother say what she needs to say."

His mother eyes him as if attempting to read his lips. She's aware he's talking about her.

"Buddy," Tyrese leans against my file cabinet along the back wall. "Some of the stuff we'd like to ask your mother might not be appropriate for your ears."

His response softens my heart for the first time. What can I say? That was a perfect age-appropriate rebuttal.

"But I know everything. My father beats my mother as you can see," He states matter-of-factly. "I'm too old to watch him hit my mother anymore."

Tyrese and I exchange glances. For a man I can't pinpoint in time, we have an entire silent-film conversation in less than a second. The few interpreters on payroll ghost the office after hours. No calls. No nothing. This is time-sensitive. We need to be aware of what Mr. Noriega has done. It's imperative to her welfare, and maybe even her children as well.

I hesitantly ask. "What happened?"

"My father hit me, too." He rubs a hand underneath his left eye. Upon peering closely, there's a grayish half-moon that I assumed was due to lack of sleep.

Juan's lips tense as he continues, "My teacher harped on about being a mandated reporter. She called CPS. That was yesterday. My mom is afraid to go to the cops. Yes, she's illegal, Rosemary is too. But we cannot go to the cops because some of those cops are friends with my father."

"Are you illegal?" I inquire.

"Nah. Dad snuck Mom over here a long time ago. They had me. Mom got caught working at a cleaner, she was sent back. But I think my dad is the reason those people—I don't know the names of them—come and get illegals."

In his haste to speak, I decipher that he means ICE or another immigration official came to get his mother at his father's request.

"Why would your father rat out your mother?" I ask, hoping my friendly jargon keeps him speaking. Much of what Juan has divulged can be verified.

"He had just beat up my mom, I was five. He had another woman on the side. Mom tried to fight him, that was the first and last time she did that." He huffs.

"So, you've stayed with your father while your mother lived in Mexico?"

"No. I stayed with my *Abuelita*. My father's mother. Then Dad went to see Mom. She got pregnant with Rosemary."

Juan continues to tell the story of how his father snuck his mother back to California. Mr. Noriega promised life would be better, and *he* would be better.

"Where's your grandmother?" I ask.

"Dead."

Shit, I keep a straight face. If CPS were involved, the grandmother would make a good relative placement due to his history in her home. My eyes light with sincerity as I reply, "I'm sorry to hear that. Does your mother have any other family in the states?"

"No. Her family isn't in Mexico either. All dead. Or maybe they don't want to see my mom because of my dad. Sometimes I wonder." He licks his lips. "I've never been to Mexico. I ain't trying to go either. Can you help my mom and sister stay? Can you keep them safe from my dad?"

His dark brown orbs plead with me to work wonders. Which is harder? Our current president doesn't give a shit about Mrs. Noriega or keeping her near her son. Her husband clearly doesn't give a shit about her in general. Mr. Noriega has a gang family to assist with apprehending his wife and punishing her as he sees fit.

"We'll speak with an immigration attorney about your mother and sister."

"Thanks. That would be great," he says.

Tyrese's gaze connects with mine. Then he stops leaning against file cabinets to lead the conversation.

I slide my cellphone from my cardigan to shoot a quick text to Vassili about arriving home late. Then I call The Four Seasons to request a room under Karo's contract. My husband would kill me for placing myself in this situation, but he's a generous man.

Tyrese comes to my side as I finish the call. The Killer Karo franchise already has an account with the hotel.

Eyebrow lifted, he asks, "A five-star hotel?"

"This office isn't in Noriega's neck of the woods, but let's have his family stay somewhere he's even less likely to frequent."

"But we have vouchers for the general area."

"Unless you're headed out for the evening," I offer him a delicious smile, "I'd be so grateful that you stop offering advice."

"*We* will lock up together," Tyrese retorts.

I t's past nine when lo and behold, I end up at The Four Seasons *with* Tyrese Nicks. Felicidad is wiping away tears as she takes in the double bed with clean sheets.

"Can you tell your mother that you all should head to the welfare office tomorrow?"

"She won't go," Juan replies. He's truly parentified. A term

I learned in child development, which indicated that the youth held on a parental role. He makes a good attorney in her defense.

"Please and thank you." I smile.

He starts in Spanish. She makes scissor movements with her hands, saying "No, mijo, no."

"I told ya." Juan huffs.

"You have the right to have food stamps, Juan. Your mother and sister are undocumented. But you have the right."

He continues to shake his head. "No. I don't care. We can go hungry together. It's happened before."

Tyrese tries. "It's against the law for welfare worker to—"

"But these are my mother's words. She's paranoid. Thinks my dad knows everybody in Cali."

"Alright," I say, dishing out a few crumpled dollars. I don't keep change around. Tyrese pulls out a money clip and gives them three crisp twenties.

Outside, Tyrese and I head through the parking lot. He'd driven Juan while the girls rode with me. He forced me to stay on the phone the entire time we searched for parking spots. Then he'd ordered us not to get out until he was at the door.

In silence, we head across the brightly lit lot. As anticipated, Tyrese doesn't head straight toward the perimeter of the lot, where he parked. He follows me to my car. The masculine scent of his cologne is so close. Yet, I'm not in the right frame of mind to ask about our shared past. Because he's not Vassili, and paranoia is creeping over my shoulders. The Loco Dios has gained notoriety in recent years. They're even more infamous since resurrecting themselves. They're a ruthless, rowdy bunch backed by cartel connections. I need some intel as to how deep Noriega is with this gang.

I know exactly the person to apprehend that information from… my father.

26

Vassili

My entire day went to shit. I assumed all the trouble Malich went through to get a message for Danushka might settle my nerves. But the logic behind what my half-sister is gunning for while in my city is still over my head.

Natasha is asleep, and I'm seated on the chair in the master suite, watching a recap of the fight from Vegas. Though there were no title matches last night, each victor keeps my attention on the 'ground and pound' they served their competitors. Shit, my very own fight held enough damage to fill an entire fight card. Karsoff and I went for blows, but as suspected, I came out the victor. My hands are clenched into fists at my side. There was a moment in the second round in which my knee started to knot up on me. Karsoff didn't use that to his advantage. Then again, fire lit my eyes. A grenade could've been tossed at me, and I wouldn't have given a fuck. Wouldn't have felt a thing.

My cell phone vibrates on my left leg. I read the message for Zariah. "I'll be home in 15. No thx for dinner."

Is she texting while driving? I call her instead of replying.

My wife's voice is cheerful as she speaks, "Hey, baby—"

"Girl, are you driving and playing with your phone?"

"*Boy*, you love to check in on me every few minutes when I'm out late." Her voice is filled with laughter, then she switches up her tone to attempt to sound like me. "Vassili, you texted, 'girl what's keeping you?' I responded about a client. Then you offered to *have borscht on the table when I get home*. Vassili, you have better luck adding a line of sugar to your cock and having me lick it up for a late dinner. So yes, the last few messages I replied to, may have been while I was driving."

"Are you hungry?" I ask. My eyes are on a roundhouse kick, on the screen. It's from the main event that sent the loser into a frozen state before he fell back.

She cackles. "I love you, Vassili. You keep me safe, I'd never go cold or hungry, so I think I'll keep you around. For the last time, no, I'm not hungry."

"Shit, salad is not dinner."

"Humph, coming from the man who tortured me with raw juice. Oh, and the man who roughhoused me enough to be afraid of entering a Jamba Juice within a hundred-mile radius."

"That fucking stuff isn't healthy, smoothie my ass." I quip, hearing the sound of the garage in the background.

"Whatever, Vassili," she says. The faint sound of music is cut off. "You can't tell me their kale drink isn't the best."

"Nyet. It sucks." Chuckling, I arise from my chair. I head down the hall and shuffle downstairs. "There's probably one bite of kale in the juice. That shit is full of lime sherbet."

"One kale leaf, a few scoops of sherbet. Stop being such a stickler? Dude, it's all for taste," Zariah says. Her voice begins to echo as she rounds the corner near the laundry room. "I had a long day at work, why are we arguing?" She asks into the receiver.

My wife is twenty yards away, glancing me up and down. Now, I need to find some fucking sugar for her to lick off my cock.

"Nyet, I'm not arguing with you, beautiful." I hang up the phone and get an eyeful of my wife. How does this happen? Every instant I lay eyes on her, she's more gorgeous than before. My hands brush over her shoulders as I remove the floppy sweater thing she's wearing, and let it fall to the floor. Yeah, that's what I think about those stupid little sweater thingies. They cover the roundness of her ass, the fatness of her hips and pussy. Sometimes she's holding the knitting over her chest and I'm not even a breast man, but I still want to snatch it off of her.

My mouth goes to her forehead, and I brush a soft kiss there. I needed her softness to settle the anxious rage within me. Her essence filters through my nostrils, and I bestow soft kisses to her neck. My nose nudges into her skin, getting an addictive whiff of her. I fall to my knees. My hands clasp her ass, and I prod my nose at the apex of her thighs, breathing in deeply. And she smells so sweet like...

"Brown sugar," I groan.

"What?" Zariah licks her lips, her chocolate gaze glancing down at me.

"You had this on during our first encounters. You were at Vadim's Gym, and then again when I visited you at home."

"More like breaking and entering. Yes, Vassili. It's my favorite from Bath and Body Works."

"Shit, girl, then why haven't you worn this in a while?"

Zariah shrugs. "I usually wear perfume these days. A little more sophisticated, I guess."

Instantly I'm standing, and I've swept her off her feet. My

wife lets out a fearful yelp before laughing and kicking her legs.

She screeches, "Can I get a little pre-warning, Vassili!"

"Okay, I'm going to feed you, then I'll eat you." My tongue weaves around hers in a breathtaking kiss. "Before you fall asleep, you still must tell me what caused you to return home so late. Dah?"

"*Nyet.*" Zariah sounds too cute telling me no in Russian. She presses a hand against my chest, though her face is beaming from ear to ear. "How about we skip part one. Let's finish the evening with you tasting these sweets. Part three is confidential, as well. I can't tell you about my case."

"Confidential, my ass," is all I say, as I carry her upstairs. There 'll be no arguing about it. I'll compromise about her dinner since she says she's not hungry. But family law or not, I prefer my wife in the kitchen and pregnant. Our house is the safest place for her. So, I'll eat her tonight, and ask about the new case assignment come morning. If it was an emergency to her, then it's a concern to me.

Only one of her gorgeous brown eyes is visible. Zariah has masked much of her face with the pillow. Her tone is delectably sultry and groggy, "Why aren't you working out?"

"I meet with Vadim at 11 am. You know the drill," I tell her.

"Humph, I'm referencing your work out before your quote-unquote workout?" She finally pushes the pillow away enough to give me that look of hers, which tells me she's about to toss a bomb my way. "Vassili, I am aware of your entire day. You're in our home gym at 5 am. Then you cart Natasha around Venice Beach to eye some hot ass, and I do mean hot. Like super-hot as in stinky, funky asses swallowing up thong-kinis, before going to the gym. What a convenient location for all you guys. And if another fighter is behind schedule, you become a big bully."

"Stinky thong-kinis you say?" I arch an eyebrow. "The fuck is that?"

"Bikini, thong-kini, don't try to be cute and innocent, Vassili!"

I lay back against the pillow and roar with laughter.

My wife straddles me and issues an assault of hooks and jabs against my ribs. "Oh, so you do check out scantily clad chicks? I hate you, Vassili."

"Fuck," I growl. My chuckles fade, and I grab the bulldozers she has for fists. She isn't that strong, but my broken rib has a few more weeks to heal. "My rib, girl, my rib."

"I don't give a damn about your rib." She pouts. "You were supposed to deny looking at hoes. Deny it vehemently!"

I reach up and kiss her poked out bottom lip. Then my tongue soars into her mouth, my hand claims the back of her neck and I send this kiss to soaring heights. Zariah's breasts rise and fall rapidly against her tight negligee as she catches her breath. My eyes connect with hers, and I decree, "There's only one woman for me. I put that on my life."

"Well ..." she pretends to cave, as I wrap my arms around her in a bear hug.

"I resent your statement, beautiful. There's only one girl I know in the entire world, whose thong can be perfectly eaten by her ass." My hand slams down on Zariah's thick flesh.

"Oh, so you're calling me a –"

"I'm calling you my little *kholodets*," I bounce my hands over her ass cheeks.

"Wait a minute, boy did you say kholodets?" Her eyes peel in thought. "That revolting Russian meat jelly?"

"I love it. That was Natasha's favorite when she first got a few teeth."

The smack against my face sends me into another hard laugh and I lay back again. Zariah pretends to lean down and choke me out for a second. She growls, "Meat Jelly? Can't you think of anything sexier? Yes, I have a fat ass. Yes, these cakes are visible from the front."

Her legs squeezing around my waist. Zariah glances back at her fatty and then her ponytail whips over her shoulder as she looks down at me again.

I rest my hands behind my head and lift my hips. My cock pierces the inside of her thigh, a reminder that too much playing in the bedroom leads to other things. I love these happy moments of joking with my wife. With her straddling me, those breasts of hers are about to spill out.

Her eyes darken with desire. Zariah rocks her hips, letting her pussy slither over my cock. There's only one problem with our current dynamic. I slept in boxers and basketball shorts. She has on panties. I don't *do* friction.

"Stop playing, girl. I want to fuck."

"Humph, you better be glad I let you have something good to eat last night." She flicks her tongue out and licks her lips.

"*Dah*, I ate this succulent pussy all night, eh? Now that sweet tasty cunt of yours can eat my cock, okay." I press my hips up, again searing the inside of her thigh with my stiff erection.

She reaches toward me, her hands go to the headboard, and her mouth goes to mine. Zariah licks my jaw as she works her lower body like a snake. My dick swells. I clasp her hair and grit, "Take off your panties."

"Mmmm, you want them off?" She leans back up, grips the sides of her thong and pulls upward. Those fat folds of her labia are on display now as the material puckers between her lips.

Shit, precum is seeping from my cockhead.

"Take them off," I bark. My hands are still comfortably behind my head. The only warning that she's in danger of me slamming her down and fucking her silly is the hardness in my eyes.

She again works the thong with her thumbs hooked at the side. "I think I might cum like this, Vassili." Her voice is trembling with desire. Zariah continues to work the material against her pussy. "It's rubbing my clit so rough, so rough. Damn, the fucking string is caressing my ass. I thought I loved Russian cock in my ass, but . . ."

I go for the takedown.

27

Zariah

Did I even get a chance to blink? Nope, not at all. For it to be a warm summer morning, the air literally chilled against my skin. Vassili swiftly had me on my back. He doesn't even snatch off my thong, nor does he take off his clothes. His boxers and basketball shorts are pulled beneath his ass, as he slams inside of my pussy. His hand claims the headboard like mine had done a second ago.

"Ooooh, shit," I scream, as his cock batters my insides. He reaches between our bodies. His thumb finds that tiny bulb of mine that always makes more of my wetness rush against his cock. He works my clit with his thumb while pumping in and out of me. My left leg goes over Vassili's hip, and he bangs my back.

Missionary never looked so good.

Our hearts drum to the same beat as his shaft glides in and out of my wetness. His cock torpedoes through my treasure, slamming against my g-spot and fucking me deep. With his hand against the headboard, I bite down on his bicep. My teeth grit down on the hard rock, releasing some tension from the pain of his aggressive cock.

"Vassili," I moan and ground down on his dick. "I'm gonna—"

"Fuck," he growls like the incredible hulk. "Shit, I'm coming, Zariahhhhh."

My eyes close and my head kisses the pillow. The raw tension dwindles, and a euphoric calm claims my body as I welcome Vassili's steel body on top of mine. I can't breathe, but I'm content. I press my arms around him, holding him against me. Delighting in his heaviness, strength, and power. He starts to roll over.

"Not yet," I moan. "Stay."

"You can't breathe."

Damn, it's a feat to give him a 'give a fuck' look that he likes to dish out on occasion. I finally murmur, "Don't need to."

Everything about him is heavy. His paws feel heavy as he rubs my face and kisses my forehead tenderly.

"I will never let you go," he murmurs in Russian.

Wetness instantly burns my eyes. His token declarations turn my heart into mush. Vassili rarely whispers adulations, but when he does our eyes connect. His lips claim mine in a reverent kiss, depleting the remaining oxygen in my lungs.

With my fingertips strumming over his biceps, I find the indention of my teeth against his hard skin. I contemplate the tiny bit of pain I offered and the even greater throbbing between my thighs.

My husband is confident. Let him tell it, and he's invincible. He's fearless. I'm becoming fearless and shedding all worry and doubt. And at this moment, we are so very connected.

My alarm goes off.

"Aw, no," I pout. It's not that I don't want to go to work.

God has blessed me with a career I enjoy, so Billingsley Legal isn't 'work' for me. But I love these moments. These moments that are solely for us.

"Turn it off," Vassili growls, getting off of me.

I reach over, grab my phone and turn off the reminder. His thick bicep engulfs my tiny waist—well, it was tinier when we met—and pulls me closer. He presses his mouth against my ear and whispers, "We can stay in bed today. Nobody has to know."

"What about Natasha?" I ask.

"Fuck, you're right. Stay in bed with me until she bullies us to move."

"Oh, she's a bully now? Like someone I know."

"When hungry, dah. When her pull-up is too wet, hell yeah. She," he nods, "is a bully. Call in, and we'll stay in bed until we're both punked."

I nuzzle my head beneath his chin. Something deep within my being just loves the nearness of this man. I can be standing on top of him, breathing his air, and never be close enough. He's my slice of perfection, flaws and all. *Thank you, Jesus, for my husband.*

While I'm thankful for my blessings, I'm totally aware of someone who needs God's love.

Eyes close, I breathe in the sweaty sex of us. Then, even though it hurts my heart, I rise into a seated position. "I have to go to work, Vassili."

"Why?" He barks. The resonance in his tone speaks volumes.

My bottom lip drops, my eyes narrow. "Vassili, you're a fucking asshole."

"Choice words, girl," he growls, sitting up, too.

"Don't throw the finger. You dismissed the hell out of my career. Tell me that my job isn't as important as playing the Neanderthal for … a lot more money."

"I didn't say—"

"All you do is ancient human grunting and tossing fists in the air. How is your work better than mine?"

He rubs the back of his neck. "Okay, Zar, I'm a bit of an asshole, that's how I was born. Sometimes you work from home. We're having the best fucking day, girl. Can't we have this day?"

I glance into his dark, genuine gaze and decide not to fault him. A bit of foreboding trickles across my heart. Something warns that in retrospect, somewhere down the road, I'll wish I had set aside everything. Set aside my so-called life for more moments with my husband. We live in a busy world. At times, the guilt I have for staying with my father at my mother's insistence during the last years of high school pervades my mind. And I'll always regret not lashing out at Maxwell for his abuse.

Nevertheless, I'm saving Felicidad and her children from Juan Noriega Senior.

"I can't, baby." I offer a weak smile. "I have a meeting this morning. We were on vacation throughout the summer already."

As I begin to create a case for myself, I ponder handing the Noriega's over to Tyrese Nick. He came through on my way home, calling during Vassili's many texts. He scheduled with an immigration attorney, who cleared her schedule for this morning. Even though Mr. Nicks is capable of handling the situation, Felicidad requested me. And dammit, I keep seeing my mother through her eyes.

With her in mind, I offer my husband an apology. "I'll try not to be late tonight."

"Okay." His broad shoulders rise and fall in a shrug. "Tell me about this new case while you get dressed, though."

For a moment, I'm silently weighing the pros and cons. Can I handle this case? Will fighting Juan Noriega place my life, my child's life, in danger? Receiving help from a Resnov would be more beneficial than speaking to my father. Hell, I'm not even entirely sure my dad is interested in being bothered with me. Although Vassili loathes abuse, he won't have it. The instant I mention Juan Noriega, I *will* lose more than this case. My husband will bully me into the stay at home career he's always desired for me. *Safety first...*

With a heavy heart, I do what a lawyer does best... I lie.

Party-girl Sarah Versa, who put down the alcohol to care for her sick, rich grandfather merges into this fresh, new assignment.

"Felicidad used to be the black sheep of the family. In the past, her mother and father spent so much money on rehabilitation centers to help clean her up. Felicidad could list off all the celebrities she partied with. Rehab was like a slumber party for grownups."

"Daddy's little rich girl?" he asks, as I head to the dresser to pull out clothes.

"Yeah. Her parents had finally removed her from their own will. They were done with her and wanted the same stance for her grandfather. Mr. Versa owned Versa Home Improvements. The place is like a top-of-the-line Home Depot."

"Dah, I know of the place. I thought about having a home built in Calabasas, but your mother chose this one. There was no fucking way I'd have it completed by our first Christmas together. Tell me more, Zar. I need to know that you're safe."

Stopping myself from glancing at my husband, I snatch out a pair of undergarments. He sure knows how to make a person feel guilty for lying to him. With a smile on my face, I subtly gulp down the lump of remorse in my throat and head for the walk-in closet. Further away from my heart.

"Ha, safe from who? The grandfather is dead. Felicidad

needs help. It's really a sad situation," I say, snatching out a pair of burgundy pants. "Her parents' mistrust has left her in a hard place."

"Keep going," he grits.

With a sigh, I continue to lie to my husband. "Alright, let's start at the top. Felicidad shared that she got so bad with her drinking habit that she also had to panhandle. So, when her grandfather became sick, she set aside the bottle and moved into his house in The Hills." I wipe a stray tear from my face and take my time choosing a pair of shoes. Meaning, I'm numb to the lies I've told, and stare at the sea of designer stilettos for a few minutes, taking deep breaths.

"I'm guessing her family doesn't believe she cleaned up to help grandpa out of the goodness of her heart. They snatched back the good life?"

"That's right. The parents had encouraged Versa to reconstruct his will when she was estranged from everyone. A few days before he died, Versa reinstated the previous clause regarding Felicidad. She gets more than her parents."

"You have to prove he wasn't coerced?"

"Yup."

"Sounds like a hard case," Vassili replies, grabbing my pillow and placing it against him.

"Yeah, this sort of litigation can be difficult. But I know what you mean by *hard* case, Vassili. You like me to debrief you regarding my cases because you worry that any of them has the potential to put me in harm's way. And no, I went to school entirely too long to become a housewife."

He holds out his hands as a sign of peace, and my heart begins to cry. Vassili plays 'nice' while mentally calculating how 'difficult' the Versa family can be. Little does he know, I feel like a piece for manipulating him.

Tyrese's dimples are deep and enchanting as he peeks into my room. And then he steps inside, holding a Harry Potter book. My eyebrow rises.

"Good morning. So it's not coffee but sorcery that gets your day started?"

"Actually, I asked Lynetta if she had a few books to spare on her way into work. She picked up a few Spanish to English illustrated library books for Rosemary. This is from the stack of her son's very own Harry Potter collection."

I blink twice. Well, damn, I learned not to ask her to file anything for me before 10 am. I sure as heck get coffee for myself on the way to work. The hoops she's jumping over, darting around and army crawling beneath for Tyrese amazes me.

"You're doing well, Mr. Nicks. Empathy looks good on you." My gaze returns to my laptop screen. "Thanks, you can drop them off."

"The meeting with Mrs. Lopez is in an hour."

While staring at the computer, I smile my acknowledgment. Why isn't he walking away?

"My car or yours, Zariah," his tone is crisp. "You're not handling this one solo."

With a smirk, I close the laptop and determine to finish the memo I was currently working on later. "How about you drive? That makes men feel like they're in charge, right?"

He offers up the sexiest chuckle he can muster. Pitiful fucker, there are plenty of other pairs of panties that need help getting wet. Mine belong only to my husband. "Alright, Zariah, I'll drive, and we can readdress the misconception that you have of me."

"I don't think so." I grab my purse from the bottom file cabinet next to my desk and rise from my chair.

He chews on his bottom lip, addressing me when I offer

him my full attention. He says, "Forgive me, I rubbed you the wrong way. I'd forgotten how easily you were set off back in the day."

"On the way to the immigration attorney, we need to keep our minds sharp." My gaze darkens, and he seems smugly satisfied that he's gotten a rise out of me. "You don't know me, Mr. Nicks. It would behoove you to refrain from 'back in the day' talk as it pertains to me. Consider what you see as the new normal."

"Okay, too soon. I get it." He steps aside and waves a hand, allowing me to exit the room first.

Later on, Tyrese and I are speaking with Mrs. Lopez as her assistant takes photos of Felicidad Noriega. The immigration firm is tinier than our own. Ms. Lopez interprets Felicidad's story as Tyrese and I practically sit knee-to-knee. Her relationship with Mr. Noriega is quite a love story. Apparently, he *was* a good guy in the past. Offering the standard 'honeymoon' phase in the typical domestic violence scenario. But even better. Juan Noriega gave her shiny diamond rings with said *shiners*.

Now, Juan Senior's not only a member of Loco Dios. He became affiliated to assist the drug trade. He ran a drug mule operation for the Cartel before his affiliation with Los Dios. Juan asserted himself when the gang was at its weakest. Their alliance with the Cartel started an army.

We are fucked.

"I don't want to know where you're keeping Mrs. Noriega," Mrs. Lopez says. "But I pray to St. Michael for protection that it is somewhere her husband will never get to her."

"Should we send her out of state?" Tyrese asks.

I had thought the same thing while the two women chatted. "Witness protection would be nice."

"You can do that," he tells me.

Mrs. Lopez has all her attention on me. "Do you have a connection that will ensure the Noriega's family's safety in another state? I fear shipping her back to Mexico will only increase the chance of corruption. Because it's either we hide her from Loco Dios in Los Angeles or conceal her from the Cartel."

Shit, we have better luck sending her to Russia than me asking my father. Speaking to my father about Noriega seemed to be the obvious scenario. But Felicidad dropped a nuclear bomb regarding the depth of the LAPD involvement with both entities.

"I can try."

"Without jeopardizing Mrs. Noriega's safety? She believes some of the LAPD are connected to the Loco Dios gang. These days, I'm inclined to agree."

"I can inquire without revealing her identity," I huff.

I step out of the room. Across the way, in an empty office, little Juan is reading a book with Rosemary. He's an attentive brother, allowing her to stumble through a sentence before helping. I smile. The girl is smart to be able to read already.

Leaning against the wall in the hallway, I slip out my cell phone and call my father.

"Hello, princess," he grits out.

"Hi, Dad. Do you have time for lunch today?"

"No, it's Berenice's birthday. What can I help you with?"

Oh, so he still doesn't have time for his one and only daughter? Leaning against the wall, I spit venom for his venom, "Help me by setting aside your bitch. I'm your daughter. I don't care if this is the day that she dedicates herself to our Lord and Savior. I need an hour of your time."

He breathes into the phone. "You've become very

uncouth, my daughter. But like I said, it's Bernice's birthday. We're in Temecula. Take this into account, Zariah Washington, it is you who has pushed me away. And I would love to be there for you, but unfortunately, I cannot in person. Is there something you'd like help with over the phone?"

"No. When do you return?"

"Two days. Where's Sammy? He's the one you run to these days when you need fatherly advice, right?"

I bite my lip. Samuel is at a conference in Washington. And I don't need him aware of the case I picked up. He's team Vassili…

28

Vassili

Today, Nestor and I are working on my takedowns. He has me pinned against the cage and the ground. This is where some fighters fuck up and get the shit slammed out of them. That's the difference between them and me. He isolates my abdomen. I've calculated my exit strategy in a split second. With my arms pressed against my sides, I jam my leg up and through his legs. Mind you, this motherfucker is padded and protected. So, the hits I'm dishing, which would otherwise hurt extremely bad, are being warded off from the Ukrainian.

"C'mon, Karo, get the fuck up," Nestor taunts.

Sucking in a breath, I continue to slaughter the padding against his chest.

"I see your fucking opening, get your way out!"

I wedge my left arm out and jab at him.

"What the fuck, you ain't killing 'em today, *Vassili*," he grunts out.

"Dah?" I finally have my leg anchored around his. Even

with his upper body padding, my positioning hocks his entire body around. I grapple Nestor into a leg slicer submission hold. "So, I ain't Karo today, eh? Just regular ol' motherfucking Vassili?"

Nestor has ceased from ranting. His breaths are slamming through his teeth as he mentally tapers off the pain.

Vadim steps over shaking his head. "Did I tell the two of you to work on submissions? *Nyet!*"

"*Dah!*" I correct my coach while tightening my thighs, in the leg slicer position. "You want me to perfect myself when my opponent has the takedown."

Nestor grits his teeth.

"Tap the fuck out, *bro!*" I order.

His hand slaps down on the canvas.

"Vassili, come see me before you leave." Vadim cocks his head to his office. He doesn't offer a chance for me to respond. The old man's back is to me as he heads to the dogface looking motherfucker, Rhy. The two of us mix like oil and water. I think Nestor put him in rotation with Vadim after me to screw us. Either I'm late or Rhy's early, and my sparring mate loves to fuck with me.

Rhy glowers like we're two gangbangers on the opposite side of the street. Vadim gestures toward the conditioning ropes. I grin and nod. "That's right, mudak."

Zariah still looks like a newborn calf when using the ropes. But Vadim has all the fighters use them during spare time. Not during training time. Vadim is cutting into his routine for not being prepared.

"You did this?" I ask Nestor as we both take our stand.

He shakes out his leg and offers a lazy smile. "Yup. Keep you on your toes, Vassili."

I chuckle, open the door to the cage, and saunter down the steps.

"What does Vadim want with me?" I glare at my cousin,

who is shaking a few more Cheetos, from the chip bag onto the tabletop in front of Natasha's stroller.

"The fuck would I know, kuzen?" He shrugs.

"You know." I glare him down hard. My cousin's gaze never wavers, but I have a drive that Yuri is more aware than he's letting on. "Okay, come," I tell him while getting behind Natasha's stroller to steer.

"Follow you to Vadim's office?" Yuri moves like an old ass man as if he's unsure about what I asked.

"*Dah*, you make a lot of money off me. It's all fun, fighting. Now, join in on the other shit," I toss over my shoulder.

Vadim intends to give me grief. Natasha's mini Jordan goes flying. I continue to cart her along, she looks back. Her pretty brown eyes questioning me. My little girl is fucking with me, too. She loves to keep me running after her shoes.

"Oh, this is fun to you?" I tell her.

Yuri catches up to get the flyaway tennis shoe. I take it from him, squat down in front of Natasha and say, "Maybe I'll start letting you dress like a *babushka*."

"Na-na?" She asks, eyes wide.

"That's right. Nana Zamora is a babushka, but I'm referring to a really, really little old lady."

Her face falls into a frown for a second and then she perks up as I slip the designer tennis shoe on her foot.

We head into the elevator and up to the second floor to Vadim's office. The place I cornered Zariah during our first encounter. MMA memorabilia still clutter each wall. Statues that reach my shoulders crowd the area, making it an effort to squeeze Natasha's stroller inside. Retired belts are even on the wall. I glance at a place where my belt will be in the future, once I'm ready to call it a day.

Yuri stuffs in his stomach and moves around me to another seat. I choose to stand.

My coach is seated in his chair. His scrawny white legs

are crossed at the ankles and propped up on the edge of his table. "Oh great, Yuri, you and Natasha can get the truth out of 'em."

Yuri grunts. There's more of a flicker of something in his eyes. One that reads he was previously aware of what Vadim has cornered me for and didn't want to be a part of telling me so.

"How's your fucking knee, Vassili?" Vadim asks. "Take a look at cutie pie before you answer anything other than the truth."

My eyebrow cocks. I glance over at Natasha, who rarely has an attitude with me. The foul with her Jordan dug under her skin. Her pretty brown eyes seem to narrow in understanding. *Don't lie to me,* my child is saying.

Fuck.

I rub a hand over my face. "*Khorosho . . . Nyet.* Okay, it's been better."

"Okay?" Vadim's wrinkly face pushes into a scowl.

"Okay as in you'll fight Rhy in October or okay as in surgery should be in the cards, first?" Yuri inquires.

" Rhy? The dog-faced fucker whose body conditioning at this very second? What do you mean, I'll fight Rhy? He's nobody. And fuck no, no surgery necessary here, *brat.*"

"Rhy's making a name for himself in this world," Vadim sits up. "He fought Laquerre."

"Fuck Laquerre, Kong is my next sub!"

"Like I said, Rhy dominated Laquerre in the octagon. Lose the big, cocky head, Vassili. Laquerre and Kong are almost toppling your old legacy! And by process of elimination, Rhy might very well put his paws on your belt before you do." He takes a deep breath. "You are both on my team. I talked to him about it first."

I point at the old man. "Then you pick. Rhy or me. You can't have both."

Vadim grits out. "You're money, Vassili. Fighting you puts money into his pockets while he guns for the belt. Son, I can recall when you first walked into my gym. I have always respected the Resnov name—"

"Oh, don't put bring the bratva into this conversation!"

"I'm not," he snaps in Russian. "You and Rhy are in my fucking gym, Vassili. I'm making the same promise to you that I've made to him. I'll be in partial."

"Fuck you, fuck Rhy. I don't give a damn how many cocks he's sucked in the cage!" I pause, noticing Natasha watching us intently.

Voice lowered, I growl, "My target is The Legion."

"Gotti will be out before you know it, Vassili. Speaking of sucking certain parts of the anatomy to get by," Vadim clucks, "Rhy isn't sitting on as many decisions as you believe. He's got Subs and TKO's. And if you close your cunt long enough to think, you'd realize this sport is like a game of chess. Any sudden movement can take the queen. In your instance, you did it to yourself. Your knee screwed you."

"I know that!"

"Can you fight Rhy? Should I hold your fucking hand and we skip like little shits to your doctor's office to see about your knee?"

"You done?" I gesture.

He grunts.

"Kuzen, are you okay?" Yuri stands up.

My dark orbs seer right through him. He's my blood, and he led me into the lion's den. Not a single warning.

Yuri groans. "Vassili, you are as much my *brat* as Igor, Mikhail, shit, all my siblings. Sometimes you say I make money off ya—"

I hold up a hand to cut off his need for an emotional moment. "I'm fucking with you, Yuri."

"But are you good, as in you can fight Rhy? Or are you

good, as in you're capable of fighting Kong in Australia in six weeks?"

I glare at him. "I'm good enough."

"Gotti isn't shit."

"That's right," Vadim agrees. "He fought a nobody after grabbing your belt. His fans are gonna call foul soon if he keeps it in the clutch."

Yuri nods. "So, tell us, Vassili should we set everything aside right now? Rhy, Kong, and have you visit the doctors? That's not the manager in me talking but blood."

29

Zariah
Two weeks later...

August sweeps in, bringing with it drier heat and mounds of luggage. I help my mother settle her items in the bedroom she's claimed since we bought our home.

"It's my birthday weekend, baby girl," she squeals. Sequence dresses and skirts go flying from the rollaway on the bed.

"Move over Tina Knowles, Zamora Haskins is in town!" I rub a hand over a sequence dress with the tags still on it.

"Patience is a virtue, my dear daughter. Thanks to your father, it only took me two and a half alimony checks to purchase that dress." She chuckles.

"Mama, where and the heck did you get this dress?"

"Kidding, it was hiding on the clearance rack at Saks Fifth Avenue. I clicked my heels together and scoured the store top to bottom for my birthday."

I smile. When picking her up from LAX, I took a deep breath and gave her the once over. The chat Martin and I had with her seems to have penetrated because the glow has returned to her face. My brother and his wife are also more available than they were in the past. And we almost have her agreement to attend counseling. Almost.

We start downstairs. Vassili is in the outdoor kitchen, grilling salmon and asparagus.

"Let's go see Maxwell tonight," my mother gushes.

With my mind still on Mrs. Noriega, I'm confused as to why she'd like to see my father. My pace falters as I look down at my oblivious mom, who's rounded the first landing. I inquire, "Mom, what exactly are you asking me?"

As I catch up to her, Mom grips my arms and gives me a shake. "Not your daddy, girl, the singer Maxwell. I got us tickets."

"Mom, I have to work in the morning." In actuality, I finally secured a spot on my father Maxwell's busy schedule. The issue of Mr. Noriega still needs to be addressed.

She pouts. "You want me to be happy, don't you?"

I groan.

"*Ascension* will make me happy. *Bad Habits*, Stop the *doggone* World, *This Woman's Work*," she says listing off songs from the R&B crooner, Maxwell. "Hell, everything Maxwell will make me happy. And when you get home, Vassili will be willing and waiting for you to pay it forward."

Later in the evening, Vassili studies MMA textbooks. My mother is content spoiling Natasha rotten with baby massage oil. So, I head upstairs and slip out my phone to call my new partner in crime.

"I expected more checking in," Tyrese flirts. There's mariachi music in the background, and I close my eyes considering how much I owe this man.

We've decided to move Felicidad and her children to a home Samuel suggested. My mentor believes I'd given Tyrese the case. Heck, Samuel is under the assumption that I was offering the newbie a little help from the start. Luckily, Tyrese didn't correct his beliefs.

For now, I have yet to have a real conversation with my father about Mr. Noriega. I reply, "Why check-in? I believe in you. Are you almost there?"

His chuckle is deliciously low in response to my sarcasm. "About an hour away. Did you finally buy your mother something for her birthday?"

I pause for a moment. The two of us have worked in tandem for weeks to help secure a safe place for the Noriega family. He had insisted on facilitating their move, U-Haul and all. Although, I agreed that it would keep my family safe —namely my daughter and my husband's frame of mind.

It took serious convincing with Felicidad to allow Tyrese to have a hand in the most precious part of her life. Her son and daughter. She still has a distrust of men but seems to be warming up to him. I'm wondering if the ride from LA to San Fran will continue to work in his favor. But regardless of Tyrese and me having an alliance for Noriega, he isn't family and he's certainly no friend of mine.

"Yes, I reply to him. "I bought her a gift. Thanks for helping out so that I can be home."

"What did you get?"

"Let's keep this strictly business, counselor."

"C'mon, this drive was... almost double the time it should've been. You know traffic."

"Okay," I reply, though part of me feels torn with carrying on a conversation with Tyrese. In college, I never had time to play. My entire life has been strictly business, aside from Vassili. Sitting at the lounger in front of my bed, I share, "I purchased the most expensive pair of ostrich cowboy boots I could find. Although, I'm not sure what possessed my mother to ask for boos."

"You got the photo album as well, didn't you?" He seems to smile through the receiver. "The one Samuel suggested."

I offer a hesitant chuckle. "The silver one, engraved and all. I highly suspect that Sammy knows my mother more than she knows herself."

"What's the deal with those two?"

"Good evening, Mr. Nicks." I hang up the phone.

"Wait a *doggone* minute, Mama." I glance my mother up and down as she saunters down the steps. A gold-toned, sequined dress skims loves each and every one of my curves. But I *ain't' got nothing on my mama!*

Her head is held high. The shimmery eyeshadow brings out the hazel flecks in her orbs. I'll be damned if my mother is stepping out of my house in a skirt shorter than mine. I order, "Put your hands down at your sides."

"What, why?" She does a 360 spin, in distressed denim jeans, a silk camisole and the boots I bought for her birthday. Lord knows she looks fit for a country concert, heck maybe even to see that Trace Adkins instead of Maxwell.

"Place your hands at your sides, Mama! I learned the game at Pressley Preparatory Academy. We outdid each other in the latest couture fashion and modified our uniform skirts. If the tips of your fingers don't exceed the hem of your skirt, it's out!"

"Oh, hell, no," she chuckles. "You have that shape. Let's even the score. Give me half your booty, and I'll exchange my skirt for a pair of jeans."

I laugh, and it takes energy for me to force her arms down at her sides. We're almost in tears with chuckles as I get her to comply. True to form, her skirt is so short, it stops at her wrists.

"Mama! Go change, now," I halfheartedly gesture for her to head back upstairs.

It's a feat for Zamora to shake her head as she's in tears from laughter.

Vassili comes to the top of the landing. My mom shouts up at him. "Look, son, she's even more of a bully than cutie pie, or you."

"You both look very nice," Vassili tells her. It's hard as hell to get him to laugh, but that sinful gaze obliges us with a twinkle. "If any man touches either one of you inappropriately let me know, I'll have it handled."

"Nope, because I wanna be touched inappropriately," My mother giggles.

"Vassili, you've learned well not to respond to my mom. I'm sure she's snuck a box of wine into her bedroom. Goodnight, baby," I blow a kiss to him.

"Oh, you think that's enough?" Vassili's bulky frame moves down the left side of the staircase. He's a lion on the prowl. His gaze locks me down like a shiny new toy. "Zamora, please turn your head."

His joke brings much more needed laughter to my mother. She's such a beautiful woman when she's happy.

My husband clutches me around the waist, his hand grabs for my ass, squeezing all the thickness.

"Will you be up when I return?" I cock a brow and lick my lips.

"If I'm not, kick me."

Vassili is reluctant to let my hand go. I reach to my tippy toes, even in six-inch heels, and taste his lips again.

"I'll be thinking of you all night long," I whisper, my lips a fraction of a second away from his. He has an impending match with a fellow fighter at Vadim's Gym. He's being trained by Nestor, and the other guy has their coach, Vadim's attention. Needless, to say, I've juggled my 'secret' case and his dwindling time before we head to Australia. I need a resolution for Noriega first, or I may not be able to attend the fight.

On my heels, I go, turning around.

"Zar, call me when you're on your way home," he says.

"Okay, baby."

"Alright, you two," My mom huffs. "Don't make me miss the comfort of a man's arms. Besides, the singer, Maxwell, is preparing Zar for the best night of both your lives. I'm the one who has to return to a vibrat—"

"MAMA!" I shout.

She stifles a giggle. White zinfandel peppers her breath as we head out to the garage. Although I'm ecstatic about the Maxwell concert, my abdomen tightens into an uncomfortable braid. I tell myself that growing up in the middle of the warzone, that was my parents' home, has made me so pessimistic. There's a saying that troubles don't last always.

Where I'm from, the opposite is true.

30

Vassili

I'm in a dead sleep when my cell phone rings. I left the damn thing on because Zariah was supposed to call me when they headed home. At a little after ten pm, it can't be them. The concert doesn't end for another hour at the very least. Placing the pillow over my head, I groan and try to reclaim sleep. Then my cell phone goes off for a second time.

"Fuck, I will murder whoever this is," I grumble to myself. Blind to the night, I reach toward the nightstand. Fingertips searching for my cell phone, I snatch it up and answer.

"Vassili, come over now!" It's Anna, Igor's wife. Her voice is heavy with anxiety. I can hear Malich shouting in the background.

Before my fucking brain can catch up, I'm out of the bed. I trip over the discarded high heels Zariah decided not to wear for the concert. "What the fuck is going on, Anna?"

There's lots of sniffling and her voice breaks with each syllable, "They shot up the house."

Lightning streaks through my veins. I stumble into a pair of jeans. "What? Who the fuck shot up the house?"

"Please come. Your uncle is talking to the cops. Oh shit, they're putting him in the back of the squad car. Mikhail isn't answering Vassili, we need you."

"Why are the cops taking Malich?" I shout. The phone goes dead. My uncle may have done bad things in his day, but he knows when to play by the rules. I dial Zariah. It rings and rings.

"Fuck," I hang up and dial her number again. What can I do with Natasha?

My baby starts crying the second I turn the light on to the nursery.

"I'm so fucking sorry, baby girl. Daddy's sorry," I grumble while picking her up. She's in some cotton footie pajamas. With the hot summer nights, I forgo a jacket for her and shuffle down the stairs with her in my arms. When I put her in the car, I tell myself to drive safely. Natasha sobs, a desperate, sleepy cry.

"Everything will be okay," I tell her.

Twenty minutes later, blue and red lights whirl in the sky, and I haven't even bent the corner. The police cruisers line the entire block. Shit, I wonder if it's half the damn police force here tonight.

Wearing a robe and with big curlers in her hair, Anna talks to a uniformed cop. I stop in the middle of the street, get out. I make a mad dash to the backseat, and scoop Natasha up. She offers a desperate little whimper. Before I can apologize again, a Mexican cop is shouting at me.

"Sir, you cannot park there!" He yells from the sidewalk. "Sir, you cannot park there!"

"Give me a fucking ticket," I tell him.

Anna comes running down the slope of wet grass. She slides and almost falls. Natasha is glancing around; her caramel complexion is already red from all the crying she's done. But she seems to be deciphering whether to continue crying or not. She yawns into my arms.

"Igor is… Igor is…" I shift Natasha into my left arm as Anna clings to my right side. Holding her 110-pound frame in one arm and Natasha in the other, I listen to my cousin's wife. She tells me something that makes me want to fucking hit the ground.

Anna sobs, "My husband is dead, Vassili."

Ice freezes my veins. I glance at her in confusion, but the cop asks, "Sir, what is your relationship to Mrs. Resnov?"

Anna sobs louder which prompts Natasha to burst into another round of waterworks.

"She is my cousin's wife. Igor Resnov is he…" My jaw clenches. Fuck, I can't say it. My pupils expand. A bloody puddle is painted on the welcome mat near the door. Yellow tape surrounds the area. A dude in a suit and more uniform cops crowd around. This is fucking real. I've seen dead bodies, mangled, tortured, all fucked-over. My father would have his enemies lined up. But they weren't Resnovs.

The drum of my heart in my ears causes many difficulties for me to hear. "Igor is he…"

"Yes, sir, pronounced dead on the scene."

"Where are Malich and Yuri?" I ask him, rubbing Anna's back, and holding Natasha to my neck. Fuck, my baby isn't to see shit like this. Never.

"A man of a similar age as Igor Resnov was also taken to the hospital."

My legs fail me. Anna crumples to the ground, I go with her, placing Natasha in my lap as we fall. Yuri is closer than blood to me.

"He should make it, sir." The Latino says more sympathetically. "Malich Resnov was escorted downtown for questioning."

At Cedar Sinai, Natasha has fallen asleep in Anna's arms. The poor woman seemed to hold my one-year-older like a teddy bear. It brings them both comfort, as I pace around, waiting for word on Yuri. Igor and Anna's four children are seated in the same row, heads all leaning to the left. The youngest, Albina was a few months younger than Natasha when I brought Zariah to the house for the first time. Albina is now a toddler; her head is rested on the side of Natasha. It's three in the morning when Malich is released from the jailhouse.

In pajamas, with a camel coat, he enters the lobby. Mikhail is a silent force at his side. My cousin who can add "God" and "church" to any scenario doesn't say a word.

I go to them. "What the fuck happened?"

"Your father." My uncle's searing glower moves away from me for a moment. Mikhail places a hand over his shoulder. But the guilt of mentioning my connection to Anatoly has gotten to his father.

"Don't touch me," Malich tells his son.

Mikhail's square jaw tenses. He gives me a nod, then heads over to Anna and the children.

I stare at my uncle. His orbs are cast to the ground. A war rages within him. He's angry at *my* motherfucking father!

Malich continues in a serious tone, "Anatoly left us wide open for retaliation. This has something to do with the government official in Italy that Danushka took out for him, I know it. They came by. Disrespectful roaches, piz'das! Drove by, shot up the house. Igor went out first. Then Yuri.

Before your cousin went down, Yuri confirmed they were Italian."

I step away from Malich as he sinks into a chair. I head down the hall to call my father when I see Zariah and Ms. Haskins rush into the double doors. My wife's face is wet with tears.

"Baby, we've called jails, hospitals! Why aren't you answering your phone?" She's angry and shaking. "I was told a Resnov was here, I thought it was you. Don't ever do that, baby. Don't ever leave me wondering."

Zariah rushes into my arms. She's hugging and hitting me. "I almost died," she says. And then Zariah sniffles rubs away her tears and looks at me. She realizes I haven't been hugging her back.

"My kuzen is dead," I say the words for the first time tonight.

"Oh," she clings to me again. "Yu—"

"Igor. Igor… is dead. Yuri is here. He's in the OR."

"Oh my god," Zamora huffs.

"Natasha is asleep, with Anna." I nudge my head. Ms. Haskins heads toward our family as I finally hold Zariah tightly. Tears burn in my eyes. The last time I was torn to tears, Sasha died.

31

Zariah

I have no words to express holding my husband, the fighter, as he cries. I'm clinging to the cold, chiseled stone. Hot tears fall like rain, dampening my hair. And then his tears turn into a roar. His hot muscles are on fire with rage.

"Vassili, baby, you have to calm down."

I hold onto him tighter. *Jesus, we need you now,* I silently pray. Vassili begins to push me away. With all the strength I have in me, I cling onto him. My grasp weakens and he wrenches his shirt from my fingertips. He starts outside into the darkness, and I kick off my high heels to hurry after him.

"Vassili, wait, wait please," I call out, almost slipping on the tile. I run across the mat and through the sliding glass doors.

The cement is warm beneath my feet. It's truly one of those heat drenching nights, but I feel cold and alone. "Vassili, wait, baby!"

He doesn't. He continues past the stretch of grass and

fountains. And then stops at the beginning of the parking lot to pull out his phone. He stops. I stop.

Vassili is calling someone. I can hear the faint sound of it connecting. My heart lurches in my throat with each ring. My eyes plead with his. But he sees straight through me as if I'm not here anymore. My stomach turns over. This isn't right. This isn't right.

He says something in Russian. The only word I can decipher as 'father.' That's can't be right. He's never called Anatoly 'father.'

I listen as he makes a threat, "The next time I see you, you're dead. If you allowed this shit to fucking happen," Vassili stops speaking. His rigid muscles contract as he roars again. "I will make do all those times I threatened to murder you with my bare hands, piz'da. You will be dead." He clicks the off button and fists the iPhone in his hand, again.

A rush of blood crashes through me. Vassili was addressing Anatoly in a voicemail. Damn, I tell myself that Vassili is not like his father, not like anyone else in his family. Tears cloud my vision as he finally stands before me.

"You promised me, Vassili," I begin, pulling away from him.

"What the fuck is wrong with you, Zariah? I need you!"

"You need me? Hello, we are a team. We need *each other*, Vassili. You threatened your father's life! You can't do that." I want to hug him, but Vassili must understand a few things. I glare him in the eye. "You cannot threaten your father's life, Vassili! He isn't any person. He might try to kill—"

"The fuck I can't," his harsh tone feels like a tornado against my skin. "If Anatoly had anything to do with what occurred tonight, then he's dead, Zar. I am a man of my word."

"A man of your word?" I wipe the tears away and step closer to him. My body wavers, as my gaze seeks his. The darkness of his eyes is tangible, and it sends fear shooting through my spirit. I need to correct this now. Vassili is better than stooping to his father's level. So, I make the discussion personal. "You told me you didn't want shit to do with what your family does! Vassili Karo Resnov, you made a promise to me! Remember? In my childhood bedroom, the day we broke up. You said that you'd never allow yourself to become like them."

"Dah! I promised." He points a stiff hand. "I won't. But I promise you, now, my beautiful wife, anybody touches my family gets what they deserve. Thus said, any other assurances I made will have to be forfeited, no matter what."

I rub the tears from my face.

Malich steps outside. Again, I become invisible. He addresses his nephew with, "Vassili, *go home with your wife.*"

His voice is dead. Gone is the always smiling man who in his generous ways loves to cook for people. The man who wants to know your favorite dish. If he hasn't perfected it, he's mastered it by your next encounter. That man has disappeared. In his stead, is a man who looks like the documentaries about … Anatoly Resnov. Someone so far gone, without a soul, that it scares me to look into his eyes. And what hurts the most? Vassili agreed to become the same type of man. I clutch my chest. These two men are better than this.

"Go home you two," Malich dismisses us.

"*Nyet!*" Vassili responds. "The girls are going home with our kids."

"You are a fighter, Vassili, not a murderer. Fuck your— stop trying to help. I don't need it." Malich turns around and heads back into the hospital.

———

My mother drives my car home, and I drive Vassili's Mercedes. Though I've been praying within my mind for the last half an hour, I navigate the streets in silence. Vassili is ramrod still. He hasn't spoken a single word to me since my mother and Natasha came outside. My heart is conflicted about him. He's seated less than a foot away and I feel him growing even further from my heart.

"I'm sure that Yuri will be okay. Time will heal him." Throat constricted, I slowly add, "M-Malich needs . . . time."

The subtle raise of his broad chest is proof that he heard me. Even if my words don't penetrate. Vassili lost a cousin, tonight. He also lost the relationship he has with his father figure. And I can only pray that I'm right about Malich. Time might help.

At home, my mother's eyes are filled with sorrow as she heads to the nursery with Natasha. I close the double doors to our master suite and turn around. Vassili is seated on the edge of the bed, his head in his hands.

"I'm so sorry, baby," I say kneeling before him. My head goes to his lap. I cry into it, reminiscing on a time not so long ago, Vassili hated to see my tears, sad or happy. He'd kiss them away. Malich's family is his family. Not Anatoly. And my husband still isn't over the abandonment by his mother at the hands of his father. It's in my heart to get the truth through to his thick skull but Vassili doesn't listen. Somewhere within him, he has to know that Malich is grieving and that he doesn't have to take actions into his own hands.

"Stop, crying, Zariah." Vassili's thick, Russian accent breaks through the silence. There's no heart in his voice, but he says the words, "I fucking hate it when you cry."

Up until tonight, we've yet to be in a situation where I saw tears in Vassili's eyes. When he mentioned morsels of time with his mother in the past, he seemed angrier at her and unsympathetic. His dark gaze is glossed.

"Get in bed," he nudges his head.

His apathetic tone and the way his jaw is sculpted in a marble scowl warns me that there's nothing left for us tonight.

"Vassili—"

"Zariah, take your ass to bed!"

Sitting back on my heels, I stare up at him. "Talk to me."

He sits there, muscles stacked on muscles, glaring down at me like I'm one of his broken ribs. "There's nothing for us to fucking talk about, girl. Everything I told you outside the hospital, I meant it. If you feel it needs to be reiterated, we can chat tomorrow."

"We are a team," I murmur, reaching up. I try to place my waist between his legs and kiss him. He pushes my hands down with such quick movements I hadn't even seen them coming. Though there's no pain in his touch. I've never felt so hurt in my life.

"Girl, we are a team when I say so. Right now, isn't the time. So, what? I've told you some shit because I wanted to have you." His calloused thumb clasps my chin, and his voice is sarcastic. "*Dah*. I made promises that I hoped to fucking God I would never have to break like I won't join teams with my father. Shit, that one's probably the only one I knew would be true. But if Anatoly sanctioned what happened tonight," he says gripping my chin, "I will deal with it."

Danushka consumes my mind. She said Horace was sweet, kind. Everything she didn't expect in a man of her nationality.

One day, she told me, "Russian men are ruthless, they don't give a fuck about anything but themselves."

243

Danny had been angry that Horace hadn't learned to split his time from his many companies with his new wife.

Only with Horace, he had never been put in the situation to choose.

What's more important?

Your wife?

Or, in Vassili's case, revenge?

Just as I had told Danny too, I speak up, ready to fight for my marriage. "Baby, you can't. Vengeance is like a seed, it sets roots. Talk to me, Vassili! Please!"

He starts to push me away. I clasp my hands onto his belt and hold on for dear life. Sex can't fix us. But dammit, it's the only thing I have of him.

"I don't want to fucking hurt you!" He screams into my face. Seems like the death grip I have on his belt is all I have of *him*. Vassili could slap me across the room, push me down on my ass, but he doesn't. I quickly undo his belt buckle and pull out his cock.

He eyes me with a dead gaze as my mouth goes to his dick. I suck for all I'm worth, for all the love we have. My lips wrap around his cock. I bang it to the back of my throat faster than someone can shout 'Mississippi!'

Sex as an advantage is new for me. I hope to God it isn't a new normal. It's dysfunctional and most certainly not how you save a marriage. At this moment, it works.

Vassili grips the back of my neck. He grunts his approval and forces my head up and down. My tonsils are bruised by the strength of his erection, and I suck vigorously.

Vassili massages the base of his cock since there's no way I can suck his lengthy shaft all the way down my throat. I'm already gagging as it is. He then pushes off the bed, and I'm back on my ass, onto the plush pile carpet, with him on top of me.

He starts to push down his jeans. I push up my skirt.

"Put that ass in my face," he growls.

I tug off my panties in a flash, reach up for a kiss. Vassili twirls his index finger. I turn over to my hands and knees. He enters my pussy with such force that my back arches.

"Fuck," I grit through my teeth. My walls begin to drench down on his cock as he clasps the back of my neck. He works his thumb into my ass. It feels good, gets my pussy quivering for more. But this is it. All the foreplay I'll get, tonight. And I know that once this false closeness we have ends, I won't be crying tears of ecstasy. I'll be crying for my husband to open up, and talk to me again.

I grip the plush-pile carpet as his cock slams through me. It's all porno action. No finesse. Drive only. Then his seed fills up my pussy before I'm alone again.

32

Vassili

Zariah is gone when I wake up on Friday morning. The moment I awaken, my mind is on the little things. Like, tell Zariah 'have a great day at work.' It's the little things that place a smile on her face. This is part of my routine. I do shit like this because for Christ sake, I can't be a man like my father. And there should be no doubt in my wife's mind of my love for her... like there was last night. I grab my cellphone off the nightstand, deciding to call my wife for virtually no fucking reason other than to say I love you.

But reality slams into my chest and the shit hurts so fucking bad. My heart isn't up to the little things. I turn on the shower, allowing it to get hot enough to burn my skin. The burn reminds me to feel . . .

I'm torn between being the monster I promised her I wouldn't be and the man who loves her. Without Malich and Yuri around during summers in my childhood or my decision to get the fuck away from Anatoly, I'd do more than *beat*

Zariah's pussy. And I would've never known true love. I'd have guarded myself with more cunts than can satisfy me.

After showering, I have a towel around myself while digging into my top drawer for my passport. I dress quickly and work over the words in my mind about what to say to my wife.

In the kitchen, Zamora has Natasha in her highchair. Scrambled eggs are on a tiny Disney princess plate.

Zamora eyes my Louis Vuitton canvas duffle and tilts her head at me. "Good morning, Vassili, I made you breakfast. It's staying warm in the conventional oven, but will you do me a favor before you leave?"

Shit, I was about to ask if she'd watch Natasha today... until I return. "Yeah, sure. Thanks for breakfast," I reply while opening the stainless-steel oven. Inside is a plate with more scrambled eggs, *kielbasa* sausage, and toast.

"Sliced fruit is in the fridge," she says, still glancing at my duffel bag. "Vassili, you are a praying man. I owe you lots for being a good husband, the recent events with Mat—"

"*Nyet*, you don't owe me anything." I cut in, although I know where this is headed.

"Alright, well, will you pray before you leave? Wherever it is you're going, pray about it."

"*Dah.*"

Ten minutes later, I've kissed my daughter and officially asked Zamora if she'd watch her today. Her eyes were expectant, so I told her I prayed. The two of us can tell that the mumble I sent to heaven landed on deaf ears.

While pressing the garage opener, I dial Zariah's number. Mid-second ring I'm sent to voicemail. I close my eyes wishing I hadn't used her body like I did last night. Shit, she sent me to voicemail on purpose.

"Zariah," I begin, still working in my mind on what to say to this woman I love with all of me. "I won't be home tonight," I start with the truth while backing out of the windy driveway. "Probably not tomorrow night or the next."

Realizing that I haven't told her much of anything I add where I'll be. And end the call.

At LAX, I took the first available flight to Moscow, through KLM Royal Dutch Airlines. There was an extended layover in Amsterdam. By the time I arrive in my homeland, it's the next morning. Grigor and Semion are posted at the terminal entrance when I arrive. My cousin's dog-ass of a face is set in a deep brown while Grigor's thin frame is in another power suit. My half-brother also has a bag, with breakfast bagels, and a cup in hand.

"Hello, brother." Grigor holds out the items.

"I didn't fucking send for you," I tell him, glancing over his attempt at a kind gesture. "Don't the two of you have a demanding job? I'm well aware that Anatoly requests alert every time I enter the fucking country. Damn, Grigor, you're the right hand, and you," I address Semion, "are the left? An equal operation, except Semion, you're a dumb fuck, right?"

The ugly fuck's eyelid twitches. He's not a fan of equality since he has the harder assignment.

***

G rigor drinks the coffee and eats the bagel all while driving to my father's compound in Rublyovka. The gates open, and armed guards on each sidetracks us as we enter.

Slurping the last bit of the drink, my half-brother squeezes next to a throng of supercars around a lengthy lap pool. Shit, this man has become a hoarder. It's like a car dealership out here for the ultra-exclusive.

Five armed men, even uglier than Semion, surround Anatoly. He meanders down the front steps of his home. His suit isn't a blinding highlighter color, but black. The many accessories he has on are all black. The clown never wears dark clothing.

"I've been in mourning," he says, holding his arms out. "Come, come, give your father a hug."

"Nyet, I'd rather not." My tone is calm and I'm my usual standoffish self with him. "Are you mourning your nephew, Igor?"

Like a missile, my fist shoots out and lands against his chin. No response was necessary. Anatoly's brain snaps in place in his legs anchor down. He timbers backward.

A bunch of hammers cocks back and machine guns are pointed into my face. A hard slam from behind goes to my left temple. As I crumple to the ground near my father, I realize that of all these mudaks, it had to be my cunt of a brother who knocked me out. Fuck, I underestimated Grigor.

33

Zariah

Two days have trickled by since I've last seen my husband. For over 48- hours quicksand has consumed me, and the devil has hold of my ankle, pulling me under. I'm torn between praying for God to keep him safe or hardening my heart to the only man I've ever fallen madly in love with. My two options encompass having faith or becoming less naïve about just who my husband is. I'd called and called him last night, each ring took the air right from my lungs.

This morning, I dipped into the expensive facial foundation I reserve for date nights. Instead of appearing flawless, it works at the crescents beneath my eyes. After showering, I opted for a yellow summer dress. The ensemble counteracts my mood for Natasha's sake.

With a faux smile, I enter the nursery. She's in the changing station. My mother has another new ensemble from Mrs. Takahashi laid beside her.

Our beautiful baby's brown eyes sparkle as she looks me over. "Daddy?"

My curved lips fall into a tensed line and no amount of rousing myself will furrow the edges.

My mom scoops Natasha onto a welcoming hip and turns around. Her face falls as she says, "Oh, honey."

"I'm okay, Mom." My voice tremors.

"You should stay home from work today."

An imaginary knife tears across my chest. Regret storms through me. Vassili suggested that I stay home so many times. Now, he doesn't seem to believe in us. I'd like to be there to help him work things out.

Rubbing a hand over my face, I reply, "No, I can't stay home. I have to work."

Zamora offers a faint smile. "I'm going to compare you to your dad now."

I scoff. "Don't—"

"Maxwell has his qualities. Resilience is one of them. Yet, balance? Not so much. Work can help get certain things off your mind. There comes a time when you still must address said things."

"Humph, save this conversation for Vassili." I place up a hand, begging her not to continue with my gaze. "I'm so sorry, Mom. We ruined your birthday week."

"How? I can't fathom how you or Vassili masterminded any of the travesties that occurred. And if you ask me to watch my grandbaby, I'll find a belt."

I sniffle at her joke, with no energy to offer a comeback.

I'm sitting in my car, across the way from my father's home. My gaze lands on a side profile of the balcony of my old bedroom and tears flood down my cheeks. Vassili climbed the tree almost ten years ago to sneak into my room as I showered. *Jesus, please, please, please,* I silently beg. *Let him be okay. You are part of my marriage, we can't do this without You. Don't let us ...*

A hard sniffle rattles through me. I flap my hands near my eyes to cool down the achy, hot feel of my skin.

Why didn't I force my dad to assist me with the Noriega case weeks ago? He blew me off after returning from Temecula with Berenice. The asshole was too busy to see his only daughter. Now, I look like shit.

I clutch my keys and get out of the car and head up the steps to the glossy black door. My fingers are crossed that he is home. Instinctively, I shift through my keys for the one I've owned the longest. Then it dawns on me how he changed the locks following my marriage. My index finger jabs at the doorbell a couple of times.

"Dad," I call out, pressing the button again. "Dad?"

The door flies open. In checkered shorts and a polo, Maxwell looms at the doorframe. The fucker does have time for golf!

"Good morning, Zariah." He shoots over his shoulder, hustling back into the house.

I step in, close the door, and follow him into the parlor. "Good morning," I grit out.

He stops at the wet bar in the sitting room and opens a chunky-crystal bottle of amber liquid. While pouring two cups, he asks, "What prompted this impromptu visit? Igor Resnov, eh?"

"No. What do you know?" Suspicion has me eyeing him with an imaginary fine-tooth comb for any signs that he's had his hands in Igor's death.

"To stave off heart failure, I've distanced myself from your mistakes!" Taking a sip of his drink, he hands over mine. Then he finally glances me over. "You've been crying?"

"I'm here about," I gulp down the fiery liquid, "About Juan Noriega."

He chuckles, sipping at his bourbon. "Russian money not good enough for you anymore, Princess? That wetback is even worse. If you'll finally take a morsel of advice, stick with the white boy. No need further slumming in the gutter. At least you'll secure the throne when Anatoly dies. Hell, they have the president in their pocket. No need screwing a roach and breeding a bunch of those babies too."

My eyebrows rise. Racist? I never pegged my father for a racist. Sexist, yes. Socialist, you betcha. But as Chief of Police, he must have some morals, right? He has *buddies* of every color on the force. I place my hand on my hip and utter one single word, "Sullivan."

My father's eyebrow cocks. He moves toward the marble mantle and readjusts a crystal figurine as if he isn't all that concerned. "Why are you bringing him up?'

"The cop turned serial killer. You and Sammy parted ways after the entire LAPD forwent good police work. Nobody offered the DA building blocks for a case. He had to use his resources for the trial!"

Maxwell nudges his drink toward me. "Zariah, check your tone."

"I remember, you and Lieutenant Sullivan were as friendly as you and Sammy in the past. Heck, he should be golfing with you right now. Why did Sammy work so hard to put him away?" I spit sarcastically. "There are a lot of questions swimming through my mind, Father."

"I don't have time for this."

"You want me to come to my senses? I can wake up, start being a bitch if you'd like. Or would you prefer I keep my eyes closed and allow you to tell me about Igor?"

"Allow! Cute, I'm being blackmailed by my daughter." My father grabs a silver case of cigars and sits on an antique chair, with his leg crossed. "Jesus! What has that fucking Resnov done to you?"

"Talk or I start digging," I threaten. "Sammy's brakes were tampered with during the Sullivan trial."

He stops attempting to light the cigar to snap, "I didn't—"

"Don't worry, Dad. I'm intelligent enough to know it wasn't you. However, you either sanctioned the request or turned the other way. Probably had your face in Berenice's sour pussy, instead of at home with your wife. Wasn't Mom leery about you then! And I don't mean due to the hits. You were jealous about mom's concern for Sammy..."

"Zariah." He points the cigar at me, voice contrite. "Shut your fucking mouth, before—"

"I beg you with every fiber of my being, *hit me*." I stand before him, as he sits there. My dad takes his first puff of the cigar. I glare down at him, arguing, "I vow, before I sic my husband on you, I'm going to jump on your back and try to take you down myself. Now, back to Sullivan. I don't need to know about that skeleton. Here's how you can keep me from pulling even more skeletons out of your closet. Two things."

I turn my back to him, feel his hard gaze stabbing me as I top off my drink. The bourbon offers the smoothest burn down my throat as I down it. Chock-full of confidence, I continue with, "First, tell me about Noriega. Second, you'll tell me what the hell you know about Igor Resnov's death!"

Too hyped to sit down, I stand at the fireplace mantel.

Maxwell runs his hand over his fresh fade. "Look at me, child. I don't know anything about Igor's death. That is assigned to a lower detective, not the Chef of police."

"Yes, you insured the assignment went to one of the less seasoned detectives."

He puffs more smoke. "Or maybe a burnt-out detective that doesn't give a damn."

"Humph, yeah, that scenario works, too. But you know more than you're letting on, father. Talk."

"Talk? Alright, let me gossip with my daughter, eh? There's talk about the Bertolucci family having done something. None of my guys give a damn. It'll be a cold case soon."

"Thank you for the name." I shuffle Bertolucci to the back of my mind, aware when my father is telling the truth "Now, Noriega."

"He has a few friends on the force."

"You allow that?"

"Me? Nope, bad for business. We have a guy who funnels them toward Internal Affairs when necessary."

"When necessary?" I gasp, a million ideas running through my mind. "What are they, scapegoats? A means to fan the flames away from . . ."

"The cops that work hard to keep the street clean. So, I wouldn't call the men in my inner-circle 'monsters' if I were you."

"So, what you do is better?"

"Are you arguing in favor of Noriega?" He snaps, although, aware that it wasn't my intention. "Princess, I don't condone drug dealing."

"You condone everything else." I shake my head at how easily the discussion diverted from the gang member and back to my father. "I'm having Noriega subpoenaed, today."

"Why?" He croaks. "You'd better luck being one of his famous baby mamas. He doesn't slap them all around."

"His wife, I'm her divorce attorney."

My dad takes a long drag of his Cuban and contemplates for a moment. "Zariah, you come in my house making inferences that I do not appreciate. In some regard, you've been spot on. We keep our own safe."

The glint in my eyes reads volumes. That sick fuck Lieutenant Sullivan would've received a slap on the wrists had my father been Chief of Police at the time.

"However, I am rigid in my ways. Unpersuaded by some fucking Russians or no good Mexicans," he spits the words, and I take a step back.

"Alright, Dad. Did you forget about the Latino political figures you golf with?"

"There's a mask for every encounter." Maxwell shrugs. His gaze drags over me again, like he did so many times in the past after I'd fallen off my first bike. "I see the ring still on your finger. For now, I'll have a police detail on you by the time you make it to the freeway. Because I love you, but that's all the love I can give, *Princess*. At least while you're married."

"I don't want it. And I have no intentions of divorcing anytime in this lifetime. So, keep your detail." I argue.

"Nah, you're gonna need it."

34

Vassili

Aside from the boulder that must've fallen on my head, I wake up on day three, away from my family, and on a bed of clouds.

The mattress I'm lying on is halfway to the ceiling, and that's speaking volumes. I'm on the third floor of my father's home, and the walls soar high.

I touch a hand to my skull. It's bandaged.

"Fuck," I grunt, swinging my legs over the side of the bed. My feet dangle because of how far I am from the floor. The room around me is fit for a king. Real gold wallpaper, antique furniture. Silk slippers are on the ground. I shove my feet inside of them and head to the door.

Once open, I'm stopped by a guard, with the barrel of his gun to my face.

My lips are in a tight line as I warn, "Move. Before you regret it."

He lowers it somewhat. "I'm going to tell your father you're up. Okay?"

"He isn't the boss of me, neither are you."

The man starts to pull a walkie talkie. My hand slams against the barrel, angling it over my shoulder, and I jab straight for his nose. Too easy.

"What the fuck!" He screams, gripping at a waterfall of blood coming from his nose.

I snatch the walkie talkie. "Anatoly, can you hear me?"

"My son, you're up. I'm in the mudroom," he says in a cheerful tone. Sometimes he gets like this when angry. Either the punch I tossed rewired his brain, or he's in a psychotic episode.

In fifteen minutes, I've made it to the basement. The room is cave-like, with dome-shaped walls, and even more shimmering 24 karat gold on them. My gaze shades to the darkness of the area. At the far side of the room, past a steaming jacuzzi, is my father, with his usual horde of model-type cunts.

One kissing his face, the other massaging mud into his back, not sure what the third is doing, her bare ass is to my face. She's down low, probably sucking his cock.

The one kissing him moves, revealing that Anatoly's eye is sealed shut.

"I'd offer you some pussy but," he gestures to his face. "My son, I regret never having attended one of your matches. That hook of yours, boy, oh boy! Semion, take notes, you ugly motherfucker. My son is a handsome devil, and that right hook of his is lethal!"

My cousin eyes me. I ask, "Where the fuck is Grigor? I'm surprised he got to me before you."

Semion grunts. "He was closer. I would have tried to kill you…"

Anatoly cuts in, "And I would have had to put your ass down like a fatted cow, Semion."

"Damn, kuzen," I chuckle. "We should switch parents.

You'd be in my spot. That's what you want, right? *My spot.* Then that ugly face of yours might not look like a dog's ass, after all those jealous days and nights."

Semion lunges for me. The men around my cousin grab ahold of him anywhere they can. Arms, waist, limbs.

I don't flinch.

"Let him go," I say, smiling at Semion.

"*Nyet.*" My father waves them away. "The two of you can play later. You all leave now. Vassili, step into my office."

He gestures toward the mud jacuzzi. The women wave me over.

"I'll pass."

Everyone aside from Anatoly's whores leaves. While fiddling with one of their breasts, he says, "Stop exciting your cousin. Semion is indispensable to me until hurts you. I'd kill him."

Semion hurt me? I grunt. "So, you're being a father today? Alright, *Dad.* How will you handle Grigor? He hit me."

Anatoly shrugs. "Grigor is my favorite. He gets as many passes as you do for being firstborn."

"Them make him your successor."

"Nyet. Grigor is pale. Skinny. Lucky me, God blessed me with brawns and brains for son's out of how many attempts?"

"I don't give a shit how many children you've brought into this world." Taking on a wide-legged stance, I grit out, "Did you allow some Italians to shoot up your brother's home?"

He laughs. The girls do, too. "I'm appalled that you think so little of me."

"*Did you?*" My shout is amplified by the structure of the cave, causing the women to jump.

"Nyet." Anatoly offers a smug frown.

"Then how?"

"Must have something to do with that public official, Albert Bertolucci. He died a few weeks ago."

"What was he up to?"

"The guy was gunning for sanctions. Bertolucci took a shot at international claims at the ports in his area. He wanted to increase the requirements for merchants and businesses entering his counter. One of the seats of the seven owns a steel company in Italy."

I rub the old scar along my jaw. The table of seven or whatever the fuck he's referring to has been mentioned before. Malich always said that Anatoly wanted him to have a seat. Even with all power, it was best to have Resnovs take every seat. Semion's mother has a seat. The rest of my father's siblings do. There are about three seats that aren't claimed by Resnov's. But each seat is claimed by billionaires.

"Then why didn't the guy handle it, Anatoly?"

"He's a bitch, all paper no balls," my father huffs.

I shake my head. "And Bertolucci's family retaliated? You've had powerful men murdered around the nation. Seems like this one—"

"His family thinks they're the mafia or something."

"Did you hear about this quest for retaliation! And why, why did they go after Malich's family, not yours?"

"What the fuck do you mean, yours? Vassili, you are *moy syn*—my son. *You are my family!*"

"Make me believe you."

"Does my word not mean—"

"*Shit.* Anatoly your word doesn't mean a motherfucking thing to me."

He stands up from the mud bath and slaps a hand against his chest. "I had nothing to do with my nephew's death. How dare you!"

I stare at him through the eyes of an unbiased man.

As if I don't have a history with this psychotic bastard.

As if I'm not aware of his dark past that revolved around my mother running away from a monster like him.

As if I haven't experienced years of being treated like shit.

As if I haven't made vows of murdering him.

Now, I'm second-guessing my father's manipulative ways. Could it be possible? Maybe Anatoly didn't remove his blessing from Malich's family. Those Italians have always feared us... so someone had to pay.

35

Zariah

After the chat with my father, I head toward Billingsley Legal. While driving, I call the hospital and am connected to Yuri's room. "Hey, Yuri, how are you? Are you hanging in there?"

"Feel like shit. There's a gaping hole in my calf. But there's no getting me down. Where's Taryn?"

I silently take a breath. "Oh my, I apologize. Vassili took off. And I never called to tell her you were in the hospital—"

"It's okay, Zariah, it's okay." He cuts into my sorry attempt for an apology. Hell, the guilt of knowing Taryn is a hoe is eating me alive. "Zar, I know you have that knucklehead to deal with. Vassili came to see me on his way to the airport. I told the mudak to stay home. Malich sent for my brothers. Mikhail is being a fucking idiot too. I never thought I'd see the day that my eldest didn't speak of peace and church."

"That sounds bad," I sigh, heading onto the freeway. Malich has bred mostly sons. Mikhail followed in Malich's footsteps. Not the part where he set roots with the bratva. He became a doctor, too. Mikhail moved from an award-winning hospital in the East Coast a few years ago to work and live near his family. Even then, Mikhail was full of goodness. Not an evil bone in his body. He always reminded me of what a 'normal' in-law would be like. Yuri had five other brothers, who've made homes throughout the states. Each brother has a mainstream job, and a good head on their shoulders due to Malich's wisdom. Igor's death has set a domino effect of ruthless antics.

Yuri continues with, "It's just that, I've been calling Taryn, not like I can do anything else, and she doesn't answer. Zar, I-I'm worried."

My heart clutches. Yuri is a big ass cuddle bear. He's lying in the hospital worried about Taryn not answering his calls. I finish the call with a bit of encouragement, then dial my high school friend and she promptly answers.

"*Ho-la*, Zariah," she sounds off in an attempt to say 'hello' in Spanish.

"Girl, where are you at?" My lips are set in a frown.

"Cabo San Lucas, heifa! It's my man's birthday, and we are celebrating."

A man in the background, with a dreamy Spanish accent, speaks. I grit out, "Taryn, c'mon, girl. Yuri is in the hospital, he keeps calling you."

She groans, "I know."

"We will be thirty in two short years, Taryn, damn. Not twenty. If you give a damn about him, answer him. See how he's doing."

The music in the background becomes muffled as if she's removing herself from paradise. A few moments later, Taryn says, "When I return, I'll check on him. Zar, I'm aware that I need to br-break up wi-with Yuri sometime, so I will."

"Are you about to cry?" My lips tense. "Seriously, I don't want to hear it. There's a man here in California who has gladly given you his heart. Heck, Yuri doesn't need tears, he needs loyalty. I'll see you when you return," I finish the call, and hang up.

Through the rearview window, I notice an unmarked cop car a few spots back. My father didn't heed my stubborn response. He's got a security detail on my six. I take comfort in the fact that he must have some sort of love for me

It's lunchtime and the drive-thru line at Hot Chili's is chaotic. Cars are illegally jamming the intersection. With a narrowed gaze, I squeeze through a tight opening and enter the Billingsley Legal parking lot.

My cell phone rings as I'm getting out of the car. The automatic tone says, "Incoming call from Husband."

I dig through my purse and apprehend my iPhone. Too fixated on answering it in the allotted time, that I didn't remember I could have pressed the radio button.

"Hello," I speak into the receiver.

"Baby, I'm sending you—"

I cut in, "Where are you?"

"Still in Moscow."

"Then save it."

"Zariah, I'm sending you a photo of my sister."

"Dan... Dan us... Danushka?" Damn, of all the times, I say the woman's name right, when my friend has the same name as Vassili's sister.

"Yes."

"Why, I have that photo ingrained in my memory. Pasty skin. Mousey brown hair. A huge nose."

He breathes into the phone. "I don't think my father allowed the Bertolucci's to go after the family. Danushka might have, and I want you to stay away from her if she ever comes around."

"Oh, so now you want to share information. Save it. I won't speak to you until you're right here in my face. If it makes you feel better, rest easy knowing that I'm an obedient little wife. I haven't forgotten about what your sister looks like. If she pops out of the bushes, I'll call you. Not sure how that will help since your oceans away." I pause. Damn, I'm acting like a brat, but there were better ways to handle Igor's death. Hell, I kept seeing images of him an Anatoly murdering each other. Fighting fire with fire as Vassili is hell-bent on doing will ruin us all.

But I soften my tone, "Hello, Vassili? Are you still there?"

"Yes, I was just taking the shit you had to offer." He grits out. Then his tone softens, "I'd never abandon you, Zar."

"I love you, Vassili." I hang up. The moment he returns home, I'll talk to him. But he'll have to be willing to be a team, and then *we* can seek out the Bertolucci family.

S amuel is standing next to Tyrese's office when I start by, with a greeting. He cocks his head at me. "You, step inside, too."

"Alright..." I follow him inside. Tyrese's tailored suit has been replaced by a short sleeve button up as he sits behind his desk. He doesn't even offer his signature dimple. Either this heatwave has him lethargic or we are in deep trouble.

"The company we commission to issue out subpoenas called me personally this morning. Our account wasn't set up to be billed for subpoenaing parties in high profile cases," Sammy says.

Crap, I chew my bottom lip. Nobody wants to subpoena Mr. Noriega. He's not your run-of-the-mill wifebeater.

Samuel's gaze tracks across us while saying, "Zariah, I'm aware you've helped Tyrese. I appreciate your assisting him with becoming acclimated with the office. But he's more than capable of handling the Noriega case."

"Alright." I glare at Mr. Nick's daring him to speak up. With no desire for Samuel to share my involvement with Vassili, I play the naïve card. "What's going on?"

Samuel huffs. "Well, I had it in my mind to commend you, Nicks, on Mrs. Felicidad obtaining her green card in such a swift manner. It takes some serious connections, and balls. But now you're suing a US Citizen for half of everything that he owns. Noriega so happens to be a known affiliate of the Loco Dios. The company refuses to submit the subpoena. Zariah, I won't have you in this mess and quite frankly, we both know that you were aware Noriega is a Loco Dios. The two of you are also aware he has ties to the Mexican Cartel. Tyrese, it's not too late to back out."

"But Felicidad was," I stop myself, and resort to a more formal response, "Mrs. Noriega was abused by her husband. She has rights."

"You *will* stay out of this, Zariah. If Tyrese chooses to continue to represent Mrs. Noriega, he's *now* cognizant of the possible consequences. He's new, so this is a warning to him, too. Zar," he pauses, glancing at me with all sincerity. "Your mother would kill me. So stay out of it."

"Well, Mr. Nicks?" I cock a brow, daring him to forsake Felicidad and her children.

"I'll pay a bum off the street to serve him, if necessary," Tyrese replies.

"That might be necessary." Samuel pinches the bridge of his nose. "Any questions or consultation required, see me."

My mentor stalks out of the room.

"So," Tyrese speaks up. "I assume Billingsley must've been so emotionally invested in keeping you away from this case, he didn't view the paperwork. Zariah, your name is all over the summons."

"Good idea about asking a transient to serve Noriega. Will you go vet one, or should I?" I arise.

"Not so fast, Zariah."

Lips set into a line, I sink back down, arms folded. "This is my case, Nicks."

"I'll see to it that the summons is delivered by this afternoon. But let me make something clear, Samuel has had conferences to attend these past few weeks. Prior to attending court, he'll know. That is if the Noriega chooses not to retaliate once he gets the subpoena."

I scoff. "Look, we agreed to have your name on the subpoena. Lynetta made the mistake of using a generic form when creating it."

"We don't have time for mistakes, Zariah. For your safety. Luckily, the company who serves men like Noriega refused. I handled Lynetta. Shit, I could fire her ass myself."

"Thank you, Tyrese." I nod in agreement.

"I can't bring up your husband, right?" he shakes his head with a laugh. "I guess, I'll be grateful he can keep you safe."

Our eyes connect. I'm too angry to read Mr. Nicks the wrong way. "Yes, he can. And I have the genetic makeup of a man who gets paid hand over fist to rub people the wrong way, too. I can handle myself. But we do not have time for mistakes."

"I'll revamp the subpoena with my information. It'll be given to Noriega this afternoon, Zariah. I understand that you're going to continue assisting with this case for whatever reason. I refuse to have you in court during litigation."

"Alright," I nod. "I'll write all the lengthy reports us attorneys aren't interested in."

He almost smiles.

"See, Mr. Nicks we're working together. Nevertheless, nobody is stopping me from communication with Felicidad and her children."

He bites his lip, then holds out a hand across the table. I reach over and shake it.

"Zariah," he says, not letting me go. "I like you, and despite the craziness of this case, I'm enjoying getting to know you."

"Okay," I narrow my eyes somewhat, as a sign for him to remove his hand.

"I'd prefer you had nothing else to do with the Noriega's, but you made a promise to Felicidad. Therefore, *I* am allowing you to have a hand in the case, regardless of the promises you've made with Samuel."

"I'm just playing cheerleader to Mrs. Noriega." With a smile, I bite out, "Now let me go."

His callused hand continues to clasp around mine. "Damn, this is the moment where I offer a wisecrack as I prefer it if you were my cheerleader."

My lips sneer like usual when he flirts. I slap at his hand and he lets me go. For a split second, genuine concern sparks in his gaze. It's my cue to head out the door.

M y eyes burn from staring at the computer screen and all the moments I was prone to tears. When there's a tap on the door, my shoulder's jolt. I pull in a sharp inhale and reply, "Come in."

Tyrese steps into the ajar door. He cocks a thick brow and says, "It's almost eight. Can I go home yet?"

With my mind on sleep and as I skim through the neurologist's statement about Edgar Versa, I mumble, "Go."

"You know exactly what I mean." He takes on a wide-legged stance.

"You chose to stay, Mr. Nicks. I've locked up shop more

times than I can count. Besides, we shook hands, you have the Noriega case. I've been consigned to Felicidad's *life coach* when she needs." A yawn breaks through my rant, so I huff. "Alright, let me finish my sentence, okay?"

"Thank you."

Ten minutes later, I exit my office. Tyrese is in the hallway, leaning against the door. He glances me up and down. The dimples in his cheek deepened. "God, you are beautiful."

"Don't piss me off, Nicks." I fork a hand through my hair.

"Look, I woke you up." When I give him a confused glare, he elaborates, "I watched you for a while, before I knocked. You were sitting in front of piles of documents, dosing. Your head kept …" He starts to chuckle, as he gestures that my head continued to dip. "Zariah, since you aren't your usual sharp, sophisticated self, I snuck in the truth. You're gorgeous when you sleep. Shoot me. It's cute, you know."

"Be respectful," I grit out, stalking to the alarm, and quickly punching in the code. Tyrese unlocks the front door, holds it open and we step outside. The air is hot. The sky is painted lilac, with fragments of orange where the sun has yet to dip over the horizon.

I've taken one step out of the door when I glance at my car. Three Escalades are surrounding it. Enough Mexican gangsters to start their own sports team lean against the sides of each SUV.

"Zari…" Tyrese's tone dies as a man comes from the side of the wall. He was hidden by the door. He's holding a sawed-off shotgun to Tyrese's head.

"*Aye Dios,* look at the two of you," Juan Noriega says. Has to be him. I googled him. He has so many tattoos on his neck and chest, if I squint my eyes, it looks like he's wearing a turtleneck. And the motherfucker is all but five feet tall. "You scared, *puta?*"

Tyrese pulls me close to his side. He barks in an authoritative tone, "You all need to disburse at once!"

I glance down at Noriega and ask, "Do you own these SUVs? I've got an inventory of all your assets. Since Felicidad is taking half, how about I take these two, you can keep the other one?"

Fuck! My promise not to attend a court hearing doesn't mean a thing now. I am truly my father's child.

He laughs, every single tooth is capped in gold. "You're a hot little piece of ass, aren't you? Isn't she Chico?"

A man-made of brick steps forward. Now him, I'm afraid of. One of his arms is bigger than the combination of my thighs! His dark gaze shoots up and down my frame.

"Alright, guys, get in your fucking rides and leave," Tyrese tells them. "Noriega, I'm sure you have a slimy ass attorney waiting to handle this case."

"No, *hombre.*" Noriega shakes his head. "I like her. Tyrese Nick's, your name is all over the paperwork, but this bitch knows my bitch by her first name. What's your name, sweetheart?"

Chico's gaze lands on mine, and then his pupils dilate. He mirrors the fear I'm internalizing. "I know this girl. Juan, we gotta go."

He nudges his chin. "Que chucha tienes?"

My eyebrows knit. I'm in the dark about what Noriega said in Spanish.

Chico says, "She's that fighter's wife—"

Police sirens ring.

An hour has passed. The sky is dark and with the bad neighborhood I work in, there aren't many working streetlights. The red and blue lights on top of the masses of police cruisers bounce a glare off the windows of each ride. I can't see Noriega's face as he is seated in the back of the car furthest from me. My stomach churns. He must be making a connection as I give my statement to Officer Greene, or I've grown paranoid. My body feels riddled with his glare.

"How long are you going to hold them?" I ask.

Greene rubs his goatee, then asks, "How long do you need us to? The guy with the sawed-off shotgun is going away for a while. But there can be drugs beneath the dash, or anywhere else you'd like them to be found in those SUV's, Mrs. Washington." He makes sure to look me dead in the eye while giving my maiden name.

Lips pursed, I shake my head. "I don't need any extra help."

"You have time to consider it." Greene waits for a beat for my response. Then he starts toward his cruiser and tosses over his shoulder, "Your call."

Tyrese comes to stand next to me. "Your husband should've texted or called you at least twenty times by now, Zariah. He had reached out to you at least five times by the time I ate my chili burger on our first night working this case."

I rub a hand over my face, glad that my eyes aren't burning with the need to cry. Fatigue weighs down on me, and my mind is too muddled to lie. "He's got a fight coming up."

"Can I drive you home, please?"

"No."

He rubs a strand of hair from my face before I can protest. "Follow you?"

"You're gonna do it anyway. You did it the night we got the case."

"So it's 'we' now."

"We did get guns put to our heads together." I smile to

keep from crying. I want to go home and hold Natasha as Vassili spoons me.

His dimples deepen. "We're friends now?"

"We're colleagues, Mr. Nicks." I shrug my usual blasé self.

Tyrese backs up toward his Jaguar as I head to my car. And then Tyrese Nicks follows me home…

3 6

Vassili
TWO NIGHTS LATER

I was flagged after returning from my homeland. A police cruiser lines up behind my Mercedes, and BLURPS the lights at me. Fuck, I thought Mr. Washington had backed the fuck off? I pull over, grab the necessary documents and zip down my windows.

"Hands on the steering wheel," a masculine voice blares through the speakers. "Both windows down."

Doing as told, I shake my head.

The beloved boys in blue step out of their cruiser and come to both sides of my car, flashing the light in.

"What did I do, this evening, officer?" I start to grab my license and insurance from my lap.

"Hands on the steering wheel," he says again, flashing the light in my face.

The illumination burns my retinas. My hands clench the wheel. He pulls out his phone and starts to make a call.

"Keep your head forward, too," commands the cop on the passenger side.

I lift my middle finger from the steering wheel as a response. A few moments later, the cop on my side holds out his phone.

Keeping my head forward, hands glued down, I argue, "What the fuck? Is it for me? Are you going to hold it to my ear?"

"Take the damn phone, Resnov."

I snatch it from his hand. I growl into the receiver, "Hello?"

"Are you keeping my daughter and grandchild safe? Why the fuck are you going on vacations to Russia for *five days*, without them? Got another family that I should be aware of?"

I groan, "What do you want, Mr. Washington?"

"You to choke on rat poison, but I'm a softy. My pretty princess loves you. When she takes her love away, Resnov," he chortles, "that's the end of you, buddy. She's a cop kid, should've married ... a cop. Should've become DA."

"This is fucking perfect, Maxwell," I laugh with him. "Your mentality is like my father. Get the entire family into the business. Zariah can prosecute the cases that you deem necessary. She wouldn't harp if you sent over investigation files with nothing on them. No reason to try the mudaks on your team, right?"

"I keep saying you were smart. Remember the first time we chatted? I came to that conclusion. You're a fighter, a strategist. Now, take your ass home. You've been gone for almost a week. Keep your family safe."

CLICK.

My chest is tight with anger. This motherfucker tells me to keep my family safe? I can handle my family! The cop reaches inside and grabs the phone. I have it in my mind to call Mr. Washington back, but I head home instead.

I n the nursery, Natasha's back slowly rises and falls as she sleeps. I place my hand on her, she's warm and soft. It takes all my strength not to pick her up and hold her to my chest. But my baby is a true fighter and a restless sleeper. She will riot if I wake her.

Feeling eyes on me, I turn around. Zariah stands at the door in a nightgown. I head toward her, she pivots on her heels and starts to our bedroom. Inside the room, she stalks past me and closes the double door. This is a signal that her mother stays. I expected loud cussing, and anger. She leans against the closed door for a moment.

I take her arm, she slaps me away.

"Zariah, I'm fucking sorry, baby," I try.

"No, I don't need your apologies, Vassili. I need you to understand something." She moves from my grasp and goes to the dresser. With her back to me, she murmurs, "Three months ago, we were in opposition of each other. Then we head to Brazil, and you had your comeback fight. We made promises..."

I'm a dick. I look like a piece of crap as I begin to grovel, "Zar—"

"No, let me finish." She has something fisted in her hands. "I stopped taking birth control, so Natasha could have a little sister or a little brother."

"I know, baby."

She flings something at me. It bounces off my arm as she shouts, "I'm pregnant, Vassili! And FYI that's from last night. This morning, I went to the doctor *all alone*. Two months, Vassili. I have a photo. Would you like to see that, too?"

"*Dah*," I nod my head slowly. Can't show I'm fucking elated, I'm still in the doghouse.

"Only if you promise to step up to the plate. What do I have to do to get a solid promise from you, Vassili? Get you to pinkie swear, sign a fucking contract!"

"Okay, Zar," I reply. "I said some shit the night at the hospital. I do my best to keep my promises to you."

"Yeah?" she chortles. "Then you tell me you went *home*. Fuck you and your damn home, Vassili. This needs to be home. Our home!"

"It is home, Zariah!"

Her look shuts me the fuck up from another attempt at an apology.

"Vassili, you go away to fight in Australia in three weeks. I dare you to runoff before then. I will find you and drag your ass home. Now, do you want to see the ultrasound? That's your gesture to me that you plan to *take care of home*."

"I'm sorry," I step closer to her. She slaps my face, again, and again. I take every hit she offers. From my back pocket, I pull out a long jewelry box. "See, beautiful, I have something for you, baby. I'm sorry."

Zariah gingerly takes the box, opens it up. It's a platinum tennis bracelet with seven-carat diamonds, I always get her seven carats. The box snaps shut.

"Save it for later, Vassili," she says, voice drowning in exhaustion. "I prefer shiny gifts on happy occasions, not as peace offerings. I'm so very sorry about what happened to your cousin, Vassili. Yesterday evening, I met with the family to help with funeral proceedings. Malich is mute, he isn't saying shit to anybody right now." She rubs tears from her face. "They're your family, damn it, and you know it! You should've been there."

I try to hug her again, but she slaps me. "I dreamed of

Anatoly murdering you, Vassili," she screeches. "I dreamt that you'd try to retaliate, and your father killed you!"

I'm stunned, stock still, standing before her. Last week, she had tears falling down her face, and I was too angry to give a fuck. Tonight, my heart shreds in my chest, from the shit she just said. She worried about me dying?

Zariah stands there, hugging her hands around her chest. She's got my seed in her belly, and I'm being a dick! My hand goes to the back of her neck, and my lips go to hers.

Zariah turns her head. "Not right now, Vassili."

My teeth grit, I can't take her tears anymore. "You want me to sign a fucking contract or something? I'll do anything for you to forgive me, Zariah." I reach for my hair, my fucking mohawk is gone. There's nothing to tug. I rub a hand over my buzz cut and then punch myself in the chest.

Zariah finally reaches out a hand to me. "Vassili, I was just talking. I love you, baby. *I love you and I'm scared.* If you ever leave…"

"Leave?" I bark. I plant kisses on her lips, more and more, tasting the soft sweetness of her mouth. In Russian, I promise, "I will never let you go."

"I know."

"No matter how much I might act a fool. I will never let you go."

"Yeah, well you can tell me more about your mother, Vassili." Her sweet voice makes my cock go flaccid. I wanted to fuck her happy.

"Vassili, tell me something! At times, you can halfway screw me out in public, and then during other instances, you play the gentleman. Why, baby, please tell me *why?*"

"Okay, I'll tell you." I nod, with a frown. My hands grope at her breast, and my tongue twines in her ear. My dick begins to stretch and harden again.

"Tell me," she folds her arms.

I press her hands back down at her sides and kiss her again. "In a minute..."

"Now," she murmurs, eyes glittering with tears. "We're not close like we were, Vassili. Let me get close to you. Tell me, now."

Fuck now, I press my mouth over hers again. This time I bite her bottom lip until she opens up for me. My cock strains against my jeans, ready to leap out and fuck her. It's been five days, and I need pussy.

My wife pushes at my chest with all her might. I take a few steps back.

"Sex doesn't fix, everything, Vassili."

"I know." I shrug, but in my mind, I declare the opposite. Sex will wipe away those tears and place a smile on that beautiful chocolate brown face of hers.

Zariah reaches up, places her hands on my jaw. "Baby, I'm not fucking you tonight. Sex isn't a means to an end. No matter how many times I've caved in the past, you're not getting any."

I close my eyes, breathe in the sugary goodness of her, and nod my head. I have to talk to her about my past, give her a little something.

37

Zariah

Vassili holds me tightly in his arms. I've showered for the second time tonight. This time with him, and without tears in my eyes. He was a gentleman and didn't try to screw me. Lord knows, I kept my gaze on his and not on all the ripped muscles of his body.

Now, we're lying in bed. He has this obsession with cocoa butter and my tummy. Although it's flat-ish, I told him during my pregnancy with Natasha that I didn't want stretch marks. Well, I had a few of those prior to, and he's kissed every one of them. But he got into the habit of massaging my belly.

Seems like the perfect slice of déjà vu as Vassili's big strong hands rub along my stomach. It's nothing short of therapeutic for him because we have deeper conversations like this.

My husband is fearless and invincible. And I'm half the

team. Now, I need to connect with him on a deeper level. I need to know more about his actions at the bar in Brazil, more about his mother.

"Tell me your trouble, my love." I sigh, sinking my head against his chest.

Vassili caresses my hair, kisses my forehead. But he doesn't utter a word.

"You promised. I'll pay in ass in the near future, not tonight though." Damn, my joke was his level of crude, and still, my husband is quiet.

"Malich told you about how my father tied my mother up to a street post?"

"Yes, baby. Tell me more."

"I'll tell you," he asserts himself. "Before she got up there, she was dragged to Anatoly's compound. I hadn't seen her in months... Had to be months. I always tried to forget about her. Then Anatoly would go look for her. Bring her ass back. Shit seemed like years since I was a kid."

"Hmmm," my finger twirls a figure eight across his chest.

"One of his goons spotted her somewhere. He tossed her out of the trunk of his car, she was in the middle of the courtyard. The sound of her screams I can still fucking hear it now. Hear her begging for them to stop, to let her go."

My skin begins to burn as an image comes to fruition in my mind.

"The bitch, Anatoly had running the house told me not to go down. I said something to Sasha, scared the shit out of her. Made her stay with that cunt. Then I went outside. My father was ..." Vassili pauses. His chiseled chest puffing with air before exhaling. "*He fucked her in front of them all.* Sometimes I can't get that shit from my head, and I don't want to disrespect you."

"Like when we were having fun, screwing in Vegas? You called me a bitch."

"*Dah.*"

I lay on my side, and place my hands on his beautiful, stone-carved face. Vassili seems so emotionless. My fingertips press against his hot skin. His past is eating at him inside. "I'm going to ask you a question, Vassili."

"Girl, ask——"

"What was in your heart?"

He blinks. This is a doggone trick question to him.

"Malicious intent? Were you angry when calling me a bitch?"

"*Nyet.* Fuck no!"

"Your father raped your mother. You saw it." I repeat to him the truth. His eyebrows knit as if the thought never occurred to him. "Rape is a means to gather power. To strip a person down to make the assailant *feel*.... good? I don't know. I'm aware that it's all in the striping down, gaining control, showing off power, and causing humiliation. Have you ever kissed me crazy at the bar to shame me?"

He shakes his head.

"We have fun, we role-play. As your wife, I am bound to make all your sexual fantasies a reality. If I don't like something, I say so."

I hold my husband tight. He has a few visible scars that increase his sexiness. On occasion, he has broken bones too. My heart cries for those scars I never knew about. It's gonna take time for Vassili to fully open up to me. He gave me one isolated incident of his childhood.

I'll have to beg, plead, and sometimes even force him to share more with me in the future. And it'll break my heart to break his over again while he's divulging the past. The pain is all part of getting to know my husband.

38

Vassili

Igor's funeral was held today and Malich still hasn't uttered a single word. Yuri walked around with a cane in his hand and a bone to pick with anybody who crosses his path. Mikhail handled everything.

Dressed in a stiff-black suit, I stand in the living room of my uncle's home, tossing Resnov Water back. The burn slams down my throat. I'm ready to hit the road. I need to fuck my wife, if she's willing, that is. It's been a week since I returned from Russia, and she's keeping those thick thighs locked. Don't get me wrong, my beautiful wife is still her nurturing self. My leaving scared her, and the threats I made about murdering my father only heightened her fear.

Yuri pats my back. "Everything has been handled." We're an in a circle, the six of us, and I feel like one of the brothers.

"You tell dad?" Mikhail asks.

"*Dah*, he's in his room."

The oldest rubs a hand at the back of his neck. "Did he say anything?"

When Yuri shakes his head, a heaviness continues to weigh further on our shoulders.

"All the Bertolucci's are dead, right down to the fucking kids," Yuri sneers. "A friend of ours owed dad a favor. I didn't think he'd do the k-kids."

I glance around for Zariah. She's seated with Albina and Natasha and has done everything to keep the toddler from crying for her father. Anna's been popping pills like candy. With Malich's medical connections, she was a zombie at the funeral.

"Good, it's done. We're family, we are fucking Resnovs," I tell them, in the words of my grandfather Anatoly Senior. "'Touch what's mine, and the funeral home becomes rich.'"

Yuri nods. Suddenly he isn't so sad about the Bertolucci kids that died. We all take a drink.

"Something bad happened yesterday?" Zariah asks as she helps me take off my suit jacket. She'd already stripped down to her panties and bra. In my anger about putting Igor in the ground, I think I've been standing at the door to the bedroom for a while now.

I don't have it in me to lie. "What do you know, Zariah?"

"More than I need to." Her eyes warm with sadness. "Anna was bragging about the Bertolucci. Bragging and crying about before she took more meds." She wants to say more. Earlier, Zariah had mentioned learning how to cope. Well, apparently Anna's big ass mouth told her exactly how we Resnovs deal.

"Are you mad?" I ask.

"No, baby. You didn't do anything."

I scoop her up, her hips go around my waist. I place her on the bed. My wife is the most beautiful sight I've ever laid eyes on. Creamy, dark brown skin. Her hair waves over her shoulder, and caresses against her bra. I push her tresses back over, pull out her breast and begin to suck.

"No more sad shit, Zariah," I say, tongue twining around the puckered bulb. "Can I fuck you now, or am I still in trouble?"

She moans. "Please fuck me, Vassili."

"Soon as I taste you, baby," I reply. After unbuckling my pants, I shove them down. I work my way down to the sweetest scent I've ever breathed in. Eager to get a whiff, I place my nose against her lace thong and growl.

"Vassili, fuck me, daddy," she groans.

My cock thumps against my thigh, begging like a panting dog for action. I tear the thong from her and dig right in. My face is so far into her pussy, nose nudging against her clit, chin riding along her asshole. My tongue digs deep into her candy core. My wife gets to cussing, and her leg starts to jerk.

On my knees, I grab the flesh of her ass and slam straight into that soaking wet pussy. All that moaning turns into sweet groaning. My tongue then presses into her mouth.

With us in a seated position, Zariah works her hips and grinds down on my cock. Damn, her pussy is as wet as her mouth.

"Yes! Yesssss!" Her long fingernails slash at my biceps as she works her hips.

"Damn, girl, you're having my baby."

She bites her lip. The perfect little fuck face of hers has me saying it again. "Girl, you're having my fucking baby."

"I'm going to have your baby," she growls slowly.

I flip her onto her back, grip the head post, and pound into her pussy. "I fucking love you. I knew this pussy was wetter than usual, you got that pregnant pussy."

"Shit," she screams, her titties are bouncing. "Vassili, I'm coming."

"That's right cum all over daddy's dick." I beat her pussy like a speed bag. Zariah's hips angle upward. She grabs hold of my ass, taking every punch to her cunt. The slickness of her walls, has me clenching my toes, and I time my release right.

Zariah
Three Weeks Later…

C hico was right about something. I'm not to be fucked
with. Drugs were pinned on Noriega and his gangster
friends, thanks to Officer Greene. However, the kilos of
cocaine wasn't "found" until their Escalades were processed.
That occurred the morning I learned that I was pregnant.
Greene had been more than happy to oblige. It was karma
for Noriega. And I'm guilt-free, well almost . . .

I've succumbed to a Fatburger with Rally's French Fries.

Natasha and I are holed up in the game room. She's at her
toddler table chewing on a Baby fat with cheese. Needing
elbow room while I eat, I chose to sit on the plush carpet and
lean against the wall. And she has some nerve, eyeing my
Rally's French Fries. Really? She didn't like them the first
time. So, needless to say, I didn't purchase her any fries at all.

"Mommy, fry, fry?" she begs.

"Girl," I chuckle, my tone is as testy as Vassili's usually is
when he calls me that himself. I pluck a few of my fries and

hand them over. "You're only one-years old. You can't eat it all."

Damn, I close my eyes and moan at the taste of my own. When who do I hear? Yuri's loudmouth. He's gotten comfortable with his cane. The other night, we went out, he was the oddball. It didn't stop a flock of women from listening to his exaggerated stories about deployment.

"Natasha, shhhhh," I tell her.

"Zariah?" Vassili shouts up the stairs.

Please don't come up...

Please don't come up...

This is déjà vu. Instead of me being almost ready to pop, I'm only three months pregnant now. At least he's at the proper weight. Gulping down a lump of food, I shout a reply, "Be down in a sec."

He's hustling upstairs now, so I slide my food over. Then my eyes lock onto our daughter's. I snap, "Natasha, we—"

"You are in so much trouble." Vassili stands at the door, arms folded.

"Why do you move so quickly?" I grumble with a smile.

He comes in, scoops Natasha into his arms and gives her crazy kisses on her neck. "So, you're the accomplice? Did she force you to eat this shit, or did you do it willingly?" He asks her as she giggles.

"Language," Yuri says, walking into the room with a gait. "Hello, Zariah. Cutie pie, don't allow that. He'll tickle you until you can't breathe."

Vassili swings Natasha high and catches her a foot before she can hit the ground.

Clutching a hand to my chest, I grit out, "Yuri, get him. Unless you'd prefer that the two of you were sporting matching war wounds."

"Hey, this cane has the pussy flying," he laughs.

"Wow, now you're cussing," I snap.

"Aw, that's not a bad word, it's a… beautiful thing."

Vassili puts Natasha down at the tiny table. He jabs a finger into Yuri's chest saying, "Keep having this conversation with my wife, *kuzen*. Find yourself waking up in that exact spot in a few hours."

My husband pulls out another tiny, wooden chair. The aggression in him dwindles as he folds himself into the seat.

"French fry?" Natasha holds the fry so tightly the center mushes in her hand.

"No, sweetheart. Can you make Daddy some tea?"

"Yay!" She hurries to get up. Falls, and then heads to the Mickey Mouse play kitchen against the wall.

"Zariah," Vassili says my name, rubbing the back of his neck. "I'm changing the flight itinerary."

"*Nyet, brat*," Yuri huffs.

"What if Danushka comes around while you and I are gone, Yuri?" Vassili spits the words at his cousin, eyeing myself and Natasha with a world of concern. The guys were heading out sooner than Natasha and I.

"Mikhail is moving in the house," Yuri says. "He and the rest of my brothers will stick around town until Danushka comes out from hiding. I can have one of them come over here until your flight, Zariah? How does that sound."

"Not good enough," Vassili grunts.

My head falls back against the wall. I sit utterly useless unsure how to respond to his cousin. I don't have any qualms with Mikhail staying here, it would be for the best. But in Vassili's eyes, he's the only person who can keep us safe. I shrug, "Sure, Yuri."

"We can push some money around, charter a plane." Vassili chews his bottom lip.

"Let's not waste any money, Vassili." I start to rub my flat stomach and remind him, "We're—"

My husband stops short of slamming his hand down onto

the tiny table before him. "Money is nothing to keep my child safe!"

"You think I'd let that cunt hurt Cutie Pie?" Yuri clutches at his cane and comes over. "Zariah, you're my sister now."

My husband isn't moved by his cousin's sincerity. "We will all arrive on the morning of the match. Together."

"No, baby, we'll not." I shake my head, climbing to my knees, I crawl over and plant myself before him. We're eye to eye, with him in the tiny chair. "You have to be well-rested. I'll be in Australia before you even know it."

I'm comfortable. Noriega is rotting in jail, for at least 16 months on drug possession—pathetic, I know. He should be in jail for the abuse of his wife, but Felicidad is still afraid of him. His attorney is so busy fighting me over his assets. This fool is so flashy that his cars are worth more than his one home, but Felicidad is stepping into her blessings. An involuntary termination of his parental rights is in the works for tomorrow. Also, the real reason I've postponed my arrival to Vassili's game. Tomorrow marks the last of the contested court hearings for the Versa family will. At least I hope.

So, the very next morning, if all things go to plan, I'll be on the plane with Natasha. Maybe I'll even sneak some Benadryl into her apple juice sippy cup so we can both get a few winks before the fight.

40

Zariah

The day death knocked at my door began like any other. Well, a little differently. Mikhail had followed me around everywhere since Vassili and Yuri had left. This morning, we both agreed that Natasha and I can make it to the airport ourselves.

I woke up with a pep in my step, reminiscent of how I did a 'takedown' to the Hollywood attorney for the Versa family will.

While dressing Natasha, I facetime my mother on my iPad, and set it against her teddy bear.

"Aw, honey, I wish I was traveling with you today."

"Mom you have your very first appointment with Dr. Jester." I hold my tongue about my wishes to be there with her during her therapy session.

"I can't believe I'm missing Australia! The men out there are made of solid gold," she joshes.

"Humph," I begin, slipping baby oil on Natasha's feet. I

grab her calf as she flips over to get away and pull her back down. "You're staying home sounds like even more of a good idea, with the way you continue to go on about it. Gushing over men."

"Tsk, because your man is made of—"

"TMI, mama, I have no desire be made aware of your thoughts of my husband."

"Vassili is still a boy. He's my son. Don't worry about this Georgia Peach! I need me a silver fox, honey. Now, let me see Cutie Pie."

"Just a sec." I'm like a NASCAR pit stop, in my endeavors to get Natasha's shoes on before she hightails it. When I sit her up on the changing table my heart melts. My little caramel drop is wearing a dress with green and pink hibiscus flowers on it. Her long curly eyelashes further make me fall in love with her. She's my everything.

"Honey, all those outfits. Seriously, you should've put her in a pair of pajamas to go to the airport. Those folks run the air condition like they want you to get sick."

"I got you covered mom." I place Natasha on my hip, move to her vast closet and pull out an 18-month sized trench coat.

"Come closer…" My mom says, squinting.

When I turn around, I laugh and say, "Yikes!" at the sight of just Zamora's eyes glancing through the screen.

This prompts Natasha to giggle.

"Oh, I like, I like. Is this one of Taryn and her whore of a mother's purchases?"

"Mama!"

"Now, Answer me, child."

"Yes."

"You know she propositioned your father. And her husband put the moves on me."

291

"There's a baby in the room," I warn.

"Natasha doesn't understand. Anywho, Taryn is a minia-ture hoe, too. But you two have always been very good friends."

"That's true." I head to the diaper bag, searching through it to determine if all the necessities are packed. "Okay, Mom, I'm headed to the airport. You have an appointment to catch."

"Time for a quick prayer?"

I pick up the iPad, toggle to the main screen, and my eyes widen at the time. "Sorry, Mom. I'll call you once I start driving. We can pray then."

When we hang up, I carry Natasha and her diaper bag downstairs. Vassili packed my car two nights ago, before his departure. Although, Mikhail offered to do it. He left at the wee hours this morning for his first shift at the hospital since Igor's death. I'd promised to call him once I left the house and before boarding the plane.

But it feels like my head is screwed on backward when Natasha and I are finally buckled in. I determine to call him one I get onto the road. *Probably should pray with Mom first*, I think.

"Daddy, daddy," Natasha babbles, as I glance back at her in the rearview while opening the garage.

"We're on our way to see Daddy. Okay, baby?" I press the shift in reverse and then sigh. The thought pops into my head to open the diaper wipe container. Vassili has a habit of using them all, but not refilling the darn thing. Pressing the shift into park, I reach behind me and grab the diaper bag. The container is in a side compartment, I pull it out and open it.

Damn you, Vassili, what the hell am I supposed to do with two measly diaper wipes? I'm out the car in seconds. I head to the backdoor and unlatch Natasha from her car seat.

"Let's put the sippy cup down, cutie pie." I give her the

look that says, this is the reason we need an arsenal of baby wipes. Her chubby fists, hold on tight. I pluck her to my chest, press the garage button, and run down the hall.

I don't hear the garage door closing. I grumble. So much for extra precautions. Juice spills on me as I take the stairs two at a time. After grabbing a fresh pack of wipes, we head back down the stairs. My cell phone buzzes in my pocket.

"Natasha, you wanna walk?" I huff, breathing heavy. She clings to my hip, as I reach around to grab the iPhone.

Vassili.

"Hey, baby," I huff, heading down the hallway toward the garage door.

"Zariah, beautiful, you on your way?"

"I'm trying. Your child refuses to walk." I again try to remove the chubby baby at my side. "I opened the garage. Forgot something. Now I'm headed back to the garage with Natasha on one hip, her favorite juice spilling on me."

"That's Natasha, mayhem with apple juice."

I chuckle. "Whatever, Vassili. I don't have time to be abused by your mini-me."

My pupils expand as I glance toward the garage exit. The sun is beaming down on Juan Noriega Senior. The way our home is built, with the curvy driveway, the tropical flowers are his background. Dressed in a jumpsuit from Twin Towers Correctional Facility, he fists a Glock in his hand.

"I'm all sticky, and we have less than an hour to..." My train of thought has smashed to smithereens. "We ---we have...."

Vassili is in my ear, saying, "Zariah, girl. What's wrong—"

"Mrs. Resnov." Noriega scratches his skull with the nozzle of his gun as he steps closer to us. "You've taken everything from me."

My baby is in my arm, a fist full of my hair in her hand,

pulling. Not a worry in the world. "Mr. Noriega... wh-what are you doing at my house? How do you know where I live?"

"My attorney, he gets paid well."

"Zariah!" Vassili shouts into the phone. "Who is that?"

"Oh, is your husband on the phone?"

It's on the tip of my tongue to beg and plead with Noriega, but Vassili's voice is louder. "ZARIAH, WHO IS—"

Noriega's lips bunch into a frown. "Tell him."

"It's Juan Noriega. I'm representing his wife in their divorce," I murmur into the phone, then I talk to my enemy. "Let's talk, Mr. Noriega, you and me. Let me put my child in the house so we can talk."

There's silence from the gang member as my husband asks, "Does he have a gun?"

"Yes..." I manage to say before Vassili orders me to give Noriega my phone.

"Okay," I reply to my husband.

When I hand it over, Noriega's cold tone churns through the receiver, "The infamous Vassili Resnov."

He proceeds to tell Vassil that he's already dead. My body wavers in disgust as he mentions his parental rights were terminated.

"Mommy? Mommy..." Natasha has stopped whacking me with her sippy cup. Her sticky hand caresses my cheek. Oh, God, I have to keep her safe. And our baby. We aren't even aware of our baby's sex. The tiny embryo in my belly has yet to mold...

"Noriega, talk to me," I speak up. My husband is adding fuel to the fire, and the man before me is shooting bullets with his gaze as he speaks into the phone. "Talk to me." I start to set Natasha down, but he cocks the hammer back.

Into the phone Noriega says, "You're capable of that, Mr. Resnov. The only problem is, I no longer have a heart. Adios, mi amigo."

He clicks the off button and drops my phone to the ground. "You're a bad bitch, aren't you?"

"I—"

Noriega steps closer to me. He's eye level with my forehead. He presses the gun against my temple and breathes in my breasts.

"How did you get out?"

"Technicality while you've been riding my cock, my attorney—" Noriega pauses, now pushing the barrel of his gun to my mouth. His dead gaze darkens further and he repeats, "You've been riding my dick, right?"

I keep my chin up, there's no denying him.

"My attorney looked into Nicks. He's new. And my bitch is so afraid of men these days, I knew it was you. So while I sat in fucking jail, my attorney made it a priority to see what Zariah Resnov has been up to. Then he got around to looking into my case. All the little technicalities." He shrugs. "I should let you have that baby, raise the little fucker as my own. Screw you a few times before you die," He says, his mucous tongue twirling across the tops of my tits. "Shit, maybe drink that milk of yours, eh? Should I, Zariah, take you to Mexico? Should I keep you locked up till that baby is born?"

His gun goes to Natasha's head. I'm too afraid to move for fear that he accidentally pushes the trigger. "Okay, let's talk this out, Noriega. You and me."

"But this little puta right here, she can go." When the barrel of his gun goes to my daughter's mouth I start to say the Lord's Prayer. There's no arguing or talking with Noriega, telling him how I feel will make it worse.

Then I hear footsteps.

"Zariah, yoo-hoo, Zariah, are you there?" A familiar feminine voice calls.

Noriega trains his gun to my belly as Danushka Molotov

walks up to my garage like it's her runway. Long silver neck-laces a draped over a couture blouse.

Her pointy stilettos resound off the fragmented stone and her face is as oblivious as ever. "I was in the neighborhood," she holds up a flowery canvas material dessert case, with both hands.

"Bitch, who are you?" Noriega glances over his shoulder.

"Danny." She offers Noriega her stuck up frown and dismisses him as if he's one of the staff members at her home.

I begin to stutter, "Danny, N-Natasha has been dying for a pla-playdate. Can you . . ."

"Sure." She continues to strut through the garage now, and toward us. "Horace has been super busy. I made tiramisu. You know, one of my new recipes. I honestly thought you were gone. I was going to drop it off on the steps out front then I heard talking. Let's all go in and have a slice?"

"Are you stupid or something?" Noriega begins to turn around.

A shot rings out.

Blood splashes onto my face and in Natasha's hair as Noriega crumples to the ground.

Danushka drops the dessert case. *"It came out dry, so I packed this instead!"* She holds up a pearl and gold-plated gun.

"You're Danushka Resnov?"

"I am."

"But you can't be. You don't look anything like her." I say, rooted to the same spot. She steps over Noriega, bypasses me and a shocked Natasha for the garage button.

"I'm filthy rich, Zariah. Let's go in the house to talk."

I walk into my home behind her, with my baby's face hidden in my neck. Natasha seems to be in tune with my worry still.

"But your name, Danushka," I say it right once again.

"Oh, you figured out how to say it," Danny offers a smile over her shoulder. She heads into the kitchen. "My logic was, why make up some name like Daria, and I don't look like a Viktoria. That would've made you even more suspicious."

"Are you going to kill me?" I ask, eyeing her gun.

"Oh, this? *Nyet.*" She gestures toward the gun and places it on the counter. "We're friends, Zariah. You are smart and rational. I took a chance by coming to you with my real name. When you conducted a search, an associate of mine had already altered my maiden name. There is a Danushka Petru. Actually, there was."

"You killed her?"

"*Dah.* Horace thought it was a good idea." She opens the refrigerator and shuffles around. "Speaking of my husband, he isn't away on business today. He's manning the jet himself. It should be fueled."

"Then what do you want from me?"

Danushka starts to open a string cheese. "Cutie Pie?"

"No," I shake my head.

"Alright, Zariah, my main goal is for us to continue to be friends." Danushka wiggles the string cheese. Natasha doesn't make a move to take it. With a frown on her face, she bites half of it. "I was a big girl, all muscle, but a big girl. I still love cheese."

"What do you want, Danushka?"

"Zar, I'm not much for repeating myself. But under the circumstances, I will reiterate. You and I are friends. Please don't have me say us much again during the entire flight to Australia. I also need you to tell Mikhail to play nice when he arrives in a few moments. That cousin of mine is such an educated man. Dr. Resnov. And he's so wise. He started to work, sheer dedication this morning. My spotter confirmed he made it halfway to the hospital before turning around."

White noise funnels in my ears as she holds the conversation.

"I anticipated his return. But there's something to appreciate in that he chose to come back prior to Yuri reaching out to the rest of my cousins. Well, not the rest of my cousins—I have many."

"His brothers . . ." I murmur, helping her out.

A hard glint shines in her eyes for a second. "You got *my* family. *Our family.* I love you, sister, you are family."

She seems to be reminding herself of that fact. I nod profusely, in agreement.

"My brat doesn't share you with the entire family, and we will need to have a reunion soon. There are more Mikhails. We have many doctors and high officials in our family. He will arrive before the rest of Yuri's brothers. He will be prepared for a fight, and so I must hold a gun to Natasha's head. A small dose of leverage until he calms down."

"Please don't," I clutch Natasha to me.

Danushka sighs. "Zariah, I love Natasha even more than I love you. She's blood. I apologize that certain tactics are necessary. We have to leave before the rest of Yuri's brothers arrive. Mikhail will travel with us like I said. Also, you will not have any side conversations with Mikhail during our lengthy travel. Neither of you is to tell Vassili that I'm here yet. I prefer to make an entrance. Oh, and one last thing, Zariah, I'd like you to help me make friends with my *brat.*"

It takes a while for me to process the many orders she gave. Vassili was vehement during the many times he told me to stay away from her.

The Danushka he 'stuffed down my throat' metaphorically speaking looked nothing like this. I had an entire rundown on *my* Danushka's background. Also, her name is as common as Mary, Brittany, or Ashley, in their culture. I wrote it off as my Danny being different from the bitch of a sister of his.

How could I be so stupid?

And how the hell do I get away from this psycho? I realize, for my daughter's sake, that I won't. We'll go to Vassili. But there'll be a religious revival in hell before he befriends his half-sister.

41

Vassili

"Mikhail is at the house, Vassil. Zariah is fine, Natasha is fine." Yuri attempts to catch my eye as he tugs on my arm. We're walking through the lobby of the hotel. He's stumbling with his cane. Streams of water are designed throughout the area. I have to give it to my cousin, for keeping up.

My passport and wallet are in my back pocket. The rest of the shit is nonconsequential. I'm on my way to the airport. I don't give a fuck if the next flight to Los Angeles is booked and I have to hand over my entire wallet to someone for their seat. I'll do layovers in every country on the way.

I'm going home.

Past regrets flood through my mind as I sidestep tourist. *I won't be home tonight... Probably not tomorrow night or the next.*

I was a dick when telling Zariah that very statement after Igor's death.

When the image of her crying fades, I'm out in front of the valet, preparing to ask one of these running fuckers to get me a taxi.

"Vassili, listen to me," Yuri grips at my collar.

My left hook snakes out, and I stop myself a fraction of a second before knocking my cousin into next week. I breathe heavy. He grips the back of my neck.

"If you fucking leave, you stupid mudak, you will miss Natasha and Zariah. They are headed here right now, do you understand?" His words are paced for my comprehension.

Did he already say this? Feels like he might have already mentioned something about them catching another flight.

"I don't want them riding alone."

"Mik-hail, my big motherfucking *brat* is with them!"

I rub the back of my neck in thought. "He's gonna—"

"Fly with them and come to the match tomorrow. They'll all be here by the time you wake up."

I start to tug at my mohawk and recall that it's gone. I rub a hand over my buzz cut and nod. "Okay."

"Okay, okay? Kuzen, are we good?" He gestures toward both of our eyes.

"Khorosho!" I shout.

He takes my hand, I snatch it away.

"Shit, I thought I'd have to guide you like my little god babies. I was gonna lead you back to your room, tuck you in like a little piz'da, the works, brat."

"How will they arrive by the time we wake up, Yuri?" I ask. "The flight they missed would've arrived at that time."

"Just shut the fuck up and thank God," he replies.

———

301

All night long, I toss and turn in the hotel bed. My dreams transform from nightmares to even worse night-terrors about my mom. About me.

Finally, I sit up in bed. It's early morning. "Fuck."

Mind racing I wonder how I'll fight tonight. I should call it a day in the MMA world. The Red Door has the perfect manager. I'll have the guy show me the ropes this time like Zariah suggested when I pulled Malich from my establishment. My wife and children are alive.

Time to be a family man....

I hear voices. What the hell is Yuri up to? In this large suite, his room is located on the opposite side of the living room. He's been hitting the porno hard since that bitch, Taryn, stopped coming around. Yet there's no moaning going on.

My eyes burn, and I stumble out of bed with a grunt. Mikhail? Is that him? My pace falters when I hear Zariah. They're here in record time, has to be under twelve hours.

"Let him sleep," I hear Yuri saying. "He fights later on."

"Okay, we will get another room for the night." This voice prickles goosebumps over my forearms. Danushka?

I finally make it around the bed and open the door.

"Shit, I said 'let him sleep'," Yuri gripes.

Zariah is in my arms in seconds, hugging me tightly. I hold onto her, breathe her in, bestow a brutal kiss to her forehead. With Zariah in my arms, I glance down at my sleeping daughter, in her stroller. Then my gaze goes to Mikhail, a slimmer, ripped version of Yuri. The woman next to him is the only other person in the room. Her skin is the color of alabaster. Blonde hair almost as white. She cocks a smile at me.

"*Moy mladshiy brat!*"

Little brother? I don't have any older sisters. Who is this bitch?

She reaches up and pats my cheek like Danushka use to... Danushka... I glance into her eyes. They're pale blue. Her nose isn't so big.

"I'm the prettiest thing you've ever laid eyes on, eh?" She punches me in the arm, her tiny hand is like a brick. Still very powerful. "Cost me a 2.5 mil for all the upgrades."

Fucking bitch is as dumb as her father—our father. She has gone under the knife.

"Alright, let's allow Vassili time to sleep." Yuri places his hand on Danushka's shoulder, but she doesn't budge.

"Hug me, Vassili, brat. I saved your wife and daughter. I deserve some respect, seeing that you hit the ground running a few days before I came into this world."

It is her! Danushka was like a broken record, all the times she mentioned how she should've been Anatoly's firstborn. I beat her to the punch by a few days.

Not feeling any emotion, whatsoever, I hug her.

She grins. "Thanks, *brat*. Zariah is still mad at me for my deception, though she's great at being cordial. And I think if you give someone a ride on your private jet, it sort of tips the scales," she says, winking at my wife. "You saved my marriage, Zar. Although you did a background check and everything, I'll admit that I can be rather deceptive at times. But nothing I said was a lie. Horace is the reason I'm so pretty. I'd like for us to continue our friendship."

"You had Igor *murdered*," Zariah snaps.

Mikhail frowns harder.

"Oh?" Danushka scoffs. "Zariah, I said I'd play nice. I'll continue to say so, but don't bring up old shit."

"What?" Yuri has changed his demeanor from being a manager to a distraught brother. He growls at my half-sister. "How?"

"I didn't, I didn't." Danushka holds up a hand. She settles down into her chair and doesn't sit with a wide-legged stance. Fuck, she's no longer the boy with a cunt between her legs. "My husband, Horace, owns Molotov Steel, an international manufacturing company. That little shit, Bertolucci, wanted to impose sanctions, even greater sanctions on Horace. He had to be put down. It was inevitable."

My eyes narrow in thought. Horace Molotov is one of the richest men in the world. He holds a seat at the seven chairs —or whatever the fuck they call it.

Danushka wriggles her eyebrows. "I may have done the job myself, you know, shopping in Milan gets boring sometimes." She offers her usual frown of disgust. "I left my Resnov card, as usual. One day, Anatoly has to notice me, eh?"

I shake my head.

"The official's family thinks they're hot shit out there. Italian mobsters, my ass. Doesn't matter now, right? Yuri, your friends showed those mudaks who's boss."

"How did they shoot up my father's house!" Mikhail snaps.

"People talk, you know." Danushka shrugs. "Malich left Anatoly. Makes people paranoid, you know. They think that Malich is going off on his own. Biding his time, taking the Resnov name."

"My father could give a fuck about the bratva!" Yuri roars.

More of a slow to burn, in anger, Mikhail bites his fist. "So, our brother died for nothing? Not our fucking name. Not a Resnov, *but your husband! You bitch!*"

Both men are torn, eyes glossed with tears. I squeeze my own eyes closed so as not to get angry enough to cry.

Danushka blinks. "I would've attended the funeral, paid my respects."

"Fuck your respect, Danny!" I shout.

"*Dah*? Fuck me? Well, let's get to the point then. I have a proposition for you, Vassili. Seeing as I saved your wife and your children." She grunts. "Heck, side note, Grigor thought you were going to murder Anatoly when you went to Moscow last. He still feels bad for popping you in the back of the head, my little brother. Isn't he the sweetest?"

I shrug. Grigor is her full-blooded brother. They share the same cunt of a mother. "What do you mean, Grigor thought I'd kill our father?"

"He went to pick you up at the airport. That ugly cousin of ours hops into the car before Grigor can leave. Semion is loyal to Anatoly. I'm Grigor's big sister. He's loyalty resides with me. We would've corrected the Bertolucci family, but Yuri's associates got to them first. Thank you for that, teddy bear."

"Okay?" My face is blank as I mentally determine how crazy my sister is. "What the fuck do you want, Danushka?"

"She wants you to be the new king," Zariah murmurs. To a round of applause from my psychotic little half-sister. My beautiful wife's eyes are sunken in with lack of sleep. This has been a long night for everyone. The only person who is elated is Danushka.

"We are a name, big brother. We are the Resnovs." Danushka grins. "Horace is one of the biggest investors for the Table of Seven. My husband has connections. And like Zar said, the world needs a king. Resnov is the perfect brand. I will, of course, be the true leader. People see pussy and run screaming." She shrugs. "Men are afraid of women. We all know I'm more than competent."

"You want to take down your father, right?" Zariah's eyes latch onto mine. "He did things to your mother, very bad things to her, Vassili."

My knees give out. I'm sitting on the ground before the

rest of me decides it has a fuck to give. My head is down, I knead the back of my neck.

"You can kill him, or I can, Vassili," Danushka offers. "Horace is a billionaire, but we can all be richer. You'll continue to fight. You attend a few meetings at the Table of Seven every once in a while, spit out my words. On most occasions, I'll appear in your stead."

Zariah goes to her knees before me, placing herself between my legs. She caresses my cheek and kisses me with fervor. Her mouth tastes as succulent as what's between her thighs. Fuck, I was so afraid yesterday. I now know what fear looks like—losing my wife and children—because I'm blown away by Danushka.

"You two are beautiful. But you don't even know how to fuck yet. There's no sex like sex when you're made of money," Danushka assures.

I stop listening to the madness. This bitch is out of her mind. Zariah's tongue flicks against mine. My dick is hardening by the second. I want them all out of here, so I can screw my wife.

This must be a fucking dream...

Zariah nibbles my jawline, and up to my ear. Her tongue twines around.

"Fuck, I'm getting hot," Danushka says.

My blood is boiling, but something tells me not to move away, not to shout, not to act in anger as usual. Let Zariah lead.

She sucks on my earlobe and whispers. "We'll figure something out..."

42

Zariah

A new king is upon us. Vassili will hit the cages in a few minutes. He will dominate his opponent and go in for the kill. And then he will work with Danushka to … kill their father.

My husband won't do it, though. He's more of a man than Danushka will ever understand. True vengeance is with the Lord. Anatoly Resnov will get what he deserves in this world, and or in the next.

Perhaps both Anatoly and Danushka will. With a daughter who was once so consumed by wanting his love that she now has decided to do away with it entirely. And him.

But Vassili and I are a team. A sea of people surrounding me. Yuri has Natasha seated in his lap, at my side, since he's still favoring his one knee. Mikhail is next to him because

Danushka claimed she had to sit next to her new "best friend." *Me*.

I shoot up to my feet in a champagne-toned designer dress that Danushka stated was fit for a queen. The silk is like warm honey to my skin as I scream at the top of my lungs. "Kill 'em, Karo!"

The same vigor stirs through her as she stands next to me. For all intents and purposes, we are good friends now. I gave her a few makeup tips while we were dressing. The devil offered her appreciation.

The commentator begs for a 'ground and pound' from Vassili and the Australian, Kong. The bell rings.

Vassili and Kong lunge from their corners. Fists go flying. They're both hungry for murder.

My teeth grit, fists down at my sides. I must look like an angry royal, ready for war myself, because I watch the match without the coiling of my abdomen. Fearlessness is soaring through my veins as Kong pens Vassili to the cage.

He catches my husband with a jab. Vassili grabs his shoulders and knees him.

Vassili's arms swing like they weigh a ton. He kissed me before entering the octagon, promised the fight wouldn't last a minute.

He tosses a left so hard that it powers from his toes all the way through his shoulder. Kong's nose is shattered. Blood pours from his face like a waterfall. Kong crumbles in a heap.

"IT'S OVER. WOW! That nose will never, ever be the same!"

As I shout at the top of my lungs for my husband's victory, I'm already at work. Internally, I'm determining who will help my team. Vassili and I.

Should I go to Samuel Billingsley? He's the proper choice, he's my mentor, and he has a great relationship with Vassili.

Or Malich? He hasn't been the same since Igor died. Yuri

mentioned that when their mother died, years trickled by before he thrived again.

We'll hold off for now with Malich. He is wise in his ways, but only when he's in the right frame of mind.

There's always my father...

Maxwell's hands can be tied behind his back, with information about Sullivan.

Vassili climbs to the top of the cage, straddling it. His dark gaze searches through the crowd. In a sea of a million people, the love of my life finds me. He pumps his fists into the air.

I blow a kiss to him, eyes burning with happy tears.

"I fucking love you!" he mouths.

SUBSCRIBE

Consider joining my newsletter to stay up to date on new releases and super discounts (especially during these holiday times). You'll also receive a free book for subscribing.

AUTHOR'S NOTE:

I hope you enjoyed the second part of Vassili and Zariah's story. Feel free to keep scrolling for Fearless III Prologue. But beware, I set the bar higher, concerning intensity, during each installment. Book one prologue started pretty damn good if I do say so myself. The prologue for this story also had me patting my shoulder. So, if I did it right, LOL, you can expect more drama for Vassili!!!

If you "ain't ready" for all the craziness, Fearless III The Finale will launch on New Year's Eve.

In the meantime, do me a huge favor and review this book. I read each and every thought that you guys have on this series. Don't forget to tell me which side character you want to see more of. So far, folks are feeling Yuri. Join my Facebook Group, so we can chat it out there, too.

Be blessed!
Amarie Nicole

CONTACT ME

Before we get to Fearless III sample, I wanted to cover a few things.

The best way to chat with me is in my Facebook Group. I'm a bit on the shy side, but I'll open up there the most. The readers give me so much good insight. Often, I'll get ideas about what to write next from my group. They get to see all the sexy ideas I come up with first! And I'll be sharing some new Fearless news with them first . . .

But check out the various buttons below, and feel free to connect with me on whatever platform you prefer.

Give a few of my buttons a click and say hi! Then, turn the page for a sample of Fearless II, or grab it now on Kindle Unlimited!

Blessings,
Amarie Nicole

#FEARLESS III

Prologue

Vassili Karo Resnov

"Here's a thousand percent of transparency for you, Mr. Resnov. Zariah's weakling of a mother and I made a beautiful girl. The first time I held my princess I thought, *God, You let us create something so gorgeous.*"

The cool evening air licks at the back of my neck. I shove my hands into my leather jacket. My wife's father, Maxwell Washington, has that cunt of a mouth of his wide open. He leans against the doorframe to his house. The inside of his home is immaculate. Trappings of success. Trappings of my family as he plays judge, jury, executioner, and mother-fucking warden. My wife is here. My daughter and my unborn son are here.

"May I come in, Mr. Washington?" I growl.

"I'll be honest, the two of you made a beautiful little girl." Maxwell points a stiff finger at my chest. I'll let him keep talking, breathing for Zariah's sake.

He's led the entire conversation, which is fine by me. He taunts, "My princess is crying for you."

"Mr. Washington, I'd like to see my wife," I grit out. "Hate me all your life. Let me talk to her."

He unfolds his arms and gestures between us. "We're having a conversation, you and me. This goes on record as our longest discussion ever. Let's keep up the momentum. As I was about to say, Zariah will pine over you. Probably more than necessary. Then when she's ready, I'll introduce her to some good guys."

My blood becomes lava in my veins as I speak. "You'll introduce her to some good guys. My replacement, *dah?*"

The laidback chit chat he was just using fades. Maxwell sneers, pointing another stiff finger at my chest. "You can bet your scummy, communistic ass, I am interviewing a substi-tute. Consider them more than worthy opponents. One of them will be lucky enough to have her. I'll vet all the candi-dates. And that one will exceed anything you could ever do for your child too."

I grab Maxwell's index finger to stop him from another

jab at my chest. But only God Himself stops me from breaking his finger. "Keep at it, piz'da, and I'll forget that you're family."

"Piz'da?"

"It means cunt. Now, I go see my wife!"

I press his hand toward his chest, twisting until he's turned around. Then I step inside Maxwell Washington's home, the house I vowed to never enter when Zariah and I were newlyweds and he'd played me. He'd played me with her bitch of an ex.

I'm in the middle of the foyer, ready to shout my wife's name when a sound I never will forget clicks in my ears.

Might as well be thousands of them.

Safeties are being removed from guns. A fleet of cops are around the perimeter of the room. Might as well all be crooked if they're affiliated with the Chief of Police. They'd been listening to our conversation this entire time.

"Which one of you little cunts will pull the first trigger." I stare face-forward. There has to be at least ten of them waiting to ambush me. "You mudaks! You all will have to take a fucking shot at me." I stop moving, pounding a hand against my chest and point a finger to my forehead like it's a bullet. "Make sure I'm fucking dead because I am going to see my wife today."

"Look at him, so fearless," Maxwell scoffs from behind me. He leans against the doorframe again, legs locked about the ankles. The bitch thinks he's untouchable.

"Kill me and . . ." I pause, offering them the rare chance of a smile. The cocky smile completes the sentence. *You die and everyone you know dies.*

"The Resnov way," someone whispers.

I stare into eyes—blue, brown, green. Maxwell has a diversified list of crooked cops ready to play knight in shining armor for him. If my blood wasn't boiling, I'd be flattered. If I weren't mad, I'd make all of them my bitches in submission—and remember to let them tap out!

"Go ahead, threaten a room full of cops!" Maxwell comes around me.

"Are they wearing cams?" I spit. "I doubt that. You want this shit to make the news? Cops shoot an unarmed man. Who hasn't threatened anyone? Who just wants to see his wife and kids?"

"No cams?" A familiar face moves to block the double staircase. Jackson, the cop who has a history of wanting to be there for my wife, stands in front of me. His nostrils are flared, light-brown skin tinged red. An image of our first encounter pops into my mind. In a police cruiser, Jackson and another cop had stopped Zariah and me. We'd been leaving Urban Kashtan, a restaurant with the best borsch, for the first time. I'd bought enough vodka to lick off all the sweet, tight spots of her body. Her ass. Her tits. Her tight, gorgeous pussy. Before we made it home, this bitch almost ruined our night.

"No cams?" I ask again, arching a brow and ignoring the pup standing in my face.

"Correct. No cams, Son. That also applies to the fact that there'll be no evidence of dead, Russian scum." Washington folds his arms. "All legalities are covered."

For every cop showing his minuscule balls by way of having a gun, I have a machine gun tattooed on my forearm. I'm confident some of them would go down with me!

I sniff, keeping myself calm. "Fuck, maybe I should finish the statement. All you little bitches know the Resnov way. I die. Everyone you know dies. The funeral home becomes rich! Is that what you want on your head, Maxwell? Before you die, knowing that you've caused the deaths of your little pups and their families? Make it clear to me."

Office Jackson snarls, "So you're working for your father, Anatoly Resnov?"

"Dah. Nyet. Why the fuck does it matter." I shrug. "No cams? No proof, right? I want to see my wife and daughter, Mr. Washington. Make that happen before I forget how important you are to *my* Zariah!"

"Don't," comes a soft, feminine voice. The walls in the room stop shrinking in.

My hard gaze pans upward past canvas pictures and rich paintings. My wife is at the top step. The chandelier hanging above. Her beautiful, brown eyes aren't as innocent as I remember. Her orbs are red-rimmed. A sweatsuit has covered every gorgeous curve that my hands, mouth, and tongue have traced over. She leans against the banister. Something flashes across her face. Sadness? Dah, that's it. But there could also be regret, disappointment.

"Zariah," I breathe. All the animosity in my chest deflates. "You got to come home, baby. You are mine. We made vows."

"With an Elvis impersonator." Her tiny laugh is almost hysterical, hopeless too.

"Doesn't matter. We made vows before God." I cock my head, hard voice as soft as can be. "You and my child have to come with me. Natasha is my blood, you are mine. You have to come home. Now."

She might as well be standing right over me. A lone tear drops onto my forehead. I don't have the power to wipe it off. Doing so would be me acknowledging my faults. I hate her fucking crying. Even the happy tears make me wonder. Makes my mind turn to dark thoughts about how my mom cried Anatoly a river. Then I contemplate on Sasha. My sister cried to so many men after they screwed her and beat me for believing she was too good for it.

I nudge my head. "Get my little girl, come down. Now."

Her sigh is heavy enough to drop her shoulders. "Vassili, did you get the divorce papers?"

Venom unleashes in my bloodstream. Keeping my cool is imperative.

"Nyet. Or maybe yeah. Maybe the papers are burnt to a crisp in our bedroom fireplace. Our bed is waiting for you." I stare up at her. The world around us has faded. All those .9mm and Glocks ready to put me under have ceased to exist. It's only she and I, which gives me a 'pass' when I'd spoke of 'bed' and Zariah in the same sentence. Yes, I have an insatiable appetite for her pussy. But I don't fucking disrespect her around people. After the way Anatoly had treated my mom, my mindset is screwed. Meaning, I would never touch my wife. Never hurt her with words or my hands. I'd rather leave MMA for good than affront Zariah Resnov. So, for now, it's only me and my wife here. At this moment as we talk.

And those motherfucking tears in her eyes. I gesture for her again. "Don't cry, Zariah. You know I hate that."

"I know," she says, voice muffled. More tears slide down her cheeks. "I can't leave."

"Okay, I help," my Russian accent falters into broken English. My 190 pounds of raw muscle has transformed into vulnerability. I start to move again.

The world crashes around me with a vengeance.

Jackson, whose been posted against the stairwell, puffs his chest up. His eyes pierce through me. I don't regard him. He's not an opponent. He's not shit to me. I want him to hit me. To get one good lick in so that when I take off on him he'll learn the lesson of his life. Shit, might even cost the mudak's life. I have zero respect for a person who dares to come between a man and his wife.

Without addressing Jackson, I look up at my wife. I order, "Save a life, Zar. I could kill him. Right now, even with them shooting me. Sweetheart, you would have two deaths on your head."

"Just leave, Vassili," she groans. "We can talk things through later."

I continue with, "You'd have my death and his death on your head, baby. You remember our first encounter. You know what the fuck I mean when I say, you'd also have more deaths on your head later."

"Vassili... go!" she screams, her voice so loud it begins to croak. "You're not going to sic Anatoly on them because they're not going to shoot you, asshole. We have kids. *Just give me a moment to think.*"

I slam my forearm into my palm and Jackson jumps; the Glock in his hands shakes. My frown sets deeper.

I snap, "You aren't shit without a gun, eh?"

He kisses his teeth, then replies, "You go up those stairs, you'll be the shit beneath my boot."

"I like that." I step closer to him. "You know what they say, those that can't back it up—talk it out. But I'll still use that little line during my next match."

"Fuck you," Jackson snaps.

"I'm a killer in the cage, so I run out of shit talk. Thank you."

So, by now, I've talked more than I ever would with an enemy. Jackson isn't aware until his body is slammed against the banister. My forearm leveled across his throat. I grit out, "Next step, I snap your fucking neck. After that, the man behind me gets a swift foot to his throat. His neck snaps too. Maybe I'll take more of you mudaks down. Maybe you all will put enough bullets in me first. But remember, I die, everyone down here is dead. That includes you, Pops."

With my tattooed forearm constricting much of Jackson's breathing, I glance over to Maxwell. My wife's father has a hand up. Either he's ready to give the order to call off this farce or he's executing orders for war.

" Vassili," Zariah stresses, from her same spot. She's too smart to come down here. Too smart to enter ground zero because if I touch her, this charade is over. All I have to do is touch her, skim my hand over any part of her body and she'll remember just who the fuck she belongs to.

Zariah's voice is raw from crying as she says, "Vassili, your entire body is a weapon. Hands. Feet. So, go. I'll send you more papers."

"Nyet. Give me a moment to talk to you. I don't give a fuck if we have to chat in front of these piz'das!" I glare at Jackson for a moment. His heartbeat is raging against my forearm; his fingers biting against my skin. But his hold is weakening, he needs oxygen. Then I return my eyes to my wife. "Let me talk to you, Zar. Baby, let me talk to you."

"Vassili, it's the end of us. Don't worry. I won't abandon our children like your mother."

All the venom in me fades. She won't see me. I stare up at her, eyelid twitching. She stays in the same spot, feet rooted to the ground. Our gazes connect. My look is enough to tell her that she crossed the line. She mentioned my mother.

P*lease leave your review for Fearless II and grab book three now!!*

Made in the USA
Coppell, TX
18 July 2020